EMBRACE THE MYSTERY

EMBRACE THE MYSTERY

Caris Roane

Formatting and cover by Bella Media Management.

ISBN-13: 978-1499501353

THE BLOOD ROSE SERIES
BOOK THREE

EMBRACE THE MYSTERY

CARIS ROANE

Dear Reader,

Welcome to the third installment of the Blood Rose Series, EMBRACE THE MYSTERY. In this book, Mastyr Quinlan pursues the artist, Batya, with only one thing in mind but soon discovers that his desire for her is just the beginning of an earth-shattering affair…

He doesn't want a woman in his life…

Quinlan must keep Grochaire Realm safe from the enemy at all costs. As ruler of his realm, a woman has no permanent place in his day-to-day existence. But when his lust takes him to Batya's bedroom, he soon discovers he's deep into a powerful experience that threatens to blow his life apart. He wants Batya with a feverish desire that makes no sense in his logical, warrior world. But when an ancient fae attacks Batya's gallery, he launches into protector mode and soon finds himself embroiled – body, soul, and fangs – with a woman he'd only meant to bed a couple of times.

Enjoy!

Caris Roane

To learn more about Caris Roane and to sign up for her newsletter go to http://www.carisroane.com/

Chapter One

What would the woman, Batya, taste like?

The question had many layers and burned like fire in Quinlan's vampire mind.

He leaned against a brick building and stared up at a wide plate glass window on the other side of the street. His pursuit of Batya Cole had taken him away from Grochaire Realm way too often, as well as his duties as mastyr. He was in charge of a million realm souls and took his job seriously.

Yet, here he was because he couldn't seem to help himself. Batya's blood called to him, like no woman he'd ever known.

His instincts warned him away from the ex-patriot who lived a bohemian artist's life in the small U.S. town of Lebanon, Tennessee. But she'd been on his radar for weeks now and he wanted her in his bed.

Nothing more.

And literally nothing less.

Once he set his sights on a goal, very little could move him.

He could picture her lying on her back, hands gripping the wrought-iron head-board of her bed, the mass of her wavy-blond hair spread out on her pillows.

He'd been through her gallery, her free clinic, her bedroom. Bastard that he was, he'd been spying on her. A couple of times in the process, he'd wondered at his obsession, only to realize the nature of his pursuit didn't matter, only that he conquered his prey.

He wanted to sink his fingers into her hair, lean close and smell all across the line of her cheek. He'd gotten near enough to her once, trapping her in a corner of her gallery, to catch a fragrance that smelled wonderfully rich, like an exotic tropical flower. He didn't have a name for her scent, but he wanted his tongue on her to find out every nuance of her deepest flavor.

He'd been seducing her for the past hour with just his telepathy and of course his mating vibration, a serious realm-ability he'd developed over the past seven-hundred-plus-years of his life. He released another set of waves.

How does that feel, Cha?

He heard her moan, a soft whimper through the window.

Stop calling me that.

His telepathy with Batya rang clear as a bell, one more reason he knew they'd be good together. He'd be able to whisper her name through her mind while he kissed her and moved inside her, working his magic.

His mating vibration, the one that emanated from deep within his body, flowed in a stream straight up and through the second story bedroom window. He loved his mastyr status in these moments that he could do things most other vampires couldn't. He could stand across the street and touch Batya low with just a thought and a vibrating stream of energy that had found the sweetest nest between her legs.

He added a jolt and heard her cry out. He extended his hearing so he could savor every whimper.

You should leave, Quinlan. Stop tormenting me.

Another jolt and again, she cried out. He liked punishing her with pleasure. *That's for telling me to leave.* For the fun of it, he added another intense stream.

She sighed, purred, and moaned, one after the other. He had her now. He'd bring her, like he did last time, but he wanted to get closer. He wanted to watch this time and he wanted her watching him. And this time, he'd let her see what he had to offer.

I want in, Batya. Now. You've kept me outside long enough. He increased the force of the vibration and she groaned heavily.

This is a bad idea, Quinlan. She panted while she pathed to him. *You know it is.*

I don't care. We'll be good together.

He levitated and drifted across the street, moving close to the window. He saw her through a haze of multicolored sheers so that she appeared as though surrounded by ripples of golden, blue-violet light. He couldn't see her clearly, but she writhed on the bed, her hands gripping the wrought iron bars just as he'd imagined.

I see you.

She rolled her head in his direction. *You bastard. I never wanted this.*

You didn't have to let it get this far tonight.

Why did you come after me? You can have any woman in the Nine Realms you want and maybe a couple billion here on earth as well.

It's all your fault. You shouldn't have smelled so good when I first came here, remember? As soon as he'd touched her, her sex had bloomed and her exotic scent had filled him with purpose.

I can't help how I smell.

And I can't help how bad I want to bury myself between your legs. Besides, you refused me and I always face up to a challenge.

* * * * * * * * *

Batya could barely see Quinlan behind the layering of sheer gold, blue, and hot pink fabric that hung in loose swathes over her window, but she caught his scent, like smoky applewood, something burning hot on a barbeque. And he smelled wonderful.

She felt him, too.

Oh, God did she feel him.

His vibration moved inside her the way other things could move, in and out, but with an added shimmer of sensation both sideways and in an erotic swirl that had her aching for more.

And he knew it.

For weeks, she'd tried to resist.

Then one night, about two weeks ago, he'd brought her slowly out of a dream state and had her so worked up that by the time she finally came to consciousness the orgasm spilled over her like a sudden waterfall.

And all he'd done was use his outrageous, built-in-Grochaire realm vibration that he'd somehow turned into the seduction trick of the century. She tried not to think about just how many women he'd bedded by using just a few flicks of that vibration.

Plenty, no doubt. He had one helluva reputation. Sensible women never got near him.

But here she was, about as close as she could get to an orgasm, only this time he wanted inside her house. And the damn vampire was honorable and wouldn't come in unless invited, so it wasn't like she could call foul-play or anything.

The vibration inside her began to slow down, easing her back from the most delicious edge.

She murmured her frustration, but still held onto the wrought-iron as though her life depended on it.

She hated having to make this decision and wished he'd just bust through the window and take her, good and hard.

Instead, she'd have to ask for it.

Let me in, Cha. Let me give you everything this time. It'll be good.

She settled her breathing down, trying to focus on why she needed to send him back to Grochaire. He represented what she'd been trying to escape for decades now. He belonged to Grochaire. In many ways, he *was* the realm he served. Of all the mastyrs of the Nine Realms, she'd never seen one more committed to governing his land than Quinlan.

But her home was here now, in the continental United States, and here she planned to stay the rest of her long-lived life. So what good was it to have Quinlan anywhere near her? No good at all.

It's almost dawn, mastyr. Go home.

I have plenty of time to find shelter and still take care of you. Let me take care of you.

She'd had enough experience with men to know he'd be as good as his word, probably better, which defined her current predicament.

It was her own fault. She'd been without a man way too long. Now she was so hungry, she'd even sleep with Quinlan, a vampire known to use up women and cast them aside like candy wrappers. He had no room in his world, his life, his heart for a relationship. She didn't know all the details, but the horrific event surrounding his parents' deaths had set him on this course, so good luck to any woman trying to overturn a childhood trauma.

At last, she released her death grip on the wrought iron and sat up. He'd given her time to think, to let her smarts work for her right now instead of her hormones.

Unfortunately, she still wanted the vampire bad.

And he still streamed his vibration, teasing her between her legs, but gently now, a reminder of what he could do to her if they were together, that he could sustain the sensation in a dozen places at once while he worked her physically with a nice list of attributes. She'd heard the rumors about him, which didn't help either.

You know we'll do this eventually. Even in her head his deep voice rumbled, another seductive layer that weakened her resolve. Quinlan had one of the deepest voices she'd ever heard, a rich bass. *So, why not tonight, Cha?*

She picked up her brush and pulled forward a heavy length of her thick hair. By long-established ritual, she started at the tips and began working out the tangles one by one. Brushing helped her to think, to remember, to coalesce thoughts and arguments, to synthesize opposing threads.

Quinlan…bad.

Grochaire Realm…bad.

Her artist's life in Lebanon…good.

She brushed and brushed, scowling and thinking, his vibration still an easy, seductive presence. For reasons she couldn't explain, she felt utterly threatened by Quinlan, that something about him could destroy the precious life she'd built for herself outside of her birth realm.

She knew who she was in Lebanon.

Grochaire and the Realm-world swallowed her up, using her combo troll-fae powers until she sank under the weight of it.

She could never go back to that life and yet here she was, about ready to open herself up to the Mastyr of Grochaire Realm himself, the legendary Quinlan and his god-like physique.

Her brush fell from her hands as she lifted her gaze back to the window, where she could see him hovering, holding himself in place through levitation alone, his vibration still a beautiful sensation.

Hang-it-all, she was going to let him in.

But just as she slipped from bed and her long skirts fell into place to her ankles, a brilliant white-yellow light flashed behind Quinlan. He whipped around, then dropped from sight as shrieking sounded outside her building, the kind that came from Invictus wraith-pairs.

She heard him shout something, maybe the word, 'run'. She wasn't sure, but the high-pitched battle screams meant only one thing, Invictus.

She couldn't believe that the Invictus had come to Lebanon. From what she'd always understood, the deadly wraith-pairs didn't have the ability to pass the realm access points and enter the U.S. She'd always thought herself safe because of it.

In the street, a red wind streamed.

* * * * * * * *

Quinlan stood on the sidewalk with his back to Batya's art gallery, uncertain what the hell he was looking at. He waited with lowered shoulders, his arms firing up his battle frequency so that he could release killing energy in streams through the palms of his hands. He even had a dagger in his leathers if this battle got up-close-and-personal.

But what the hell was he looking at?

He could almost make out the shape of a woman held within a bright yellow glow, a sight that made his vampire eyes ache. He smelled the female though, a dark rancid scent that he knew from a battle six months ago in Bergisson Realm. An ancient fae had cursed the area and dammed up the waterfall at Sweet Gorge. Together, the Mastyr of Bergisson and his blood rose, Samantha, had created a new paradise there and the fae's stench was gone.

But Quinlan would never forget that smell and it was here now, in Lebanon.

However, it would appear she'd shifted her attention to him, or maybe to Batya. But what would the ancient fae want with an ex-patriot, living at the Tennessee human earth access point, and running a free-clinic for other disenfranchised realm-folk? Batya wasn't exactly a threat to the Invictus, the deadly wraith-pairs that many now believed the ancient fae had created.

But whatever this was, Batya was no match for the powerful fae, which was why he'd shouted for her to run.

From the shadows behind the golden glow, four figures emerged, levitating just a few feet above the ground.

Invictus wraith-pairs.

Yet something more.

Bigger.

Deadlier.

Two female wraiths each bonded with Guard-sized vampires, as big as him. But they weren't regular vampires at all. Holy shit, each was a mastyr vampire. The Nine Realms had over two dozen mastyr vampires beyond those, like him, who ruled each realm. Only the most powerful mastyrs became rulers, a law that had been part of the Nine Realm world for millennia.

His nostrils flared. A bitter edge reached him, emanating from the Invictus, something cloying that reeked of the ancient fae and both pairs smelled of it, like wet ashes, a sure sign that this new version of the Invictus was her creation.

Great.

The battling vibration of both Invictus pairs swarmed toward him and in this moment he knew he was dead.

He could have fought a dozen normal wraith-pairs, but not these two together. Maybe not even one alone because the bond between wraith and mastyr vampire had created unimaginable power between each couple.

He thought of Batya in her studio. What would happen to her if he couldn't stop them? He didn't want to think about that.

A woman's voice called out. "This is all wrong. He's not supposed to be here." The ancient fae drifted sideways, her features indistinct, her glow still hurting the backs of his corneas. He shaded a hand over his eyes.

And why wasn't he supposed to be here?

Her words meant only one thing, that she'd come for Batya.

The thought of her in the hands of any of these monsters increased and focused his battle energy. He lifted his hands. "All right, motherfuckers, which of you wants to die first?"

* * * * * * * * *

Trembling, Batya made her way to the lower gallery floor and hid behind one of the pillars. She couldn't believe what she was seeing and her heart beat so hard in her chest she thought it would explode.

A soft, feminine voice called to her from behind. "Batya, what's going on?"

Batya turned toward the doorway that led to the back rooms and her assistant's apartment. Lorelei had been her solid right-arm for two years now, helping her run both the gallery and the free-clinic. "I don't know, but I think Mastyr Quinlan's in trouble."

Lorelei drew close. She stood just slightly shorter than Batya as she stared out at the strange golden light and the massive wraith-pairs that looked ready to eat Quinlan alive.

"He'll never stand against her."

"Against who?" Batya could vaguely make out a woman's shape.

"She's the one, the ancient fae."

A serious shock ripped through Batya's body. "Holy shit. You mean the one that caused all those problems in Bergisson, at Sweet Gorge?"

Lorelei nodded. "I know her."

Batya felt as though she'd been kicked in the stomach. "What the hell do you mean *you know her*? You know the ancient fae?"

Lorelei sighed heavily. "Yes. I can see her plainly, too. Can you?"

"No. I see a female figure. That's all."

"Mastyr Quinlan won't survive this attack. She has too much power."

Batya didn't know what to do. She could sense Quinlan's battle frequency gearing up, but she could also feel the other vampires, that they were super-charged. She understood then that Quinlan showed nothing but bravado, that he knew he was going to die.

"We only want the woman." The ancient fae's voice sounded rough.

"You can't have her." Quinlan's deep voice roared along the street, easily breaching the gallery window.

"I have to do something. He can't die. I can't let this happen."

"But what can you do?" Lorelei asked. "We're lost. All of us. No one can withstand the ancient fae. Even now, her power ripples over my skin."

Batya turned to Lorelei and saw that tears tracked her pale cheeks. She trembled head-to-foot. Fear reeked from her as well, but not a sudden kind of panic, something that tasted metallic on the air like she'd lived with it for decades.

She didn't know very much about Lorelei. She'd shown up a couple of years ago and stayed to help, but Batya didn't ask questions, one of her rules in the ex-pat community. She believed it was important for all ex-patriots, those realm-folk who chose to live in the U.S apart from their birth-realms, to feel like they could start over without having their histories made public.

Suddenly, the air outside the gallery lit up and streams of killing energy passed from Quinlan to the hovering wraith-pairs. Quinlan rose into the air as well, at least three feet off the ground.

He looked magnificent, even from behind, because he held his arms wide and flung impossible arrays of battle energy at the enemy, something that would have destroyed a normal wraith-pair with the first blow.

Yet the Invictus couples barely moved as they slowly advanced on him, pressing their joined energy hard at him in brilliant streams of alternating red and blue light.

The golden aura of the ancient fae grew brighter as the battle raged. Maybe she gained energy from the sight of destruction.

Probably.

The woman was evil.

Batya heard Lorelei's soft sobs, but her own inclination leaned away from sadness or even pity in this moment. She'd grown up with the destruction that the Invictus pairs could inflict, which was one of the reasons she'd left Grochaire in the first place. She'd had enough of the war.

The other reason began to forge a heavy vibration through her body, the part of her that was monumentally and powerfully fae. For a moment, she even wondered if she could pull this off, because she'd kept her power dormant for the past century.

Yet with one man's life hanging by a couple of blue streams of energy, she gathered her power. Quinlan belonged to her, not to these vile, wraith-vampire Invictus pairs and he sure as hell didn't belong to an ancient fae who even she could detect smelled like rotting garbage.

"Stay back, Lorelei. But don't worry, this won't hurt you."

Batya moved forward and began accessing one of her powers, a realm frequency that many fae shared that made use of enthrallment in many different forms. The canvases and easels all around her began to vibrate and shake as she gathered her power. Some of them even fell to the floor.

Damn the Invictus anyway and if this ancient fae had charge of them, damn her as well.

Everything happened at once.

Both massive wraith-pairs charged Quinlan. A brief flash of red and blue light flew into the air on impact, then Quinlan crashed through the window.

"There she is," the ancient fae called out. "Get her."

But without giving it too much thought, Batya sent her enthrallment power outward and wrapped her gallery up inside a shield, like she'd just set a hard cement wall all around the perimeter of the entire building.

Beyond the shield, the woman ensconced in the golden light writhed. "Where is she? What happened? Where did everything go? What the hell is this?"

"Mistress we don't know. But we hit Mastyr Quinlan with everything. Wherever he is, he's probably dead."

"Do you think that's any consolation? I don't give a ripe fig about his ass. I wanted the woman." Her voice vibrated with rage.

Lorelei joined her. "What did you do, Mistress Batya?"

Normally, Batya didn't allow anyone to address her in the ancient realm way, but she let it pass for now since she had a bigger problem. She had one half-dead mastyr vampire lying on a bed of shattered glass.

She dropped to her knees beside Quinlan. He had burns all over his body and most of his heavy battle leathers and Guardsman coat were gone. His long, thick, black hair remained intact, but she wasn't sure how.

"Will you help me, Lorelei? I need to get him to the healing room."

"Of course, but will your shield hold?"

"Yes."

Lorelei glanced toward the broken window. "But how are you maintaining it?"

Batya met her gaze, staring at her hard. "The same way, I think, that you were able to see that bitch out there."

A blush crawled up Lorelei's cheeks. Batya had suspected for a long time that Lorelei had many secrets and tonight she'd put a spotlight on at least one of them.

Lorelei merely nodded. "Fair enough."

"Now do you, or do you not, have levitation powers here?" Batya's own abilities in that area, much to her dismay, left a lot to be desired. Many powerful fae could fly, but even with her three-hundred-plus years, she still couldn't lift her feet off the ground. But she could raise other things for short bursts, like near-dead vampires.

Lorelei sighed. "I do."

"Then you take one side of this big Guardsman and I'll take the other."

When Batya slid her arms beneath Quinlan, he moaned heavily. She sensed that a number of his bones were broken and that left alone, he'd die.

She sent a calming vibration through his mind and somehow that did the trick. He dropped into a much-needed coma.

When Lorelei worked her arms beneath Quinlan as well, and she opened her levitating power, some of it zinged against Batya.

I've never felt anything like that. Who the hell are you?

Lorelei's lips quirked. *An ex-pat, like you. That's all.*

Like hell. But Batya smiled.

"On three." She counted down and together, two Grochaire ex-pats, levitated a near-dead mastyr vampire, weighing in at a heavily muscled two-forty and not an ounce less, and carried him through the blown-apart gallery to the infirmary off the back hallway.

The healing room held a large bed so that family members could often sleep beside their loved ones, or just be near them when they passed.

Mostly realm-folk survived whatever trauma or disease came at them, one of the perks of being long-lived.

Yet Batya had noticed that sometimes the spirit of her fellow realm inhabitants gave out when a human spirit didn't. That was one of the mysteries of her world.

As she and Lorelei worked to get the blood-feeding-tube down Quinlan's throat, she doubted he'd succumb to a loss of will, or anything else like that. Only these levels of burns and physical destruction could take Mastyr Quinlan out.

For the next several hours, she and Lorelei took turns donating blood to the feeding-tube apparatus. Vampires were excellent self-healers and more than anything, blood would do the trick. So together, they donated and watched as minute upon minute his skin knitted together and his broken bones stretched out and re-formed properly.

She kept him out cold so that anytime his powerful conscious mind tried to rise back to the surface, she'd send a reassuring vibration, from her healing frequency, straight to the center of his brain. He seemed to know her and to acknowledge her presence, because he didn't fight her, but each time settled back into his unconscious state to let his body do the work.

Lorelei brought her a tray of food of fresh fruit, an orange muffin, and a vanilla yogurt. Batya didn't speak as she ate, but she did inspect the enthrallment shield she'd created. The preternatural wall held and wouldn't budge unless she made a decision to release it. She could also open up small portions in order to let people come and go if necessary.

Though the wraith-pairs had left at dawn, an elven female, wearing protective sun-gear, stood guard across the street within a faint enthrallment shield so that the humans couldn't see them. The ancient fae was having her gallery watched.

By nightfall, having been up for twenty-four hours, Lorelei needed some sleep.

Quinlan was well on his way to healing and she'd removed the blood-feeding tube. He'd be waking up in the next few hours at which time she'd give him a solid wrist-feed.

For now, however, with Quinlan's skin mostly restored and sleeping as he was on his back, she stretched out on the bed, pulled a separate blanket over her and turned on her side to look at him. With all the lights in the room off, she altered her vision and saw him in a soft glow.

He had an incredible profile. His nose was slightly crooked like it had been broken in some way he couldn't repair or maybe he'd been born that way, but she'd always thought it his sexiest feature. He had thick black brows, and his hair lay twisted and matted beneath him. She didn't envy him that brush-job.

Her hair was similar so she knew exactly what he faced when he finally recovered.

She tucked her hand beneath her cheek and sighed. Not a bad night-and-day's work, saving a mastyr vampire from an ancient fae and two uber-powerful Invictus wraith-pairs.

Was this the future then? An army of wraith-pairs that could defeat even a powerful mastyr vampire?

If this were true, then what would happen to the Nine Realms? How could Grochaire or any of the other North American realms stand?

Well, she couldn't solve all the world's problems, at least not tonight.

She smiled as she fell sound asleep.

* * * * * * * *

Quinlan woke up slowly, his mind cluttered with images that he couldn't quite make sense of, like huge vampires and wraiths, snowfields, and a deadly net flying through the air.

But beneath the revolving spin of scattered sights and sounds, rode a sense that he should be up and doing something. He just didn't know what.

His eyes took their time opening and they hurt in a strange way, like he'd been staring at the sun, a very bad thing for a vampire.

He recalled seeing something gold and glowing, but what?

Some of his bones ached, especially his ribs, and he could feel them reforming, which meant he'd been hurt recently, but how? Why?

A weight across his upper thighs and another across his chest stung a little where his skin hadn't completely healed.

So he must have been burned as well.

He reached down to remove the first weight and found a woman's arm.

An arm.

He smiled. Though he wasn't sure why, he liked the woman's arm over his chest and he could live with the moderate pain it caused.

He sighed and his mind drifted back into oblivion once more.

Sometime later, he awoke again with a new weight pressed on his chest, something heavier this time and his nose tickled.

Opening his eyes, which didn't sting nearly as much as earlier, he lifted a hand to rub the tip of his nose. He found several strands of coarse hair curled just so to make his skin itch.

Blond hair. Very thick and wavy.

He knew this hair. He was sure of it.

Ah, the woman again.

She lay on his chest, the cause of that heavy weight.

His ribs still hurt, but not that much, not enough to make him want to wake the woman up and tell her to move.

Instead, his lips curved once more. Oddly, he felt more relaxed than he had in a long time, in decades, maybe even centuries. His stomach didn't even hurt.

Weird, that.

He wanted to explore why his stomach wasn't all cramped up with blood-hunger, but he drifted off once more.

When he finally woke up for good, the first thing he realized was that he was in a fully aroused state and the woman lay partially on top of him.

He opened his eyes and found that no aches remained in or near the sockets, but his stomach warned him that he was low on fuel and not the kind that a meal could provide.

He needed blood.

The woman was still on him, only this time she lay completely over him, snoring gently.

He cradled her with one arm. She wore a skirt of some kind and a blouse. A bra.

He wore nothing and the sheet that had once covered him hung around his knees.

Shifting slightly, the woman snuggled closer, tilting her face into his neck. She found the skin at his throat and slowly started nibbling, then she began to suck.

His cock loved what she was doing, but somehow the whole thing seemed wrong. If only his brain would pull together and work properly, then he could figure this out, like who she was, where he was.

He looked up at the ceiling and saw a beautiful painting of a woman with wings, an angel perhaps, in flight. The colors were navy and a violet or purple. He wasn't sure about the names for the different hues.

She seemed happy and somehow the painting made him feel at ease, which he supposed was the purpose, if someone was in what he could only interpret as a kind of healing facility. Glancing around, he recognized fae-paraphernalia, some scented candles, a blood-feeding tube.

At that, he frowned. He needed to feed again, but given the severity of his injuries, the woman must have already donated through the tube.

And just like that, the images coalesced. He recalled flying through Batya's art gallery, having been thrown through the window. He remembered a painting of a snowfield, and another in a meadow littered with the unique camping tents that his troll brigade used in the mountains. There were other images like streams and maybe a river, of a trail through a fall forest, almost brilliant orange, and burning or maybe it was just the colors of fire.

Batya's paintings of course, remembered in vivid detail.

Batya. Yes.

He held her in his arms, the woman who suckled his neck softly in her slumbers. He squeezed her and his cock moved against her abdomen.

He drifted his nose, as he'd been wanting to for weeks, along the line of her cheek. He dragged in air and there it was, the scent he now associated with her, an erotic, flowery fragrance, like something found in the tropics.

For a moment, he thought about moving his hips on a downward trajectory, until he could position himself between her legs. He knew her sleep-style a little, since the first time he'd brought her to ecstasy, she'd barely been awake, just coming out of her slumbers. Very wicked of him, but it had been worth it.

On the other hand, he didn't feel right about invading her like this. Seduction was one thing, but taking advantage of a vulnerable female was not his style, despite that she sucked his neck and now rolled her hips into his with matching need.

He groaned then squeezed her waist, shaking her just a little. He needed her to wake up, to stop moving on him.

She cooed in her half-sleep. "Quinlan?"

"I'm here."

"Oh, that voice of yours, as deep as the ocean, and you smell so good, like wood-smoke."

"I know what you mean."

She swirled her tongue over his neck.

"You need to stop doing that."

"But you taste so good."

"Open your eyes."

"They are open."

"No, they're not."

She chuckled softly. "Yes, they are."

He drew back just enough to look at her, wondering if he was mistaken, but her eyes were fully closed. Yep, still half-slumbering and he knew he could take her. Was ever a woman more accessible at this point in her sleep than Batya?

"Wake up." He spoke in a sharp tone, which snapped her eyes open.

"Quinlan? What are you--" She broke the question off mid-sentence and blinked several times. "What am I doing here?"

He chuckled softly. "It's okay."

"Did you pull me on top of you? Quinlan, is that you pressing into my belly?"

"The answer to your first question is, no, I did not pull you on top of me like this. I awoke in just this position. Several times in fact, and each time you were sprawled over me, but this is your latest arrangement." He cleared his throat. "As for the second question, yes, that's *me* pressing into your abdomen."

She didn't move for a very long moment, though her limbs had stiffened slightly. She just kept looking at him, and blinking rapidly. He couldn't imagine her thoughts and he had no idea what she would address first.

But a faint smile made him hopeful as she said, "Well, the rumors about you are exactly spot on, but I won't say more about that."

He smiled. He knew what she meant and damn him for loving that she'd just said it. His cock twitched appreciatively.

She drew back a little and searched his face. "How do you feel? Any pain? You'd been fried to a crisp and had a bunch of broken bones when we brought you in here."

"I'm fine. Just a little soreness here and there, but I'll need to feed soon."

At that, she relaxed against him and offered her wrist. "Go ahead. Take what you need."

Quinlan stared at her for a good long moment. He'd expected a lot of things, but not Batya offering up her arm. He knew she was generous: she had a free-clinic and had brought in some kind of ex-pat to help her out, a woman who lived in an apartment on her premises.

He also knew he was the last man who deserved that kind of generosity. He had no illusions about who he was. He'd spent his life trying to atone for his father's death.

But that Batya would donate so freely when he'd been harassing her for weeks about needing to get into her bed, crushed something inside his chest.

He didn't press her either about finding another *doneuse*. To refuse her wrist would have been tacky after all she'd done for him.

When she curled her arm so that he could take her wrist at a good angle, and without giving it too much thought, he lowered his fangs and struck to the exact, practiced depth and began to suck down the sweetest tasting blood, flowery and erotic, just as he'd imagined.

However, given that she still lay on top of him, his other problem suddenly got worse.

* * * * * * * * *

Batya realized her mistake when she watched Quinlan's eyes roll back in his head with his first draw at her wrist. An involuntary flex of his hips followed so that she felt his cock glide up her lower abdomen in one long erotic stroke.

Sweet Goddess, I'm sorry, Batya, but you don't know what you taste like. Don't worry. Just ignore my response.

But Batya couldn't. He'd been working her up for weeks. He'd brought her to climax several times with just his vibration and he looked so good close up, with his golden skin and sexy crooked nose, his full lips plundering her wrist.

A simple idea came to her given their shared level of need, so with her free hand, she carefully drew her skirts up so that when she turned back to him, she felt him skin-to-skin, the base of his cock pressing against her mound.

Heaven.

What are you doing? He pathed. His eyes looked frantic as he watched her.

Caris Roane

Just keep taking what you need. She held his gaze as he sucked and she pressed herself against him and began to rock into him.

He groaned as he sucked. *Can you come like this, even though I'm not inside you?* His deep voice in her head almost brought her.

She nodded. *Oh, yeah. Can you?* She searched his dark eyes.

Fuck, yeah, especially with your blood flowing down my throat.

She reached around and grabbed his ass to keep the pressure anchored. He shifted just enough and began to push against her as well, quick upward jabs, holding her gaze.

Come for me, Cha. Come for me. His voice. Sweet Goddess, that rumbling bass voice.

And before she knew it, he added his vibration which pushed her over the edge and she groaned as ecstasy poured through her. She cried out, grinding against his cock. He left her wrist and held her close, his cock jerking repeatedly as he came. He grunted heavily as he pushed his hips into her over and over, extending the moment.

"Your vibrations, Quinlan. They get me every time."

"Your response gets me."

Her breathing slowed. His as well.

"Short but sweet."

She smiled. "I love your voice."

He drew her against him, cradling her again, rocking her just a little.

Thank you, Batya. That was a double kindness. I owe you one.

Well, you took care of me, too, so maybe we're even.

He chuckled.

After a couple of minutes, she leaned up on her elbow to better see him. "Your hair's a mess."

"Hey, I almost died."

"I'm not making a comment on fashion or tidiness, just remarking that you'll have a couple of tangles to clear up once you shower. I have a really good crème rinse, though. You're welcome to it."

He reached up and touched the matted hair at the nape of his neck, then winced. "You weren't kidding."

"Look at it this way, you didn't lose your hair though half your body was burned bad."

He frowned suddenly and looked around. "Can you explain to me why I'm still alive, why you're still here and not dead? How did you survive the attack?"

She looked anywhere but at him. She'd known this moment would come, that she'd have to tell him the truth about her radical fae powers, but she didn't want to. She slid off him, pulling her skirts away.

"Where are you going? Batya, what's going on?"

She kicked the blanket off her legs and sat at an angle on the side of the bed, mostly away from him. Time to confess. "When you crashed through the window, I gathered my power and set up an enthrallment shield."

"You did what?"

She waved her right hand. "Can't you see that? Feel that?"

He looked around, then settled his gaze on the window that overlooked the alley. The blinds and drapes were drawn for privacy.

She watched him as his gaze scanned the window, the drapes, the wall. He closed his eyes for a moment then opened them. I sense a very faint vibration, nothing more.

"Good. I'm glad. For me it's like an air-conditioning unit that's been running full bore, all night, right next to my head and I wish I could shut it off. But the ancient fae has one of her minions stationed across the street from my gallery, about where you were last night. She's a pretty elf who's been chain-smoking for the past several hours.

"She's watching your home?"

"She's waiting for me to lower my shields so she can bring in the big boys. You know those wraith-pairs you fought two nights ago?"

His brow rose. "Two nights ago? Sweet Goddess. I've been out that long?"

"Do you remember the pain?"

"Not really." He shook his head slowly. "Just, I don't know, I remember something entering my mind, a kind of ease."

"That was me."

"No wonder I slept and healed so damn fast. I really do owe you, don't I?"

"Kind of. But do you think the ancient fae was really after me?"

"I do remember her words. She wasn't expecting me to be there, so if it wasn't me, then it had to be you."

"I guess. I just don't know what to do next. I mean if they were after me, because of what I can do, and they could take you down like that, where will I ever be safe?

"Besides, I've built a life here, one that I love." She lifted her chin and met his gaze straight on. "I don't ever plan on living anywhere else, either."

He crossed his arms over his chest. "A real ex-pat."

"Absolutely, and proud of it."

His gaze skated away from hers. He sounded almost reverent as he said, "I can't imagine living anywhere but in Grochaire."

She felt a familiar twinge of guilt when she thought of the Nine Realms, especially in the face of Quinlan's dedication to her birth-world.

"So let me understand something, Batya. You've got sufficient power to sustain an enthrallment shield around your entire building, for what appears to be an indefinite amount of time."

"Pretty much."

He released a sigh. "I had no idea you had this kind of power, but then it explains why the ancient fae would be after you."

"I suppose."

"I'll pay for the window, of course."

"It's not necessary. The Invictus did this and that she-devil who created them. "

He rubbed his thumb over what was now a crevice between his thick black brows.

Even upset he looked sexy as hell and it didn't help that the sheet he'd just pulled up hung below his navel. She had a perfect view of a spectacular chest, tight abs, and heavy pecs that she wanted her mouth on.

His gaze shifted toward her and his hand dropped away from his face. "What's with all the scent now rolling at me?"

She looked up at the ceiling. "You know, I've been thinking of changing that mural."

"Well, it shouldn't be a problem since you changed the subject as quick as lightning."

She laughed and met his gaze once more. "You look good to me right now and before that goes to your head it's only because I've come to realize that I've been without a man for too long and as soon as we get this situation sorted out, I'm going to start dating again."

"Date me."

She laughed. "That's not dating. That's sex."

"Then sex me. Use me. I can handle it."

She tilted her head. "I want more and I know you can't deliver what I want."

He sat up, grabbed her arm and let some of his wicked vibration float over her skin. She shivered, a full body shake that made her gasp. "How do you do that?"

He released her and sank back down on the bed, his hands clasped behind his head. He looked so smug, so self-satisfied. "I've had lots and lots of practice. Now just imagine all that vibration, elsewhere, in conjunction with other things. I wouldn't dismiss a purely sexual relationship, Batya, not one with me." His dark eyes glittered.

She stood up and let her skirts fall where they may. "I've been trying to avoid exactly this kind of liaison since you first started sniffing around here. But we don't need to settle anything right now. I don't know about you, but I'm starved."

"You changed the subject again."

"Yeah, I'm pretty good at it."

She didn't wait for him to make another suggestive remark but headed toward the door. But before moving into the hall she said he could use Lorelei's shower, that she'd find him some clothes, and bring him her special crème rinse."

"Thank you, Batya. I mean it. You saved my life."

Her throat tightened as she nodded. "Anytime, mastyr. Anytime."

As she moved into the hall, she drew a deep breath. The ancient fae had intruded in her world and right now she had no idea how long her siege would last, or if her life would ever return to normal.

Chapter Two

Quinlan showered, washing the mass of his hair twice then applying Batya's crème rinse so that he'd have a half-way decent shot at getting the snarls out.

Using her blow dryer, he cursed as he watched his long, thick hair fly around. Why couldn't a vampire, especially a Guardsman, have some kind of preternatural power to remove tangles and dry his hair without electricity?

"Want some coffee with your 'shits' and 'damn-all-the-elf-lords-to-hell'?"

He met Batya's reflection in the mirror, and saw a mug extended in his direction.

He shut the dryer off, turned around, and took the cup. "Guess I wasn't holding back much."

Batya chuckled. "No, you weren't."

She had dimples, two of them. Not deep, but they were definitely there. He'd never really noticed before, but on the other hand most of his seduction work had taken place at a distance.

But right now, he sipped his coffee and had a good, long look. Her large, hazel eyes had to be her best feature, although her straight nose and striking cheekbones took a powerful second-best. Her chin angled to a lovely fae point.

Her gaze flicked over his hair. "Turn around. I'll work the back section."

Since she reached past him and grabbed the brush, he decided to take her up on the offer. That he didn't hesitate resonated in his brain as a serious warning of some kind, but he wasn't sure in what way.

She picked up a thick section and started at the tips. He couldn't even feel the tugs so he drank his coffee and released a sigh.

His thoughts turned, as they so often did, to Grochaire. "I need to get word to Rafe, my second-in-command, to warn him about what he might be up against. But my telepathy isn't working through your shield and my phone got blasted by one of those wraith-pairs."

"You can try my phone, but I can't guarantee you'll get through, not with the shield I have in place. I can reach my Lebanon people, but I doubt you'll get through to any of the realms. And, sorry, but I'm not letting the shield down, not for nothing. Staying alive has priority here."

He smiled because he couldn't have agreed with her more.

She brushed through another long length, hit a snag and started working it. He could see her in the mirror, brow furrowed. He'd seen that look already, more than once just conversing with her. She had a seriousness about her that he approved of, maybe because it matched his own.

He sipped some more and watched her. She was a beautiful woman and tall, maybe just under six feet. He wouldn't have to lean too far down to kiss her. She wore her hair loose with clips holding it away from her face.

He knew her ancestry, half-fae, half-troll, her genetics having fallen on the fae side. Realm-DNA did that when the species mixed. The offspring landed one way or another, the same if more than two lines made up the code. Genetics always picked a lane.

But perhaps above all, Batya was an artist.

"Have you ever done a self-portrait?"

She picked up another long hunk of his hair and once more started at the tips, working swiftly. "I don't really do faces. I've always been into landscapes and the occasional still-life if the objects intrigue me enough."

"Do you go out, snap photos of woodlands, that kind of thing?"

"Sometimes." She stopped brushing and scratched her cheek with her thumb. "But more often than not I'll get these rich images in my head and that's what I'll paint."

"Sounds fae."

She started brushing again, making quick work as he continued to sip his coffee. "Maybe. Probably. I don't think about it. I just paint and let the spirit move me."

He smiled. "The spirit, huh?"

"It's a good earth-saying, don't you think?"

"I suppose. So you really like being here on human earth."

"I do. In fact, I love it. I didn't know what happiness or freedom was until I moved here." She met his gaze in the mirror. "And I don't plan on ever returning to the Nine Realms. The day that we made our treaties with the US turned out to be the best day of my life."

"You run a free clinic. I know that much. What else?"

She shrugged. "I have my gallery and I teach classes on assimilation for ex-pats, currency, lingo, that kind of thing. Most stop saying 'sweet Goddess' by the end of the first year and use the more typical 'OMG.'"

"And you really don't miss Grochaire? Not even a little?" He couldn't imagine how anyone could feel like that. Grochaire lived in his bones.

"No." Strident tone, too strident.

"So, what happened that set you against your own world?"

"I'm not set against Grochaire." She ran the brush down his hair, top to bottom, one section at a time. "I think I'm done."

"What? That was damn fast."

"You'd done most of the work already. You just don't have enough patience."

One side of his mouth curved. "You got that right." Turning toward her, mug still in hand, he added, "Now tell me what happened, subject-changer. Why did you leave Grochaire?"

Lorelei called out that the food was ready.

Batya smiled. "Good-timing because I think the inquest is over for now. Get dressed." She waved a hand over the towel wrapped around his waist, then left the room.

"I'll be asking again," he called out as she disappeared down the hall.

"Whatever."

He set his mug down and drew his hair back, securing it in the traditional Guardsman's woven clasp. He experienced a sudden and powerful need to get the hell out of Lebanon.

He didn't like being away from Grochaire for any length of time. All his responsibilities were there, his commitments, his devotion. He would never understand the ex-pat mentality of those like Batya who turned their backs on the realm-world. And knowing the level of her power, that she could create an enthrallment shield strong enough to keep an ancient fae and uber-powerful wraith-pairs from busting through, meant that she could have been useful to their ongoing war against the Invictus.

Still, there was a story there and he liked enough about Batya to want to hear what she had to say to justify her decisions. Generally, as closed-minded as he was about ex-pats, he wrote them off.

But Batya broke the mold. She wasn't into earth-based drugs, looking for a fix as many ex-pats were. She used her abilities for good and looked after the realm-community in Lebanon, she volunteered her powers, and she had a thriving business.

But what could have driven her out of Grochaire?

* * * * * * * * *

Batya didn't go immediately to the oversized kitchen and dining area of her downstairs gallery rooms. Instead, she paused about ten feet down the hall and put a hand to her chest.

She realized suddenly that she felt oddly fatigued this afternoon and more than once her heart seemed to labor in her chest.

Maybe she was getting some weird version of a human virus, something that happened occasionally in her community, though rarely for her. She had a superb constitution, otherwise, and came from extremely long-lived stock. Her father was over two-thousand-years old, a famous troll in the Nine Realms, so she was a little surprised that she wasn't in top form.

Of course, she hadn't exactly gotten a lot of sleep over the past two nights and she'd donated quite a bit of blood to bring Quinlan back from the brink.

At least she wouldn't be taking her usual appointments. As soon as Quinlan had been out of danger, she'd contacted their sister clinic across town. She'd told the administrator about her supposed 'burglary', unwilling to upset her community until she better understood what needed to happen next. She could bring people in by extending her enthrallment shield, so food wouldn't be an issue.

Lorelei, on the other hand, was strangely calm about all that was happening, which somehow didn't seem right to Batya, as though Lorelei knew something she wasn't sharing.

But as her heart continued to beat erratically, she tried to sort things out, to determine what if anything she could do about the ancient fae and the danger she presented.

Yet, as she rubbed her chest in a slow circle, she knew another kind of danger had invaded her gallery and it stood about six-six, had the body of a god, and smelled so incredible that the whole time she'd been brushing Quinlan's hair, she'd wanted to sink her face in the mass, burrow through, then bite the back of his neck.

He just smelled so damn good, like wood smoke. Yes, that was what he smelled like, the burning of a rich bonfire.

She knew the rumors about his early life, that he'd killed his father. The Sidhe Council had exonerated him all those centuries ago, but the story still circulated and gave her pause. Quinlan had a darkness within, an almost tangible quality, maybe as a result of what he'd done, she didn't know. She also didn't know if she could trust him.

The level of attraction she felt for Quinlan mystified her. She'd known him since she could remember, but something must have changed recently to have brought him chasing her skirts. And why was the sudden attraction so mutual?

But if she was honest with herself, she'd always been drawn to him like most of the women she knew. However, until he'd begun this ridiculous pursuit, wanting to bed her, she'd always supposed her interest in him had its source in his obvious physical prowess. The man was built, gorgeous, and carried a kind of deadly air that got to her. If he became determined, she wouldn't be able to fight him off, a thought that sent a shiver down her back and tightened things very deep.

Now, however, that she'd brought him back from the dead, shared a brief but lovely orgasm with him, and actually brushed out his really magnificent hair, she felt more in danger from him than ever before. He had the capacity to strip something vital from her, from her life, from her self-purpose as a troll-fae and as an ex-pat.

Quinlan threatened her way of life and he had to go, the sooner the better.

* * * * * * * *

His temper on full throttle, Quinlan entered the dining room and glanced around the rectangular space. Batya sat with her back to the far wall at a long table decked with ten upholstered chairs in a dark purple fabric. She looked so serene, as she stared back at him, as though the joke she'd played didn't exist at all. The clothes he'd been given to wear put a thunder cloud over his head, and he let the full range of his emotion fill his eyes as he glared at her.

She met his gaze and quickly pressed her lips into a tight line, no doubt biting the inside of her cheek.

She swallowed hard and with false admiration said, "How well that shirt becomes you. Do the pants fit?" Her gaze dropped to the cuffs that landed about six inches off the floor. "Oh, well, you are tall, but I see the tie I left you is holding them up."

The white silk shirt had been made for a man of ample proportions who had a preference for red sequins patterned in a series of red rose buds. Oddly, the cut fit across the shoulders but from there the fabric ballooned out to a grotesque size.

Lorelei frowned at Batya and clucked her tongue. "How could you do that to him?" She turned her soft brown eyes on Quinlan. "That's part of a Mardis Gras costume. I laid out a perfectly reasonable t-shirt and I can get it for you, if you want." She even offered Batya a disapproving shake of her head.

"No," he said, feeling stubborn, eyeing Batya once more. "This will do nicely."

Batya pathed, *Sure you don't want the tee because that deep voice of yours has an edge.*

I'll give you an edge.

Batya sipped her coffee and met his gaze over the rim. *Promises, promises.* She gestured for him to take the seat at the head of the table.

He growled softly in what he hoped sounded menacing. Lorelei's eyes widened but Batya laughed. He experienced a sudden, strong desire to teach her that whoever she thought she was in this absurd little world of hers in Lebanon, he was the Mastyr of Grochaire Realm and could take her apart if he wanted to.

When he sat down, however, a strange odor met his nose. He looked around first, wondering where it was coming from, maybe something rotting in the basement, then realized that it came from a soupy-looking bowl of what had to be an attempt at scrambled eggs.

Sweet Goddess, was this his meal?

He met Batya's gaze but she stared back as though not understanding, daring him, probably. "Lorelei was kind enough to cook for us."

He glanced at Lorelei. A flame of pink suddenly covered her cheeks. He took the ladle and scooped the eggs onto his plate. Seasonings floated in the lumpy, watery mixture. His nose twitched.

Using his fork, he took a bite and only with the strongest effort stopped from spitting it out.

Batya's voice pierced his head as she pathed, *I should have warned you. Lorelei isn't the best cook, but she tries very hard.*

Okay.

She ladled out her own eggs, took a bite and washed it down with a swift gulp of coffee. He should have brought his mug with him.

If you intend to eat this, I'll follow your lead.

It'll be a kindness. Lorelei has issues.

Got it.

That's when he noticed that Batya's color was high, almost feverish. Was she ill?

Are you all right?

Her gaze shot to his. *Why do you ask?* She even frowned slightly.

Your coloring. You don't look so good.

I'm fine.

A little too hasty, Cha.

We're being rude to Lorelei, conversing like this in front of her. And by the way, she may be a gentle spirit but she's got some power I haven't yet figured out.

He glanced at the ex-pat, who also pushed her eggs around on her plate.

Lorelei lifted her gaze to his. "It's okay. You can keep pathing with each other. I don't mind and I'm sorry about these blasted eggs. How about I make some toast?" She rose as she spoke, grabbing up the bowl before either of them could protest. "I'll cut up some apples and cheese as well. I don't think I can screw those up too badly." Her smile faltered.

"Thank you," he said.

When she left the room, his gaze followed her. Something wasn't right about Lorelei, beyond her 'issues', but he couldn't quite figure out what bugged him about the woman. She was tall like Batya, almost the same height, maybe an inch shorter.

She had beautiful dark brown hair, layered past her shoulders. Her brown eyes had a large fae look, yet she wasn't fae, though Quinlan had no idea how he even knew that.

"What is it?"

"What species is Lorelei?" he asked quietly.

Batya shrugged. "I think she's part fae, but I never asked. It's a rule in the ex-pat community here. You can volunteer all the information you want, but no one is going to interrogate you about why you're here, where you've come from, or what you might have done that brought you to the States."

He grunted. He had issues with the existence of an ex-patriot community period, but he ignored his disapproval and stuck to his current curiosity. "The thing is, I can always tell a realm-folk's lineage. Like with you, I sense fae and troll, although somewhere in your DNA is a small piece of witch. I get that big-time."

"Witch. You are so funny," she said sarcastically, shaking her head. "I'm just dying of laughter." The concept of 'witch' belonged only in fables, although some of the more powerful fae did work with potions and spells.

But the response pleased Quinlan. "Just tell me I'm right. Fae and troll."

"You're right, but that's common knowledge. Everyone knows who my father is."

He tapped his fingers on the table and shook his head. "I can always tell. It's one of my powers, I can identify the species in anyone, but not Lorelei."

At that, Batya leaned back in her chair. "What the hell does that mean?"

"I don't know, only that whatever realm species she is, she's hiding it from the rest of the world. Take that one step further and it means she also has the power to hide it. So, what exactly has she shared with you about who she is? Anything?"

She shifted her gaze to the chair that Lorelei had just vacated, then frowned. "You know, Lorelei and I chat all the time, but we've never talked about the past, not specifically, only that she said she grew up in the mountains, but not which mountains."

"And we have at least five realms with big mountains."

"Exactly, including Grochaire, but you and I would have known her, or at least of her, if she'd grown up in your realm."

He nodded. "You're right about that." He searched Batya's eyes. "And you were never curious?"

"Oh, I wanted to ask. Remember, I'm part troll so it's often hard to control the gossip-loving bent to my genetics, but it is one of my rules, so I stick by it."

He nodded slowly, trying to make her out. He still didn't know what could have driven her out of Grochaire. She had an excellent father as well, a revered troll considered by many to be a sage. Another mystery. But he respected that she stuck by her rules.

"We have ex-pats from all Nine Realms here. Did you know that the three eastern tribes have even worse problems than Grochaire?"

"Yes, I know."

"You would do well to take some time to talk to our people here."

"You seem to have built a community around your gallery."

She shook her head. "It's the free-clinic. We have a big drug problem here, homelessness, lots of stuff to deal with. Which I must say is part of my beef with you and Grochaire"

"You're going to blame our realm for drug-addiction?"

"No, I didn't mean that. I mean that we all aren't like you. We all don't just fit in. You've had your role laid out for you in Grochaire and you seem really happy about it like it suits you perfectly."

"It does."

"Then why are you scowling?"

"Because I dislike what you represent here."

"So the truth comes out. Yet, you've been seducing me, so what does that say about you?"

His smile quirked. "That I like beautiful women."

She rolled her eyes, not buying it, so he grabbed her hand. "And I like you. I may not approve of your life choices, but I approve of you, how you conduct yourself."

She batted her eyelashes. "How you flatter me."

Rather than putting him off, her un-impressed response struck a chord, that she wasn't the least moved by his rank in the Nine Realms, or his power, or anything else. If he wanted to win her, he'd actually have to make an effort and that was new to him. Besides, he loved a challenge, maybe more than anything, and Batya had challenge written all over her.

So, what would impress her?

He looked away from her and crossed his arms over his chest. He didn't need an answer to that question. Batya couldn't be anything important in his life and finding a way to gain her respect and approval had no meaning for him. All he'd wanted before the attack was to take her to bed a few times and slake his lust.

After that, he would have moved on to his next conquest, but here he was sitting at a table next to her, wearing a mardis-gras shirt and saying provocative things to her.

When Lorelei returned with a fresh pot of coffee, mugs, and a heaping platter of chunks of cheese and fruit, he breathed a sigh of relief. She whisked away their plates of now-congealing eggs, then poured out more coffee

"Sorry, but I burned the toast."

He repressed his laughter. "This will do nicely and thank you."

Curious all over again, he focused his identifying ability on her, even adding a slight vibration, but he got nothing in response. For a split-second Lorelei paused in pouring Batya's coffee, as though she knew what he was doing, but continued without so much as a flick of her doe-eyes in his direction.

He still had no clue what she was.

Just as he bit into a slice of red apple, a strange, very realm, sensation crept over him, something he'd experienced only a few times in his life. Fate lingered at this table, hovering over the platter, the coffee, and three unlikely people. They were meant to be here tonight, like this, the three of them.

Mentally, he uttered a string of curses, one after the other.

This wasn't good.

* * * * * * * * *

Before Batya had finished half her coffee, she received a phone call from the jack-of-all trades service she used that had done initial clean-up and now returned ready to install the plate glass window that had already been delivered. She excused herself and while keeping her enthrallment shield strong but manipulating one section, she let them in the back door, something Batya could do at will.

They were three powerful shifters, working in demolition, clean-up, and repair work and seemed well-suited to the work.

None were as tall as Quinlan who made a show of standing at the doorway between the hall and the dining room, arms folded over his chest in part probably to hide the sequins, and nodding to the men as they passed by. He eyed them closely, his lips compressed in a hard line.

"Mastyr." Each offered a half-bow as he moved by.

When the last worker disappeared into her gallery, she glared at him. "Would you lighten up?"

His upper lip curled as he turned back into the dining room.

She rolled her eyes wondering just how soon she could get rid of him and get on with her life. Reality, however, seemed to indicate she'd be stuck with him for a while. For one thing, she couldn't let her enthrallment shield down completely without inviting another attack and for another, if the ancient fae was really after her, then what was she going to do long-term? She couldn't sustain her gallery or the free-clinic with a shield intact and she really wasn't sure just how long she'd be able to support it. She felt fine now, but what about in another twenty-four hours or even a week?

Besides, she didn't feel like herself. Even Quinlan had picked up on her complexion. She felt overheated in a way that spoke of 'virus', but she'd always been so healthy.

As the shifters went about their business, Batya took some time to assess the damage to several of her canvases. One of them, a more modern piece made up of an island of trees and a flame-like wind, would have to be tossed. At least three would require repair and might even sell better among the wealthier ex-pat customers because of the provenance of having been involved in a battle between Mastyr Quinlan, two extraordinarily powerful Invictus wraith-pairs and an ancient fae.

The rest, especially a series of four along the brick north wall, were untouched. She glanced at them now and felt a shiver go through her, of fate or some kind of fae-recognition unfamiliar to her. The first was called, *The Leap*, a picture of a lovely fae woman, looking a lot like Lorelei, who stood on a precipice, the wind whipping her hair wildly. Her expression of uncertainty yet excitement had prompted many gallery conversations.

The second was a meadow with a river and a stream, the third a golden forest that rose high into a mountain range, and the last a painting she called, 'Snowfields', depicting a vast stretch of snow, distant lavender hills, and the sun barely cresting the horizon. Just looking at all four paintings brought something from her realm-soul rising to the surface and tears rushing to her eyes.

"I saw these." Quinlan's voice rumbled next to her. She jumped a little, because she hadn't known he was there, but he put a hand on her shoulder and murmured an apology. His gaze remained fixed, however, on the paintings.

"You mean when you first came into the gallery about two months ago?"

"No, I mean when both wraith-pairs attacked in unison with that final blow and sent me through the window. I saw these paintings in slow-motion, one after the other. These feel like some kind of story to me."

She glanced up at him. "I know what you mean."

"So you didn't write it as a story?"

She shook her head. "Not at all, and I didn't paint them in this order, but this sequence just feels inexplicably right to me."

"Was this a vision then?"

She shook her head, looking back at the paintings. "No, no vision. Images, like I told you before. I've had dozens of offers, mostly for them as a set. But I won't sell. I can't explain it but they mean something to me."

"I'm tempted to make you an offer myself. I'd put them in my mountain home." Most of the mastyrs had more than one home for security reasons.

"Really?" She pivoted toward him slightly. "You are a complete enigma to me."

His smile curved on one side, something she'd begun to associate with him. "You think that because I'm a Guardsman, and I battle the Invictus for a living, that I couldn't appreciate fine art?"

"I guess that's a bit of a stereotype."

"Yes, it is."

"Huh." He was so damn handsome and she loved that he could meet her gaze and not look away. She knew she had something of a dominating presence and frequently the men she met couldn't always look her in the eye.

Quinlan had no such problem, another reason *he* was a dilemma for her.

She was about to turn away, to shift her attention anywhere but at him, when a familiar and oh-so-welcome voice ran the length of her gallery.

"What happened here, most beloved daughter of mine?"

"Papa," she called out, whirling.

Davido stood at the top of the room, near the entrance to the back hall, his arms wide, waiting for an embrace. He was an ancient troll and had more power than Batya would ever understand that he could have passed through her enthrallment shield so easily.

She crossed the gallery quickly, and though she stood several inches taller and had to lean down to hug him, somehow she felt like the little girl he'd loved and raised all those centuries ago.

He didn't release her but looked at her with strong affection glowing in his light blue eyes. "How is my favorite one, my most beloved of all?"

She giggled. She must have lost at least a century of her real-age hearing that comment. "Papa, you say that to all of us." Because he was over two thousand years old, Davido had several dozen children, grand-children, and innumerable 'greats'. But he loved his offspring more than life itself and it showed.

"My sweet love, I feel that way about all of you, so why shouldn't I be able to say each is the most beloved? And how could I feel anything less?"

"It makes no sense." She grinned so hard, her cheeks hurt. She hadn't seen him since Bernice's birth nine months ago. "And how is your new most-favorite daughter?"

"Beyond splendid, growing into her third little baby troll ridge. But how are you, my darling dove?"

She rose up and quickly looked around. "Papa, how did you get past my enthrallment shield?"

He chuckled. "I closed my eyes."

She shook her head at his dismissive response. However, she now feared that the ancient fae could do the same. "I just need to know if we're at risk from the enemy. We're holding a very powerful woman at bay with my shield. If you could get in, maybe she could as well."

"Trust me, daughter, you have nothing to fear. Your shield will do its job."

As secretive as he was, he rarely answered questions pertaining to any of his powers. So, from long experience she chose to trust him and let the subject drop. "Fine. I don't care how you got in, but

I'm so glad you're here. You know Mastyr Quinlan, of course." She gestured with a sweep of her hand toward him.

Davido pretended to block a strong light by holding up his hand. "Is that Quinlan? I thought it might be a bonfire. What the deuce are you wearing, my good man?"

"What your daughter provided for me."

Batya didn't know why it was that Quinlan's voice always surprised her. Davido had an excellent resonant voice, a nice baritone. But Quinlan's timbre sank into the deepest registers, which in turn affected the ability of her knees to hold her upright.

Davido lifted his brows and met Batya's gaze. "Indeed? You gave him this shirt?"

Batya smiled. "As you know, Quinlan can be very provoking. He'd had his clothes burned off in the battle, you know." She then told him about the attack.

"Ah. Vojalie is so wise. She'd been troubled for days, insisting that I come to you, that something terrible was afoot. And now we have Quinlan wearing a clown's costume, workmen replacing your plate glass window, and you having created a very fine and exquisitely powerful enthrallment shield. I'm most impressed, daughter."

Batya wasn't fooled by her father's light tone since the three ridges of his forehead had become compressed—a sure sign that he didn't like the current situation at all.

"But come," he added. "I'd like to go elsewhere so that your workmen can finish their job, I can enjoy a cup of tea, and you can tell me in greater detail exactly what happened." He glanced at Quinlan. "Both of you. My talented wife insisted that each rendition of events would be important."

"Of course," Quinlan returned.

Davido sounded so serious that a new shiver went through Batya. Some part of her must have been blocking all that had transpired until she could assimilate what the recent attack might mean for the future.

She knew one thing for certain, she was not going to like what her father had to say.

* * * * * * * *

Quinlan stunned Batya by telling her he would make the tea. One of his reasons was very selfish, however, since he couldn't bear the thought of Lorelei preparing anything else. He felt certain she'd add too many bags or not enough, or something.

Of course the real reason was much closer to his sense of self-preservation. He wanted time to think.

If he'd been bothered before by what seemed an impossible situation, Davido's sudden presence, urged by his wife, one of the most powerful fae in the Nine Realms, cemented the idea that the recent attack and continued surveillance had huge realm implications.

Not that his thoughts had been much different, since the sheer size and power of the radical mastyr vampire wraith-pairs told him that a new threat had entered the war.

But when visionary elements intruded, like Vojalie's, brought here by one of the most enigmatic and powerful trolls in his world, Quinlan's heart had turned to stone and started sinking.

Sweet Goddess, what was going on here?

He took his time making the tea, then finally carried the tray into the sitting room adjacent to the dining room. Batya, he'd come to discover, owned the entire building.

Davido stood with her next to a large north-facing window that overlooked a small enclosed patio garden. They were discussing weather control options and planting some specialty roses that would bloom all winter for her.

Davido was a renowned gardener.

He set the tray on the coffee table, the sound serving as a call to tea since both turned and headed in his direction. Father and daughter kept talking while Batya took charge of the teapot and poured out three cups through a strainer.

As Batya and Davido sipped their tea, Quinlan told his side of things in as much detail as he could recall.

Since he remained standing, his audience looked up at him while he spoke.

"Could you see her face?" Davido asked.

"No. Just a powerful glow but I could smell her, like something that had been rotting for a long time. I remember the smell from Sweet Gorge."

"Sounds like an herbalist of some kind," Davido remarked. "And the quality of her smell might be an effect she created on purpose, like a dramatist. After all, a pleasant fragrance wouldn't incite fear, would it?"

"No. But what's her game? What does she want with your daughter?"

Davido's brows rose, which in turn deepened the lines between his three forehead ridges, typical troll features. "Nothing. She wasn't here for Batya. Vojalie was very clear about that."

"You're mistaken, Davido, or your wife is. I can remember the ancient fae stating, 'He wasn't supposed to be here', meaning me."

"Then we have a mystery." Davido sipped his tea.

"Did Vojalie say anything else, some detail you might have forgotten?"

"No, that was it. Wait, there was one more, small thing, but it didn't exactly make sense. Maybe it will to the two of you. She said, 'speak to the siren'. But what could that mean? Were the police here?"

"'The siren'? Are you sure?" The stone in Quinlan's heart sank farther still because he thought he understood, which meant that Batya wasn't the object after all.

"No," Batya murmured, shaking her head. "No, no, no."

"What's going on, my children?" He looked from one to the other.

At that moment, Lorelei appeared in the doorway, only she wasn't walking, her soft brown eyes were now almost lavender in color but darker, her limbs had lengthened and thinned, and she now wore a long flowing black gown made up of gauzy strips of fabric. She floated several inches above the floor. "Your wife meant me. I'm what the ancient fae wants. I'm what she's after. I've hidden all these decades, but she's finally found me. I just don't know how and I don't know what to do."

"Lorelei." Batya's large hazel eyes widened. "You're a wraith. But that's impossible."

Chapter Three

Batya knew she stared at a wraith, but she couldn't believe her eyes, couldn't believe that sweet Lorelei was a wraith. On the other hand, given that so many wraiths had chosen to become Invictus pairs, she wasn't surprised that the woman hid the truth of her DNA.

Yet not all wraiths were bad. She knew that a large portion of the wraith population had long ago either gone into hiding or now lived on an island colony off one of the eastern realms.

Whatever the truth about the location of the wraith community, Batya had been living side-by-side with one all this time. Unbelievable.

In her wraith form, Lorelei's skin was the color of chalk, her lips a dark hue, the whites of her eyes pale yellow, and her irises violet. Her long hair floated around her as though moving underwater, almost weightless.

She drifted slowly into the room.

Batya's cup had frozen halfway between her mouth and the saucer she held in her left hand. Two other cups hung midair as well.

"You really are a wraith." Batya still couldn't believe her eyes.

"Part of me is." Lorelei frowned, a pained expression crossing her face. Then suddenly, the wraith became a blur, transforming into a lean white wolf that leaped high in the air, landing on the coffee table to snarl in Batya's face.

The tea tray and pot slid over the edge, clattering to the carpet below.

Lorelei howled.

Batya dropped her teacup and saucer and covered her ears, not because the sound hurt but because the emotion behind the plaintive cry pierced her heart. She felt Lorelei's pain, an old wound fitting for a wolf's howl. Batya wept because of the pain.

She didn't know what to do. She squeezed her eyes shut and shook her head back-and-forth. She needed the sound to stop.

Suddenly, it did.

She opened her eyes, and saw the cause. Her father had embraced the wolf, from the side, softly around the neck and spoke into Lorelei's ear.

Batya recognized the cadence of the old language. Davido had used it to calm her more than once when she was a child.

When Davido drew back, releasing the wolf, Lorelei whirled through another transformation, resuming her fae form. She sank down into a chair across from the table, her feet turned in like a child as she shaded her face with her hands.

She'd finally unveiled her secret, but Batya still didn't understand. "You can shift, but you're a wraith?"

Lorelei nodded.

"Yet you're also fae."

"Yes. My mother was…is…fae and wraith. I carry all three strains."

"That's not possible." Quinlan, still standing, flared his nostrils. "No such thing exists in our world. You can't exist. The wraith gene can't exist with more than one other strain."

Lorelei chuckled bitterly. "And yet, I do. A product of extensive experimentation."

"How old are you, child?" Davido remained nearby.

"Ninety."

"And who is your mother, though I believe I already know."

Lorelei lifted her gaze to Davido. "Do you? I've always wondered if you or Vojalie or some of the mastyrs had ever known her."

"Yes, I knew her but she disappeared from the realm world for several centuries. Now it would seem she has decided to make a reappearance. And for your sake, I've very sorry my dear."

"Who are we talking about?" Batya glanced from one to the other, but got a sick feeling in her stomach as though her body already knew what her mind did not want to accept.

"Fuck." Still standing, Quinlan set his cup on the table and turned his back to Lorelei. He shoved his hands through his hair, dislodging the woven clasp.

The sick feeling worsened. Batya turned back to Lorelei and held her gaze. "Who's your mother?"

"Quinlan knows. So does your father. Can't you guess?" Tears now rolled down her cheeks.

Batya once more shook her head over and over. "It can't be."

"Her name is Margetta, the ancient fae, the one who smells of a land fill, the one who enlisted Mastyr Ry, turning him against

Bergisson Realm, who caused all that misery at Sweet Gorge six months ago."

Davido drew close once more, standing behind her. He petted her head with his short, thick fingers. "My dear, you are among friends."

"Am I? But for how long? And where will I go now? I was so happy here." She glanced up at Batya, tears glistening on her long lashes.

Lorelei then stood, shook out her hands and straightened her shoulders. Drawing in a deep breath, she blew it out slowly. "Not your problem. I know that. If I leave, Margetta will not bother any of you again. I'm the one she wants. I'll pack up now."

Batya rose to her feet as well. "Well, eff that, Lorelei. You're not leaving, so don't even think about it. We're family here."

Davido nodded, an approving light in his eye as he met Batya's gaze. "Listen to my most beloved daughter. She speaks the truth from her heart. You have a home here."

Lorelei glanced from him to Batya. She nodded several times but kept her lips pinched tightly together. "Thank you. I don't know what to say."

Quinlan, whose hair now hung about his shoulders, scowled at Lorelei. "Help us to understand what's going on here. Is she behind the Invictus?"

"She and my father, yes. You've probably heard him called the Great Mastyr, he is both vampire and shifter."

"Sweet Goddess. Then you are vampire as well. Why didn't you tell us that?"

She shrugged. "Because I'm a disappointment to my father. My vampire genetics are the weakest part of who I am. 'Negligible' is the word he used. I believe they've been searching for the right mate for me, that because I'm also part wraith, I'd be able to form an incredibly powerful Invictus pair."

"This is insane."

"Yes, it is. Papa considers himself to be a scientist but my mother carries the ambition in the family, though she's happy to use my father's abilities. Margetta wants to rule the Nine Realms. She has desired nothing else for the past thousand years."

Batya's mind spun, question after question rolling through like leaves swept along by a brisk wind.

Lorelei met her gaze. "Maybe, if I told this from the beginning."

Quinlan sat down on the couch and Davido moved behind Lorelei to sit in the chair next to her. Batya picked up the teapot and tray, as well as the cup and saucer she'd dropped, putting them back on the coffee table. She sat down at the opposite end of the couch from Quinlan as Lorelei slowly resumed her seat.

Over the past two years, since Lorelei had served in the clinic, Batya had imagined several scenarios to explain who the woman was, even a past that involved Lorelei being a professional, high-end thief in one of the Nine Realms and that she'd moved to Lebanon to escape capture.

Never in her wildest imagination could she have pictured that the delicate woman opposite her, teardrops brimming once more in her eyes, was the product of gross genetic manipulation and the union of a shifter-vampire and a fae-wraith.

"Excuse me if I stare at you."

"I understand." She settled back in her chair. "I suppose for you to understand how I ended up here, I need to tell you about Genevieve." She spoke of her troll governess that Margetta had kidnapped to serve Lorelei over sixty years ago, forcing the woman to school Lorelei until she was eighteen.

Margetta had erred, however, because the woman had been the salt of the realm-world and had imbued Lorelei with the values she held so close to her heart, of love and personal liberty, of realm-service, of kindness to strangers, all good things.

At the very moment that Margetta had come to take her daughter out of the mountain prison and put her to work in the family business of scientific evolution and Invictus pair creation, Genevieve had concocted a plan to escape with Lorelei.

All had gone well until Margetta arrived just a few minutes early, and Genevieve had died helping her charge make good her escape. "I didn't know until I was well away, hidden by the disguise I could create, that she'd sacrificed her life for me." She shook her head as though, even after all these years, she still couldn't believe what happened.

"Where did you go?" Quinlan asked.

She smiled and glanced at Davido. "I lived in Merhaine for a long time, in Vojalie's shadow. I was a troll servant in your home for twelve years from 1952 until 1964. I think you might have recognized me when you saw me in the doorway."

"Of course I did. You called yourself Jenny."

"I did, after the one who had saved my soul, altering my life forever. Did you know what I was?"

Davido shook his head. "No. Only that you were special, but even I couldn't figure out what you were. I was intensely curious, of course, but Vojalie-the-wise told me to mind my own business and to let you be, that you needed to find your own way through life."

"Your wife is one of the best women I've ever known."

"Except perhaps for my beloved Batya's mama, I would have to agree with you."

Davido smiled sweetly at Batya. Her mother had died in childbirth, a rare occurrence in the Nine Realms.

Shifting his attention back to Lorelei, he said, "Then Margetta must have found you there. In our home."

"Yes. Do you remember the night that you lost all those cucumbers to an inexplicable frost?"

"I do." He leaned back in his chair, stunned. "And here is a mystery solved. Amazing. Eighty years later, I finally have the answer to the strange phenomenon that destroyed only the cucumbers."

"I battled Margetta then fled. After that, I never lived longer than a year or so in any one town except Lebanon. I don't know what it is, how she can find me, but I must emit some kind of signature that Margetta eventually locates, despite all my disguises and shields.

"After the first year passed in Lebanon, I thought maybe the earth-world would be my salvation. You can't imagine how happy I was when I marked my second anniversary."

"Oh, my poor child. If only you'd approached me or Vojalie. We could have done something for you."

She smiled and extended her hand to him. "Knowing you both was enough."

"Jenny," he murmured. He took her hand, covering it with both of his own.

"It's good to see you again, Davido. Truly."

"Where did you go after Merhaine?"

She detailed much of her wandering life, from realm-to-realm, which meant that she knew a lot about all nine realms, more than most realm-folk would ever know.

"So now I'm here." Her gaze shifted to Quinlan. "I'm so sorry, Mastyr, that I brought Margetta here and that you suffered."

His brows drew together as he stared at her. "You are not responsible for the evil either of your parents inflicts on the world. You are as much a victim here as I was of the recent attack. Now all we need to decide is what needs to happen next."

Lorelei slowly rose to her feet. "Please don't worry about that. I know what to do, then you can get back to business as usual."

She turned as if to leave the room, but Davido met Batya's gaze and gestured with his widening hands. *You can't let her go. This must stop now.*

"Wait," Batya said. "We won't let you leave."

When Lorelei got to the doorway, she turned and blew them all a kiss, shifting afterward to her wraith form and sped away, floating swiftly through the air.

Batya's entire being stiffened with sudden, powerful resolve. She tightened the enthrallment shield as she never had before.

At the same time, she followed after Lorelei and found her in her bedroom punching at the shield with energy blasts from her palms. "Let me out," she shrieked, sounding more wraith-like than Batya would have ever thought possible.

"I can't let you go," Batya said, moving into the room. She knew both Quinlan and her father had followed her. She held the enthrallment shield with an iron grip, the value of a strong will in times of preternatural exchange.

Lorelei floated in the air, her hair weaving madly back and forth, her long black gown floating around thin spindly wraith-legs. "Let me go, Batya. You've done enough, given enough."

"No, I haven't. You're my friend. I don't desert my friends. Let me help you. We all want to help and we can. There's a helluva lot of power in this room right now."

For the next few minutes Lorelei pounded hard on Batya's shield and a couple of times Batya flagged, but either Davido or Quinlan put his hand on her shoulder and revived her.

In the end, exhausted, Lorelei resumed her fae shape and slumped to sit down on the floor. She fell apart at that moment and wept.

Batya would have gone to her, but Davido was before her. He gathered Lorelei up in his arms and jerked his chin at Batya. She took the hint and left the room with Quinlan.

She made her way slowly upstairs to her studio and crossed to look out the window. On the other side of the street, Margetta's spy leaned against the opposing brick wall, puffing away on a cigarette with a pile of butts scattered around her feet.

Night had fallen.

She glanced back at Quinlan. "Didn't you used to smoke?"

"Why do you ask?"

"I remember you always had a cigarette in your hand. Our friend down there smokes like crazy."

"Gave it up. My *doneuses* didn't like it so they ganged up on me about it."

She laughed, then took in the absurd shirt and went to her closet. She pulled out the long-sleeved, black ribbed tee she'd chosen earlier from the stockpile the free-clinic kept on hand, and which she knew would fit him, then tossed it his direction. "Can't have you battling with that on."

He smiled and shrugged out of his shirt.

Rather than watch him disrobe and endure temptation all over again, Batya went back to the window to stare down at the spy once more. She worked to assimilate all these new, extraordinary things, from Lorelei's strange DNA, to her immense power, and finally to the horror of the woman's parentage.

"Monuments should be built in honor of women like Genevieve."

Quinlan joined her by the window. "I couldn't agree more."

"She gave up her life for Lorelei."

Quinlan sighed heavily.

"What are you thinking?" She looked up at him, his scowl as dark as she'd ever seen it.

"That my life has been very small."

She snorted. "You've served Grochaire for how many centuries, without question? No, your life hasn't been small, Quinlan, and you lay it down every damn night."

"It doesn't feel that way, not with the Invictus still operating in each of the realms. I should have done more, found a way to get rid of them once and for all."

She thought he expected too much of himself and would have said so, but Davido arrived holding Lorelei's hand.

"Lorelei thinks she knows where she can go next, a place she's been trying to find for a long time, where Margetta won't be able to touch her. Tell them."

"Ferrenden Peace. I believe it lies on the border between Grochaire Realm and Walvashorr."

Batya shook her head. "But that's a place from childhood fables. It doesn't exist. Tell her, papa."

Davido shrugged. "I have reason to believe it might and that it's been hidden behind an impenetrable wall of enthrallment, similar to your own, for a millennia. You can't even see it on the maps, the enthrallment is that good. Just remember that most myths have some basis in fact, in history."

Batya's lips curved. "And did you once visit this fabled place, papa, in a previous millennia, perhaps?"

"Shrewd, very shrewd, daughter, but I'm not saying."

Everyone tried to find out Davido's true age, but he'd worked hard to keep it a secret. Batya thought it possible that not even Vojalie knew just how old he was or even half of the things he'd experienced over the course of his long life.

Quinlan, now looking magnificent in the snug tee despite the too-short pants, drew close to Batya and touched the back of her arm. She thought she understood. They both felt it, the need to do this thing. Yet she knew he wished himself anywhere but here and she hated the thought of going back into the Nine Realms.

But here she was with a mastyr touching her supportively, her father's eyes expectant and glowing, and Lorelei struggling to control her emotions.

"We can get you there," Batya said.

Had she really spoken the words aloud, committing herself to this path? And what would it mean that she'd be traveling with Quinlan for who knew how long?

Lorelei's eyes brightened. "You can?"

"We can," Quinlan added, his voice rumbling around her studio, taking command of the space. "I just wish we had a map."

Davido snapped his fingers. "I'll be right back." He moved on quick troll feet, running from the room and down the stairs. Trolls had active, expressive feet.

Batya waited, her heart thudding in her chest. Was this to be her future, a journey with Quinlan, a vampire she'd been trying to get rid of for two months? He still held the back of her arm, his thumb rubbing up and down, more comforting than seductive, for once.

She might even have thanked him for his support, but Davido's steps sounded up the stairs once more and he all but ran into the room. He carried his satchel, a worn leather case to which he was profoundly attached and which none of his children had been able to replace despite multiple attempts.

"I have the most beautiful and the most visionary of wives." He lifted the side flap, pulling out an oversized, yellowed map. "She said I'd need this. It's very old and covers Grochaire and Walvashorr Realms, just the two. What do you think of that?"

"Vojalie has always amazed me."

* * * * * * * *

Quinlan released Batya's arm and reached for the parchment-like paper. "I don't think I've ever seen this one."

"Probably not. I had to search the storeroom of my library. It took me a full day before I found it, Vojalie having been exceedingly specific about which one to bring with me."

Quinlan's biceps flexed as he carefully unfolded the ancient document. He made his way to Batya's worktable, situated midway between the east wall and the foot of her bed.

Glancing over his shoulder at her, he waved a hand at the table. "Is the surface clean? I know you do a lot of your art here."

Batya frowned at him slightly, though he wasn't sure why. "Yes. Very clean."

"What is it? Did I offend you by asking?"

She shook her head. "No. It's just that, I've never seen you like this before. So … engaged."

He felt torn. He might have asked what she meant, but the map carried a vibration and he wanted to find out if he could actually locate the fabled Ferrenden Peace.

He had several hundred maps of Grochaire, made throughout the ages. He'd followed many of them through his realm over the centuries, climbing down hillsides that weren't supposed to be here or there. He'd found an old copper mine and later had it refitted and made safe.

Of course, other dark memories surfaced, that even as a child he would leave his house for days at a just to escape his father's brutality. But the hours he spent exploring Grochaire had helped make him the man he was today.

He loved maps and he loved his land.

He spread it out and asked Batya if she had something that might hold down each of the corners.

She returned with four pewter dragons, making quick work of securing the map to the table.

He leaned over it, smoothing his hands slowly across Grochaire as though bringing forth his physical memory of the contours of the land. He began at the ocean in the west, Maris Sol, to the sloping plain in the center and the Mountains of Ashur that bordered the access point to Walvashorr Realm.

A strange vibration met his palm when he covered the northeast area of Grochaire, which then ceased when he moved to the Walvashorr side. He repeated the process. His heart hammered in his chest because he knew that a section of Grochaire, his home realm, had been kept hidden from him his entire life.

"What is it?" Batya asked.

But Lorelei responded. "The enthrallment is there, at the point where Mastyr Quinlan slows the movement of his hand. I can feel it."

"I, as well," Davido added.

They all drew close, heads bent over the table, staring down at the map. Each pressed fingers over the area above the access point. Batya gasped. "The vibration is so strong."

"Yes, that's Ferrenden Peace and I know that Margetta wouldn't be able to reach me there. I would be safe, for once, behind that level of enthrallment."

Quinlan glanced at Lorelei, who now stood next to him. Her entire being radiated something he couldn't place at first, then finally realized that the woman felt hopeful, something she must not have experienced for a very long time. For that reason alone, he knew he had to accept this challenge. If only he could actually see the location on the map.

Batya stood opposite him, her long fingers continuing to drift over the hidden space. He glanced up at her. "You have similar enthrallment powers. What do you suggest? Is there a way we can break through and look at the terrain here?"

Davido drew close. "I think I know how it might be done."

Still leaning over the table, unwilling to move away from the map even a couple of inches, Quinlan shifted his gaze to the left and met the troll's glowing eyes. "How? Tell me. Whatever is it, I'll do it."

"Good." He even smiled. "I've always liked your spirit Quinlan. Always. Just thought you had too broad an eye for the ladies."

Quinlan's lips quirked.

At the same time, he picked up Batya's hand and laid it over Quinlan's. "This is the way. You touched my daughter's arm earlier, and I felt her power increase, not just doubling as might be expected, but a real flare of her fae ability. Didn't you feel it, either of you?"

Batya shook her head. "I was comforted, but I didn't notice a shift in my power."

Davido frowned, the three ridges of his forehead rippling slightly. "Odd. Well, perhaps it was because of your enthrallment shield."

"I saw the shield flare and brighten with a red hue," Lorelei offered.

"That's it," Davido said, lifting a finger in emphasis. He shifted back-and-forth sideways on his feet several times, a trollish sign of his excitement over what was happening.

Quinlan met Batya's gaze and for a split-second, because her hand touched his, all he felt was his need for her, a surprising response in the middle of staring at a map and trying to uncover a millennia-old mystery. But desire was what he felt, a hunger for what came from her neck and what he'd been pursuing for weeks now.

Was there more to his pursuit of her than he understood?

Her breathing hitched and her chest rose and fell.

He blinked, forcing his thoughts and his needs away. He focused instead on their joined hands. Taking her fingers in a light clasp, he lifted them above the map.

"Do your enthrallment thing here."

She nodded. He felt her focus hard on the map and on their joined hands. He saw the reddish hue light up the shield around the property, just as Lorelei had said, but all he felt from Batya was a soft humming sensation against his skin where their hands met.

But it was Lorelei who directed them. "Shift your hands to the right no more than an inch." He moved their joined hands slightly.

"There," Davido cried out. "I can see more of Grochaire. It's working."

"How do we sustain it," Batya asked, "so that we can all see?"

Davido tapped the top of Quinlan's hand. "I think your devotion to Grochaire might just do the trick. Use your other hand and caress the map, in the same way you've been doing, but while you do it have Batya cover that hand as well."

Quinlan didn't question the troll's suggestion. The Nine Realms had thousands of forms of magic, one of the things he loved about his world, one of the mysteries, something that changed with each succeeding generation.

When Batya covered his left hand with her right palm, he felt a cool vibration travel up his wrist, all the way up his arm to his shoulder. He focused on the map and in slow circles pressed his fingers over the newly created area. He could see the land unfolding before his eyes, the symbols for mountains, for streams, for caves, everything. The names stunned him, however, because they could be found in the age-old children's tales of the Nine Realms: the Great River Caverns of Pickerne, Gem Meadow, the Dead Forest that continued through the Pleach Mountains, and the Snowfields of Rayne. All on this map.

At the same time, he worked their joined hands east, pushing toward Walvashorr in small increments, until at last an entirely new section of map emerged, a bordered space called, of course, Ferrenden Peace.

Davido offered, "Vojalie said that once the location has been revealed, that you should contact Mastyr Seth."

Quinlan turned toward Davido. "Then you knew Ferrenden Peace would be revealed in this way?" His temper shot up a couple of notches as Davido shrugged. "Anything else, old man? Anything else you've got in your satchel or any other words from Vojalie-the-wise? Any more instructions? Should we call on the eastern mastyrs and involve them as well?"

"No need to get snippy, Mastyr Quinlan. I do as I'm bid and part of that means holding back until the moment is ripe."

Quinlan lost the rest of his patience. He lifted a brow, crossed his arms over his chest and waited.

"Oh, very well. Here is what my beloved wife told me. I'm sure she wouldn't object, especially if she knew her dearest husband was being threatened by a powerful vampire."

These taunting words slid right over Quinlan's thick skin. "Spill, troll, or I'm likely to turn you upside down."

At that, Davido, rather than being offended, laughed heartily. "I have not been troll-turned in a donkey's age. Ah well, but I can see your nostrils are flaring now." He glanced at Batya and Lorelei. "You must each pack several changes of clothing, sturdy footwear, and of course a toothbrush. Vojalie was not certain how long the journey would take."

Batya's brows rose. "These are very specific instructions."

"She also said you weren't to worry about warm clothing, that what you needed would be amply provided along the way."

"Warm clothing?" At that, Quinlan turned to the map again and once more caressed the new section. A new reality emerged, "Sweet Goddess, will you look at that."

"What?" three voices intoned.

"Do you see this section of the mountains?"

"Yes?" Three voices again.

"Two hundred years ago, I built a stronghold right here, right at the edge of the hidden section. Some part of me must have known."

"Did you feel a connection to the place?" Batya asked.

He met her gaze. "Only that I thought it rugged and magnificent." He glanced down at the map once more. "Holy shit."

Again, three voices, cried out. "What?"

He met and held Batya's gaze. "Your paintings, the ones you won't sell, I think you laid out the entire journey for us."

* * * * * * * *

Batya's flowered canvas satchel rested beside her right foot on the solid wood planks of her gallery floor. She stared at all four paintings and knew Quinlan had called it right. Each subject indicated some aspect of the places they'd have to go through to get to Ferrenden Peace. Traveling through the air, a meadow, a forest, and finally dense snowfields.

In the space of forty-eight hours, she'd gone from artist, gallery owner, and clinic healer to an adventurer trying to save a fellow realm-woman from enslavement, on a journey she'd painted years ago. Incredible.

Very realm.

Lorelei drew close and took Batya's hand. "Are you sure you want to do this?"

She met her friend's gaze, then smiled. "This is the right path."

"And you're happy about it?"

At that, Batya laughed, pivoting toward Lorelei. "Hell, no, but it's still the right path."

Lorelei's eyes grew bright in the way that Davido's did quite often. Still holding Batya's hand, she gave her fingers a squeeze. "Then, thank you." She swallowed hard and drew in a deep breath. "But there's something else you should know."

"Oh, sweet Goddess, there's more?"

Quinlan, having reached the bottom of the stairs and still barefoot, called out, "Are you two ready?"

"Almost." Batya stepped back so that he could see them both. "Apparently, Lorelei needs to share one more bit of news with us."

Quinlan's brows grew together in a tight, concerned frown, a familiar look for him. "What now?"

Davido moved up beside Quinlan. "It's probably about Margetta. Vojalie said we'd get one more surprise. Tell us, child."

"My mother will be here in a few minutes and she's bringing a powerful wind with her, as well as a few chosen wraith-pairs."

Batya turned to stare at her. "But how do you know that? A vision?"

"It's a mother-daughter thing, part of the reason she wants me under her control. I can, to a small degree, predict her movements."

Quinlan hurried toward them. "Then we'd better go."

Davido joined them, leaning up to kiss Batya on the cheek. "Farewell, daughter. We part here. I must return to Vojalie. We have a strict agreement about the first year of a child's life."

"I know. I love you, papa."

"And I you, my most precious, most beloved offspring."

"Hug Bernice for me."

"Of course I will." His gaze moved past her. "But I fear your visitor has arrived."

Batya glanced at the plate glass window and saw that a red wind flowed down the street. Margetta had arrived in a glow of golden light accompanied by a formidable array of wraith-pairs. She hovered beyond the window ready to attack surrounded by a thin enthrallment shield of her own making, which would in turn keep her Invictus brigade invisible to human eyes. The original mastyr vampire wraith-pairs flanked her.

She would have moved into action, but Davido gripped her elbow gently and pathed, "*Give Quinlan a chance. There's a mystery here with him that you must pursue and don't be afraid of Grochaire. But above all, remember the breadth of your heritage, that you are both troll and fae.*

Before she could say anything more, her father vanished. He rarely did that, which sent a shiver through Batya. Davido had so much power, which he kept hidden from everyone and rarely used. That he could get past her shield as well as the ancient fae still stunned her. She might have asked for his assistance, but Davido had come only to support her. She knew his realm philosophies well, that each must face up to his own challenges.

Batya must deal with the ancient fae, now also known to be part wraith.

The next second, the new plate glass shattered and the high shrieking sound of Invictus wraiths punched through the air. At the same time a severe wind blew into the gallery, through her enthrallment shield, gathering up all the paintings and easels and carrying them past Batya, Quinlan, and Lorelei.

As she turned in the direction of the window, the golden glow of light softened in increments and Batya could see Margetta. But the one she knew to be evil turned out to be very beautiful with a complexion as smooth as glass, a straight nose, wide-set eyes and the faintly pointed chin of the fae.

"Mother," Lorelei whispered quietly. "No."

Margetta shifted her violet eyes from Batya to Lorelei. Her gaze narrowed as though directing her thoughts, but Lorelei lifted her chin and looked away.

Cocking her head, Margetta turned her attention fully on Batya, and not just her gaze but the force of her will as well. Ambition ruled Margetta more than anything else, to where she planned to dominate the Nine Realms at all costs, including the subjugation of her daughter.

But like hell Batya would give in to Margetta without a fight.

On instinct, she drew the enthrallment away from the building perimeter and into a tight protective shield around the three of them. "Quinlan, we're ready to go." She picked up her satchel and threw her arm around his neck. Lorelei did the same overlapping Batya's arm. Quinlan gripped both waists.

"I have you both," he said. "But Lorelei, would you do better to shift into your wraith-form?"

"No, I'm at my weakest as a wraith, especially if I fly."

"Okay, then. Let's go."

Batya rarely flew with vampires, especially from the time she'd moved to Lebanon, so she wasn't exactly used to this kind of flight. But Quinlan had muscles on muscles and held both women securely against his side, maneuvering them swiftly up the stairs to a side window.

Releasing them for a moment, he jerked the large double sash out of the molding, then dove into the air. He returned swiftly to pull Batya from the building, then Lorelei.

"Margetta!" Batya shouted. The woman's gold light bloomed suddenly and her wind frequency struck hard, pressing them back against the brick just to the side of the window.

Batya pathed to Quinlan. *We've got to get out of here.*

* * * * * * * * *

Quinlan closed his eyes. He focused on his essential physical prowess and battling vibration. Gathering his warrior strength, he shunted Margetta's wind aside, but only for a few seconds. The wind returned stronger than ever, despite the fact that he pressed back with all his might. She'd created a formidable wind, something he'd never experienced before and it felt inexhaustible, the way Batya's shield felt, as though the ancient fae could sustain the hurricane indefinitely.

Batya, I can't hold against her. Can you add your own abilities? Your battle frequency? Most realm-folk carried all the known frequencies, to lesser or greater degrees.

I'm not sure. I'm not trained like you.

He met Batya's gaze and saw her fear, the untried nature of her latent abilities. *You can do this. I've felt your power. Just connect your battle frequency with mine. It's there. You know it is.*

She stared back, searching his gaze. His power shook now, barely holding against Margetta.

His voice rumbled once more through her mind. *You can do this.*

He felt her invitation to search her power and directed his frequency to dive within her.

She groaned as though his invasion hurt and maybe it did. She'd never opened her battle-frequency before. But when he found it, and tapped in, he felt a rush of energy flow out of her.

I don't know if the shield will hold now.

We'll soon find out.

Power flowed through him as never before. He let it engage his levitation abilities, and like a rocket he flew straight up, through the wind, angling to fly faster than ever toward Grochaire.

"Don't let up," He called to Batya. But she'd slumped against him, only half-conscious. Damn, he'd hurt her. He could feel it now, that she was in pain. But her battle-frequency flowed like a quick-running river.

Once at the access point, he called to the Guardsmen on duty, but nothing returned. Two seconds later, he saw why. Both men were dead, split apart, blood everywhere.

There was nothing to do but press on, knowing as he did that Margetta would follow after them.

The moment he crossed the plane-border to Grochaire, he turned in a northeasterly direction and added even more speed.

He felt Batya's growing exhaustion yet at the same time, he sensed Lorelei's excitement, like a dog kept in a kennel and suddenly allowed set free.

"Grochaire," she murmured. He heard awe in her voice.

He felt the same way. Love for his homeland pulsed within him, maybe enhanced by the ferocity of Batya's battle frequency, he didn't know. But he loved his land, his realm, his world.

Can't hold on, Batya's voice sounded faint.

I have you.

My satchel.

Lift it to my hand.

She raised her arm and with just a little shuffling, he grabbed the handle, while still holding her tight against him.

I can't sustain both frequencies, Quinlan. Which do you want me to keep going? Battle or enthrallment?

He thought for a moment, then decided it would better to have the increased flight speed so he chose to let her drop her shield. They were far enough into Grochaire that he knew their trail would have already grown cold to Margetta. It would be no simple thing for her to find them now.

When he told Batya that she could release her enthrallment, he felt her shield fade then vanish, but her battle frequency remained at full-bore which kept his power steady.

The immediate danger was now over and he finally breathed a sigh of relief.

He was damn proud of her. She'd come back to Grochaire, a place she'd never wanted to return, for reasons she had yet to tell him. He approved of her sacrifice, and her willingness to share her power to get them all safely to his stronghold in the Mountains of Ashur.

The last time he'd stayed at his heavily fortified dwelling had been three months ago.

Tonight and through the following daylight hours, he'd bed down with Batya, recoup his strength. His stomach had started cramping and he would need to feed. He wasn't surprised. He'd been using up a phenomenal amount of energy during this flight.

Grochaire was one of the larger realms, five hundred miles across the middle. The flight would take some time.

An hour came and went, then another.

Finally, the Ashur Mountains appeared in the distance and he rose higher and higher into the air, which in turn grew frigid. Lorelei began to shake.

"Can't be helped but we'll be there in just a few minutes. Hang on." Fortunately, Batya had passed out.

Three minutes later, he flew over a thick fir forest and saw the rooftops of the town of Ashland that bore at least a thousand realm families. His stronghold was only ten miles away.

He often brought his *doneuses* in from Ashland, though he hoped that tonight Batya would be willing to service him. His body heated up at the thought of taking from her neck. He drew in a couple of deep breaths to steady himself. "Not long now."

Lorelei's teeth chattered.

He pathed to his brigade leader, Henry. *Incoming, you old goat.*

Quinlan, you fuck of all fucks. You back? Where have you been? Rafe has been out of his mind because he couldn't contact you. Rafe was his second-in-command, in charge of his Grochaire brigade made up of vampire Guardsmen.

I'll contact him soon enough, but we've got a situation and we'll probably see some action in the next twenty-four hours, so put your Guard on alert. He gave a brief explanation of events in Lebanon without going into issues that related to either Lorelei or Batya, only that the ancient fae had attacked the gallery and that she'd slaughtered the Guardsmen at the access point.

Shit.

You said it. Now get the front gates open. I'm in flight with two powerful women. Have the housekeeper light up her enthrallment shield.

On the double.

Henry signed off and had no doubt already begun issuing a string of orders.

The next moment, the stronghold came into view, a massive timber and iron structure set against the mountain on a wide jut of land that dropped off steeply to a forest below. A narrow road allowed vehicles to drive to his gates, but he rarely had visitors. His stronghold served as an emergency refuge and a private retreat. He had two other homes in Grochaire that he used on a regular basis, one in the largest city of his realm, Chape Fawn Hills and the other at Bright Sea, on the western side of Grochaire.

The heavy, massive doors to his stronghold started to open as Quinlan made his descent. The thick, black wood, reinforced with iron, pushed piled-up snow out of the way.

He slowed down and entered the outer enclosed courtyard of his building. When he cleared the opening, he levitated above the stone pavers, pausing midair to turn and watch the gates close behind him. He knew he hadn't been followed, but it never hurt to catch a visual. If he needed to escape, he wanted to be in motion.

But they were alone, no one had followed them.

He adjusted his vampire vision as he dropped to the stone pavers of the courtyard.

At the same time that he touched down, the space began to fill with his highly trained and experienced troll brigade, who'd fought the Invictus wraith-pairs for decades now, making use of long spears in addition to battle frequency streams. They wore the typical Guardsmen uniform of long, leather sleeveless coats, leather pants and boots, and woven shirts. A thick belt angled over the chest ended in something new, sheaths for daggers.

As the entire brigade assembled, Henry flew in to stand in front of Quinlan.

Lorelei stepped away from him and stretched out her arms and rolled her shoulders. Batya was still unconscious, so he held her against him.

Henry frowned, however, his gaze moving from one woman to the next. He was as handsome as Davido was ugly. All realm-folk ranged on the full spectrum of beauty and Henry was known to bed a lot of women with very little effort. He also had a heavy dose of charisma, like Davido, a specialty among the more powerful trolls.

Slowly, Quinlan pulled out of Batya's battle frequency, but immediately his own energy faded and he had to work to keep from dropping her.

Henry, understanding the dilemma, grabbed Batya. But the moment he made contact, something came over Quinlan, a fierce protective compulsion so that his voice filled the courtyard. "Release her or die!"

Sweet Goddess! Had he just yelled at his brigade commander?

Henry let go of her, the three ridges of his forehead raised in tight, surprised folds.

"Leave her to me," he said quietly.

"Understood." But Henry's eyes narrowed as he looked at Batya. Finally, he said, "Your Guard is present mastyr, for your inspection."

He glanced around at the highly trained brigade, one hundred strong. He nodded his approval. Henry had one of the most disciplined brigades in the Nine Realms. "I want an around-the-clock watch set up for all areas of the stronghold and Guards posted outside the ladies' doors. Is that clear?"

"Yes, mastyr." Henry nodded to his unit leader, a tall troll, at nearly five-seven, by the name of Vincent.

A strong shout hit the air as Vincent ordered the brigade to fall out. Four Guardsmen remained in the courtyard, one to take up a post on a short flight of stairs to the left of the gates. He opened a viewing window and peered outside. The other three took up opposing positions. Each Guardsman stood with feet far apart, spears with points up, and one hand behind his back.

The remainder of the brigade filed out and despite the distance, Quinlan heard the echoing shouts as various squads broke away to guard the more vulnerable points of the stronghold, any place with a window and any of the inner doorways.

The only simple way into the stronghold was by the front gates.

He nodded to his housekeeper who stood by the doorway, a formidable elven woman who wore her long dark brown hair in four braids that hung down her back. She stood taller than Batya. "Anthea, we have guests."

"Of course, Mastyr." She bowed slightly. Some of the older realm-folk held to ancient traditions. Anthea was very old.

She cast her gaze first over Batya then Lorelei. Her eyes flared at the latter. "And you're very powerful."

Lorelei nodded. "I suppose I am."

Quinlan looked down at Batya, whose eyes were closed. He felt her weakness and his need to take care of her deepened to an almost painful level. He didn't quite understand why he'd felt desperate to get Henry's hands off her or why, even now, his sole concern was seeing her restored.

He'd hurt her by invading her battle frequency.

Now he needed to heal her.

To Anthea, he said, "I want soup brought to my chambers and bread. Some cheese and white wine. She'll be with me through the daylight hours."

If Anthea's eyes widened once more, he drew a long breath ignoring the truth that for the first time ever a woman would share his stronghold bed.

"Please take Lorelei to the best guest suite and give her whatever she needs. She's under my protection." To Henry, he said, "I want you to have one of your men work to contact Mastyr Seth and as soon as you're able to make contact, tell him I need to talk to him. After that, get Rafe on the line. We've got a disaster in the making."

"Yes, Mastyr." Henry inclined his head, and on swift troll feet disappeared into the arched stronghold doorway.

He slid an arm beneath Batya's knees and lifted her up, cradling her against his chest. Anthea preceded him, her arm hooked around Lorelei's as the elf spoke in low tones, asking about her preferences for food, sleeping arrangements, bathing needs, everything. Her warm, confiding nature had already set Lorelei at ease.

With everything taken care of, Quinlan turned his full attention to Batya, who still hadn't regained consciousness.

Chapter Four

Batya reclined against soft pillows in a fairly upright position, but her eyes remained closed.

She couldn't seem to open them.

Something in the center of her realm-ness hurt like she'd been battered for hours. One of her frequencies cramped and seized, the one Quinlan had accessed earlier. Her battling frequency.

Something delectable, however, reached her nose and her brows rose. Her eyes almost opened, but another slice of pain gripped her and she gasped, breathing through, trying to get past the spasm.

"You must eat." The words rumbled over her.

Quinlan.

A shiver went through her and a different frequency began vibrating.

"Eat," the voice commanded.

She parted her lips and creamy soup slid into her mouth. She drew every drop off the spoon. She tasted potatoes, onion, celery, a bit of ham and the finest cream. "Oh-h-h-h. More."

A bass chuckle floated over her.

The spoon tapped her lips again. She opened and the savory goodness slid once more into her mouth.

She kept parting her lips. More soup arrived.

Heaven.

And the more she ate, the less her frequency spasmed.

"Wine?"

"Yes, please."

A cool glass touched her lips. She drank cold, sweet white wine.

More heaven.

A bite of bread with the best butter ever created.

Soup, wine, bread.

Repeat.

Eventually, the pain in her frequency ceased altogether. Sometimes a good meal made the miracle.

Eventually her eyes opened and she met Quinlan's concerned gaze, while his brows pulled together in a tight line. She lifted a hand and pressed her finger in the furrow between.

She felt so much better except for the heaviness in her chest that in the last few days kept turning into a thudding heart. She suspected she'd begun having serious feelings for the vampire at her bedside.

"Better?"

"Much. Did I pass out?"

"Yes."

"How long?"

"Two, three hours. No more."

"Then you started feeding me. Wonderful soup, by the way."

"Anthea has an excellent staff. She keeps the household running and the brigade well fed and content."

She glanced around. The room had massive proportions, the ceiling rising at least thirty feet. "Great space. Is this your stronghold?"

He nodded. "My rooms." He gestured with a flip of his wrist. "Right against the mountain."

Her realm vision had taken over and everything looked lit as if in an early evening glow. She saw two long and very narrow windows, not even a foot wide but rising fifteen feet in height. A rocky hillside was right there, just a few feet beyond the glass. The windows were too narrow to allow anyone to enter.

She could see stars at the upper portion. "Doesn't the snow pack against the windows?"

"No. This portion of the structure overhangs a warm spring."

"I see a slight rising mist."

"Exactly."

"Well that's just brilliant."

"Thank you."

She turned toward him. "Do you stay here often?"

"Not as much as I'd like."

She wondered how many women had shared this room. But her faeness kicked in and she knew she was the first, the only.

Dear, sweet Goddess…

Panic set in and she closed her eyes once more, leaning against the pillows. What was she doing here?

She forced herself to breathe. She tried not to make too much of what was happening but even Davido had encouraged her to embrace the unknown, which in this case meant Quinlan.

She'd never been good at relationships. She was too opinionated, too self-determined to be of much use to a man. She wanted what she wanted and experience had taught her that most men needed their women more compliant than she could ever be.

"I'm feeling it, too." Quinlan's deep voice rolled over her, sending a shiver through her, striking her mating frequency with just the right note. She was so damn attracted to him, even his voice.

But she had to get hold of herself, of whatever this was, so she turned her head and met his gaze straight on. "Feeling what?"

He scowled again and took her hand. His vibrations ran up her arm and she arched her neck, gasping. "Quinlan, sweet Goddess."

At that, he smiled. "Not, 'oh, my God'?"

She chuckled. "That, too." But her amusement slid away as fast as it had come. "I'm not good at this, you need to know that. I'll want my own way."

He nodded. "We'll lock horns over the next few days. Then we'll part."

"I couldn't bear a life in Grochaire."

"And this is my home, my heart."

"I know that. I watched you while you looked at the map. You slid your hand over the entire stretch of Grochaire with the most loving caress. I don't think I'd ever understood you so well before, or known how much a mastyr could love his realm."

"She's been in my care a long time. Centuries."

"Do you think you could ever have a wife?"

"I doubt it and not to malign the married state, but I've never wanted that kind of relationship."

"And what am I?" She wanted things out in the open.

One side of his mouth curved. "The best seduction ever. You intrigue me and I like you."

She covered his hand with her own. "That's a compliment coming from you. That much I do get. So thank you."

"You're welcome." He searched her eyes. "And I want to apologize for how hard I hit your battle frequency."

"It hurt."

"I know. It was a virgin breach and for that I'm sorry. A warrior usually breaks in his or her frequency over a period of weeks with serious training and care."

"I don't regret it, though. We wouldn't have made it here, otherwise, would we?"

He shook his head, giving her hand a squeeze. "I couldn't have gotten away from the wind Margetta had created without your help. She's incredibly powerful. She could have killed me outright."

"But that might have injured Lorelei and she wouldn't have risked it."

"No, she wouldn't have, but she's very determined."

He winced slightly and her heart kicked in a couple more heavy thuds. "You need to feed, don't you? Have you eaten?"

"I had some soup." His gaze had grown hungry, though, and now slid over her throat.

A soft vision of what the next hour would hold for her rolled through her. "I'd like a bath, Quinlan. Do you have one here?"

"I do."

"And will you bathe me?"

* * * * * * * *

Occasionally, Quinlan could use his brain, which he did right now. "Yes, I'll bathe you."

He rose from beside the bed, his stomach cramping but the rest of him flexing in anticipation. He was almost dizzy as he slipped into the adjoining bathroom, another large space with an enormous, made-to-order, black ceramic, claw-footed tub smack in the middle. The tub faced another stretch of rocky hillside, patches of snow, the feathering of fur needles and a dark starry sky above.

He ran the water and lit several candle pillars.

"Anytime you're ready," he called over his shoulder.

"I'm ready."

Her voice, closer than he'd expected, startled him as he turned in her direction. She stood in the doorway completely naked, her long, thick, wavy hair hanging almost to her waist.

He rose, his gaze falling to her large breasts and peaked pink nipples. Dizziness returned because he could smell her sex and she was ready.

This wouldn't be simple, not this joining, but he didn't care, not right now. He would bathe her, caress her, savor her.

She had a large clip in her hand and slowly drew her hair up, twisting it around and around. Of course his gaze stayed close to the swaying of her breasts that these movements caused. His mouth watered.

With her hair clipped up on top, she finally moved forward to stand in front of him. He froze, not because he was intimidated by her, or by having her so close, but because he didn't know what to do first. He wanted to kiss her, touch her, pull her against him, play with her nipples and suck on her neck all at the same time.

But Batya had a different idea entirely. She took his hand, spread her legs, and planted his palm against what was very wet.

She closed her eyes, her lips parted and she groaned. "I have been wanting you to touch me so badly all these weeks. Your vibration was one thing, but your flesh, any part of your body, how I've longed for you, needed you."

He groaned heavily, surrounding her with his free arm. Pulling her close, he slid a finger inside her. At the same time, he crashed his mouth down on hers and kissed her, driving his tongue deep, then plunging in and out.

Quinlan, sweet Goddess. Quinlan.

He could have brought her right then, a few quick strokes and a jolt of his vibration, but he didn't want to. He wanted to draw this moment out. He'd worked her up for weeks, now he wanted to savor every moment.

He released her, rinsing his hand in the water. "Bath first."

She nodded, her lips still open, waiting.

He held her hand to support her as she stepped into the tub. She stretched out, facing the window. He let the water run until her breasts were two floating islands. The water could have risen higher, but again he used his intelligence and shut the tap off.

Her pale skin looked exquisite against the black of the tub. He rarely chose a bath over a shower, except when he'd been battling for days and needed to work some of the stiffness out of overused muscles.

Again, no woman had ever reclined in the oversized vessel, a small boat really.

Big enough for two.

"If I'm going to bathe you, I'll need better access."

"Good idea. I might get lost in this ship."

He smiled. "We wouldn't want that."

He stood up and stripped off his shirt, his gaze fixed on her, watching her. Her eyes dilated, taking in his arms, his pecs, his abs and lower, as he shrugged out of the absurdly short pants, held up by the ridiculous tie.

"Perfect," she whispered, her gaze on his fully erect cock. "Now come join me."

She moved back, away from the side, as he climbed in. What foresight he'd shown to have the dimension of this tub made so big.

From a nearby basket, seated on an ancient, dark polished stool, he took a washcloth and a large bar of soap, imported from the U.S., made in France. There were many excellent perks to the opening up of the Nine Realms to their access points.

He dipped the cloth in the water then soaped up. "Why don't you turn around, let me scrub your back."

Batya shifted in the water and, spreading his legs, he pulled her toward him, working the cloth over her shoulders and back, her neck, her arms.

"That feels so good."

"Thought it might." He scrubbed in circles, working into the muscles and little by little, he felt the tension drain from her.

He soaped up again, and made his way up and down her arms slowly encircling her and leaning forward to wash her upper chest and gradually descended to glide the cloth over the swell of her breasts.

She leaned into him now, nestling in the curve of his neck so that he had the best view.

He let the cloth fall into the water, soaping up his hands this time as he massaged her breasts. He had big hands but she was built, more than he'd realized. He caressed down her tips and massaged them both, tugging in rhythmic strokes. The sight and feel of her breasts hardened him all over again.

She writhed against him, pushing against his chest.

Quinlan, that feels so good. Everything you do feels so good.

Love your voice in my head.

Slowly, as he worked her breasts he started adding his vibration. She gasped, then moaned.

He nuzzled her hair as he massaged her, licking a line at her temple, flicking his tongue. *I want to do this between your legs.*

She cried out and he gave her a jolt of vibration.

Then he took the vibration in a line down her stomach, lower and lower, like he had so many times while standing across the street from her loft.

She lifted a hand to caress the side of his face, her body turning slightly in the water, her breathing harsher.

He plucked one of her nipples and took the vibration straight to her sweet spot.

"Quinlan. You're here. Oh, do it please."

He closed his eyes, flicking his tongue against her cheek and drifting toward her ear. His hands pulled and pushed her breasts and his vibration now stroked her deep between her legs.

Do you want to come like this?

Yes, but don't let it be the last.

Sweetheart, we're just getting started.

He ramped up the vibrations and she cried out. *I'm coming. Sweet Goddess--*

He kept everything up until her hips grew quiet. He dialed down the vibration and let his hands rest on her breasts. He took careful breaths because he was closer than he wanted to be. He knew when he wanted to come and it had to be inside her this first time.

She shifted slightly to look up at him. "I want to feed you, just a little right now. I know you need blood. I can sense your hunger. Take some at my wrist." She met his gaze. "And you can feed me at the same time."

His cock jerked against her. He forced himself to breath and once more, showing intelligence, he nodded.

* * * * * * * *

Batya turned inside the tub so that she was on her knees. She'd seen the built-up lip at the back of the tub and knew exactly how this should go.

She extended her arm. "Now rise up and balance yourself on the ledge behind you because I'm really hungry."

His eyes had fallen to half-mast. His beautiful full lips were swollen and parted. His breathing seemed rough, which made her smile.

She inched closer between his knees. His cock was right in front of her and straight up, ready for what she wanted to do.

Planting her left hand on his hip, she slid her other palm up his chest taking a moment to play with his thick pecs, to caress his muscles, to feel the curves of him.

When she reached his chin she drifted her fingers over his lips. "Open."

He parted his lips and she slid a finger inside.

"Now suck."

He obliged her.

"And that's what I'm going to do to you."

His eyelids fluttered.

After a moment, she withdrew her finger, but held her wrist close to his face. "Turn your head to the side, get a good angle, and when you're ready, bite me."

His whole body shivered, like he was cold but she knew it was just latent energy leaking out of every muscle because he had to sit there and hold himself together.

He closed his eyes and licked over her wrist several times. His nostrils flared.

She watched, waiting for the moment. She'd had vampire lovers over the years and this part always got to her, straight into her core where all the good things happened.

He pulled back his lips and his fangs emerged. She watched as he struck.

Her body arched with intense pleasure.

Then he started to suck.

As her blood began to leave her body, more pleasure followed, different this time, invading her chest, intensifying her lower pleasure.

Yes, she'd had vampire lovers, but not a man like Quinlan, not such a big man, a powerful one, a dominant creature, sucking and lapping and moaning as he took her blood.

She eased toward him now and looked at his cock, at the thick staff and broad head.

She leaned near and once more swirled her tongue, easing over the head first then drawing him into her mouth, the soft skin, thickened and toughened with desire, full of purpose and strength.

She sucked, a long savoring draw of her mouth, her tongue rippling at the same time. She moved her head to take as much of him inside, drawing back with suction, then descending once more.

She accessed her own vibration this time letting it flow through her tongue. She didn't suck hard, just enough, and let the feathery vibrations float over him

Oh, fuck. I didn't know you could do that.

She added a little more.

Fuck. Me. That feels incredible.

He drew harder at her wrist.

She didn't do anything more than that. She just wanted to work him up, to let him feel the pleasure, but she didn't want him to come, not yet.

When she felt his agitation increase, she let go of his cock and leaned her head against his abdomen.

He stopped drinking at the same time, but moaned in short grunts. "Don't touch me."

She'd taken him straight to the edge, just where she'd wanted him. He deserved to be there, suffering a little, because that's what he'd done to her for weeks.

She smiled.

When his breathing seemed more normal, she drew back, took his hands and pulled him back into the warm water.

He slid down into the tub and she stretched out, floating on her stomach, her legs behind her.

When he was settled with that half-smile of his on his lips, he stroked her arms and shoulders.

"Good?" she inquired, almost taunting.

"You know it was. Nice vibration, by the way. Never had a woman do that before."

"Someone taught me the trick."

"Somebody smart, I take it."

"Too smart for his own damn good."

He caught her arms and pulled her toward him.

She snuggled against his chest, sliding her arms around his waist. He lifted her chin and as she leaned back to look up at him, he kissed her, a soft plucking of her lips at first, then deeper until he possessed her mouth with his tongue.

But he used no vibration, at least not yet, he just entered her, searching her mouth, then plunging a few times, making the age-old promise of good things to come.

He kissed her for a long time, then paused, waiting, calming down perhaps, or maybe just savoring, taking his time. A slow build could be extremely erotic at the end.

He held her chin this time and looked into her eyes. "My turn to do as I want with you."

"Uh-huh." Like she'd argue with a man who could bring her to climax with just a vibration.

Her internal well seized with anticipated pleasure at the idea that soon what she'd taken into her mouth would be inside her body.

He shifted sideways, took her hand, and pulled her back toward the perch he'd sat on. "Put both your hands there, flat, and hold on."

Her breath caught as she sloshed through the water, bringing her knees up while he got behind her. "Now lean over the side."

She did as he told her and stretched out, but she was fully exposed, her bottom in the air.

Then he split her legs wide, pushing them apart. He leaned over her and started at her waist just kissing her and flicking his tongue. But gradually he began moving lower covering each of her ass-cheeks, licking and kissing, lower and lower, until he spread her down low with his fingers.

Her breaths grew quick and shallow as the depths of her began long slow pulls on what needed to be there.

He added a vibration as he reached her lower lips and kissed her.

She moaned heavily. He flicked all around her entrance, teasing her with his tongue and occasionally sucking with pulls of his lips.

Then he French-kissed her, his tongue vibrating softly as he penetrated her.

He slid his hands around to the front of her hips holding her in place, then tongue-fucked her hard from behind, pushing his face into her body.

Quinlan, it's never been like this.

He grunted as he pushed. *Come for me, Cha. Loud. I want to hear you come.*

She was so close again and her hips responded rolling into him each time he pulled out.

She felt a new level of vibration on her hips first, emanating from his fingertips. The sensation poured through her abdominal wall, and reached the center of her.

Oh, Sweet Goddess. Are you really going to do this?

Yes.

He connected the vibrations, one that went straight through her body to meet his pulsing tongue. It was like a shock wave that invaded her well, tightening her body.

Pleasure erupted and she screamed as she came.

He moved faster, driving his tongue into her harder still, the vibrations reaching a crescendo that kept her own pleasure coming and coming, rising, falling a little, only to rise again so that her screams echoed around the room repeatedly.

Finally, as he stopped the vibrations, she began to ease back and what followed was a sweet lethargy that made her hips fall against the side of the tub and her arms dangle over the edge. Her breasts were now smashed against the ledge but she didn't care.

Quinlan rubbed a hand up and down her back and chuckled softly, a smug sound that she damn well thought he deserved to make.

"That was amazing. Let's do it again about a thousand times."

Once more, his laughter flowed over her body.

He leaned his hips against her, his cock a hard missile.

"Do you want to come like this?" she asked. Right now, she thought she'd do anything for him. He could tell her he intended to tie her into a knot and she'd say it was a great idea.

"No," he responded instead.

He got out of the tub and dried off then took his time peeling her away from the side of the tub. She was still in a state of post-coital heaven and didn't care what he did. "You can drop me off the flat end of the earth now if you want. I'm ready to go."

He laughed once more. He made her stand on her feet, but only to dry her off, then carried her into his bedroom and laid her out on a thick layer of soft furs, another piece of heaven.

She watched as he lit a fire, one piled high and layered with wads of newspaper, a lot of kindling, and several small logs. It lit up quickly and burned hot, something the room could use, made of stone as it was.

When he was certain the screen contained the blaze and the damper worked properly, he came back to bed. He lifted her once more, shunting the furs aside until she rested on silk. He took the clip from on top of her head and pulled her hair around her shoulders.

"You're so beautiful. I think that's part of the problem, and why I want you so much. No woman should be so pretty."

He kissed her then, like he had done before, as though he meant something by it. She wasn't sure what, almost as though he wanted to take as much as he could because their time together had an end-point.

For the same reason, then, she responded in kind, taking her time with him, caressing his face between kisses, savoring the shape of his lips, even kissing the sexy crooked line of his nose, his strong cheekbones, and eyelids that often lay at half-mast because pleasure had taken him over. She slid her hands into his thick, long hair.

His dark eyes glittered as he looked down at her. The fire blazed beyond the bed, lighting up the room in fiery glow. He'd ignited her kindling for weeks and now she blazed for him, needing him in every way, taking pleasure in stroking his arms, the swell of his back, his narrow waist, his tight buttocks.

Slowly, he made his way inside her, pushing his cock inch by inch, sliding easily into her wetness, the state he'd put her in, driving her close once more to the pinnacle.

She looked into his eyes and fell into all that he was, his strength, his command, his power, his dark sensuality, all that was lethal and fierce about him. Her body weakened for him, submitting and surrounding him, holding him fast inside her, savoring.

"Oh, Quinlan."

That half-smile emerged and her heart drew into a tight knot of something she really didn't want to think about.

Damn him.

* * * * * * * *

Quinlan's arms quivered as he pushed inside Batya. He had her on her back, the place he'd been wanting her for weeks now. He just never thought it would be because of a shifter-wraith, who was also part fae-vampire, now ensconced in his guest room for the rest of the night.

But right now, he didn't care how this had come about, only that her lips were parted and swollen and he'd made her that way. He flexed his hips, which brought her chest up and a slight gasp rising from her throat.

Sex had always been a thrill, but right now he stood on the peak of a tall mountain ready to fly. His chest felt buoyant and yes, her wrist-blood had helped, but this was more about conquest and he loved it. He'd conquered all her reservations, despite the circumstances, and now he took his prize with another deep thrust.

She writhed in response, pleasure evident on every twist of her lovely face and every moan from her long, pale throat.

He drove steadily now, lowering himself to balance on his forearms, her fingers clutching at his biceps in a way that made his balls tighten. Pleasure accompanied every stroke, especially the ones where her hips pushed back in response.

Quinlan.

He loved her feminine voice in his mind.

Her head rolled back and forth over the pillows and her breathing grew labored. But each roll revealed the sides of her neck where more goodness lay. He'd taken her wrist twice, but not her throat and there was nothing so sweet, so erotic as neck-blood.

His body started to hum with increased desire, but he had to hold back so he slowed things down, which left her panting. Finally, he stopped and leaned close to lick up the side of her neck.

"Yes, sweet Goddess, yes," she whispered. "I've been wanting this from the time you trapped me in the gallery."

"Same here."

He tilted his head, then released his fangs. Saliva dripped. He struck quickly creating two punctures then retracted his fangs and began to drink.

He had Batya in the most vulnerable position possible, his mouth sucking down her blood, his cock buried deep. His body shook with pleasure and just for her, he started up the vibrations she liked so much, pulling his cock slowly toward her entrance then pushing back in.

Her body convulsed and a series of achy sighs left her throat.

So much pleasure, Quinlan. I could die like this.

He wanted to respond, but couldn't. His body had locked onto its target and as he drank down her blood, and drove into her, his hips took over.

Yet somewhere in the center of his being, he felt his mating frequency join with the pure sexual vibration he'd developed so long ago, and a fire burned through him.

He pounded now, sucking hard at her neck, his mating frequency seeking entrance.

Let me in.

Your voice sounds hoarse, even inside my head.

Cha, let me in. Sweet Goddess, I want inside your frequency.

I want to, but is this wise?

He didn't care. He kept pushing and his balls were so tight. Still, he wanted all of her.

Let me in.

He felt her give way, so he rushed inside and that pushed him over the edge. He released her neck and rose up shouting as his body rocked and pleasure streaked through him.

But it was the frequency joining that kept sending thrills up his cock, his abdomen, his chest, and that kept him shouting and coming, releasing all that he had into her.

Somewhere he felt her body writhing and heard her crying out then screaming as she came. His vibrations were a heavy pulse through him and at the same time through her body.

He eased back but he wasn't done. He continued to thrust into her, stroking her, feeling her.

"Look at me."

She opened her eyes. She looked almost panic-stricken.

Quinlan, my God.

"I'm going to make you climax again."

Her neck arched and he pumped her harder, his body winding up once more.

"Faster," she called out.

He didn't hold back, but pumped into her with his warrior strength, his vibrations at full bore, his mating frequency inside her own, possessing her, conquering her yet again.

"Oh, God." She arched her neck and screamed, clutching at his biceps, digging her fingernails in and it felt so good.

Pleasure rushed through his cock once more and his shouts lifted to the rafters of his stronghold all over again, the cry of dominance, of command, of having his woman beneath him, whose blood eased him, whose blood took away the cramping.

In stages, his hips settled down. Her hands swept over his arms, his shoulders, his back, the way his hand had moved over the map earlier, a kind of claiming of her own, her land, her territory, his body.

And right now he was exactly that, without reservation.

He rested on top of her, his head joining hers on the pillow. She slid her arms around him and held him fast. She breathed hard, catching her breath. He did as well.

He remained joined to her, his cock inside and both frequencies bathing in what he perceived was the warm nest of all that she was as fae and troll in their world of vibrations.

* * * * * * * *

Batya lay beneath the wonderful weight of Quinlan's vampire, Guard-sized body. She'd never really made love before, or had sex before, that's what she decided.

Quinlan had done exactly what he'd been promising for the past several weeks. He'd given her the ride of her life.

And she wanted more, the greedy fae-troll that she was. Oh, Sweet Goddess, had he just ruined her for other men? How could sex ever be the same for her? And the way he'd broken down her mating frequency shield—she'd come hard with that one. His vibration had streamed through in a way that sent pleasure all the way to her fingers and to her feet, rushing back and forth in heavy waves up her body then back down. And the whole time ecstasy had been a thrill inside her where he'd plunged in and out with vampire speed.

Ah, well, he'd definitely ruined her, but it had been so worth it.

Yet a small ignoble part of her needed revenge. If he'd ruined her, then at some point on this journey to Ferrenden Peace, she intended to do whatever she could from her vast array of fae-trollness to serve him with his own sauce and to take him down.

The mere thought of it, of bringing Quinlan to heel, lightened her heart, so much so, that with her arms wrapped around the big bastard from Grochaire, with his cock tucked inside her, she fell contentedly asleep.

She slept hard, her dreams barely there, just faint distant images held back by a pleasant mist.

She slept and slept. When she finally awoke, she had a soft linen cloth pressed between her legs and a warm fur tucked up snug against her bare body. Oblique northern light lit the space, which told her a new day had broken or more likely, was about to end. She'd no doubt slept the day away.

But where was Quinlan?

Hey, she pathed softly, reaching for him.

I'm with my stronghold brigade. Bathe if you like, ring for your first meal. Anthea is an excellent cook.

Do you need me?

No, not yet, but soon. Take care of your needs first. We'll be traveling at full dark.

Got it. Thanks. She closed down immediately because she had felt the tension in his voice, even a sense of urgency.

She saw that her flowered satchel sat just inside the door and a funny sense of relief struck her. A woman always needed her things close by.

She showered and dressed in jeans, a tank and a long-sleeved sweater, socks and running shoes. By now she felt urgent as well. Knowing Margetta's level of power, she would have divined something about where her daughter meant to go, that she'd enlisted Quinlan to help her, and just what kind of force she'd need to destroy the enemy.

She found Lorelei and Anthea in the kitchen, on adjacent stools at a large island of black marble. Each sat in the same position with elbows on the marble, hands cradling coffee mugs.

"Oh, coffee. No, don't get up. I can see the cups and you have everything ready."

She helped herself, filling a heavy red mug three quarters full, then adding two teaspoons of sugar and enough cream to create the exact shade of caramel that she preferred. She took a sip and her lips parted. "Anthea, this is the best."

The housekeeper grinned. "Nothing better than coffee after a night of gymnastics."

Even Lorelei smiled.

In ordinary circumstances, Batya might have been embarrassed because it seemed her lovemaking with Quinlan had been a little loud. But thoughts of what had transpired, of the blood-giving-and-taking, of his vibration, of breaking through her mating frequency, of having his beautiful girth inside her then at the end, his weight on her, flowed through her mind like a never-ending stream.

She shivered.

"Are you all right?"

Batya shifted her gaze to Anthea. Something nagged at her, but she wasn't sure what it was. "He's pretty amazing."

"Yes, he is." Anthea took another sip. "I've served in many homes over the years as housekeeper. Mastyr Quinlan is very demanding, but he's just, and he always has an eye to everyone's comfort. No, that's not the right word, because sometimes we're uncomfortable. He has an eye to our well-being. Yes, that's more what I want to say about him."

"Well-being." Batya brought her mug to her lips and turned to lean against the island, slightly away from Anthea and Lorelei. From the beginning, this time with Quinlan had been full of mystery. She narrowed her eyes. "He started coming around a few weeks ago, intent as men like him often are, on getting me into bed. I always knew his reputation. But look where it led."

She pivoted, resting her hip against the marble. Meeting Lorelei's gaze, she continued, "One night, Margetta shows up and nearly kills him, but if he hadn't been there, hadn't been doing what men have always done, you'd be enslaved now and my guess is I'd be dead."

"I think you're right." Lorelei tucked her dark brown hair behind her ear. "I owe Quinlan and you so very much."

"Has he been here, earlier I mean?"

"Only to eat," Anthea said. "He's in his library with the map he brought from Lebanon. Henry's with him. They had conference calls with both Rafe, his second-in-command of the Grochaire vampire brigade, and Mastyr Seth of Walvashorr." She set her mug down and slid off her stool. "But I have strict orders to feed you a big meal and I will, if you're hungry."

Batya had fed a vampire last night. She planted a hand over her stomach. "I'm starved."

Chapter Five

Quinlan stared at the upper central portion of the map, at what he and Batya together had uncovered between Grochaire and Walvashorr Realms.

He shook his head. "I don't see any other way. We're going to have to find the Pickerne Caverns if we want to make it to Gem Meadow alive, any of us."

Henry kept touching the region that actually said, 'Ferrenden Peace', and the long section before the area called the Dead Forest— another mystery. "I can't believe I'm looking at the real deal, but I can feel the place right here. The vibrations are powerful." He let his hand rest over the words. "This wasn't supposed to exist. I read these tales as a child, of a queen who secluded herself to keep her people safe. Do you think she's real as well?"

Quinlan shrugged. "Hell if I know. But at this point, anything seems possible."

Once more, he ran his left hand over the western portion of the map that encompassed his realm. The concept of a straight up battle had always appealed to him, of fighting for the health of a people, for the rights of the individual, for justice. He fought the Invictus wraith-pairs because they destroyed the innocent, often drinking them to death and casting them aside. The poor made excellent targets living unprotected as they did in those tracts of land where the Invictus hunted on a regular basis.

But he could count on one hand the times he'd functioned as prey rather than predator and he didn't like the feeling one bit. Margetta sought to bring her daughter under her control and his job meant staying one step ahead of her, not getting caught by her extremely powerful vampire-wraith Invictus pairs, and somehow getting her safely to Ferrenden Peace.

For that reason alone, he felt a profound urge to move, to take the women under his arm, and fly them straight over the newly uncovered Pleach Range to safety. But both the map and Batya's paintings had illuminated the way and he was realm-enough to know when to submit to the whims of the Goddess and when to push back.

Earlier, he'd made contact with Rafe and relayed all that had happened. Fortunately, Rafe had seen no signs of what he now described as the mastyr vampire wraith-pairs that had attacked Quinlan in Lebanon. With any luck, those pairs would stay on Lorelei's trail and away from the regular Grochaire population.

Rafe had taken care of the dead Guardsmen at the access point and had set up a small force of twenty in their stead. He'd offered to support Quinlan on the trek to Ferrenden Peace, but his mastyr instincts told him that his Grochaire Guard needed to keep going out, as they normally did, to battle the Invictus, town-by-town.

When he'd finally reached Seth, who served as the Mastyr of Walvashorr Realm, he'd listened without offering either comment or question. In the end, he'd affirmed exactly what Quinlan knew in his gut to be true. "This whole situation has serious realm undercurrents. And I am at your service."

Seth didn't express amazement at the discovery of Ferrenden Peace either, or that the ancient fae had managed to create a new brand of super-powerful wraith-pairs, making use of lesser mastyr vampire, or even that the ancient fae now had a name. Of course, Seth had always been stoic by nature.

However, he agreed readily to track Quinlan's journey from the western reaches of Walvashorr, to hopefully meet up with him in Ferrenden Peace just in case Margetta should find her way there as well.

With his own realm secure in Rafe's hands, and Seth ready to move toward the land of fables as well, Quinlan had only one issue to settle, namely, where to begin.

According to the map, the Great River Caverns of Pickerne led to Gem Meadow. However, Quinlan had no idea how to get to them. With his finger, he traced the symbols for the caves. He peered closer. A smudge lay to the left. He rubbed, but nothing came off.

He used the magnifier once more and saw that what he'd perceived as a smudge was actually the shape of a shallow bowl. "What do you make of this?"

Henry took the magnifier and bent over as well. He extended the glass, then drew it close.

Rising up abruptly, he snapped his fingers and the three ridges of his troll forehead rose and rippled slightly. "I know where this is, mastyr, and it's not far from here.

"What is it exactly?"

Henry shook his head. Some of his blond curls had escaped the woven clasp that all the Guardsmen wore and for a moment he looked a bit like Ethan. He had a broad smile like the Mastyr of Bergisson as well. The ladies enjoyed Henry, no matter the species. Henry, like Davido, excelled in charisma.

He turned his right hand palm up. "I'm not sure. It's really too small to be called a meadow or anything like that. Besides, in the summer it's dry like it can't collect water to grow things though it's a depression in the earth."

"Is the ground bad there, unfit for growing things?"

"Maybe salt deposits. I'm really not sure, not being into horticulture."

Quinlan grinned. Henry had been his wingman on dozens of trips to the nearby town. "No, that you're not."

Henry's smile dimmed bit-by-bit until he tapped the magnifier against the map a couple of times. "We're in some serious shit right now, aren't we?"

"Realm shit, like nothing I've ever experienced."

Henry scanned the map once more. "Wait, I've just realized something." He placed his hand on the map at a location some thirty miles from the stronghold. "This section doesn't contain the same vibration and if my calculations are correct, I know this meadow well. A river and a stream converge there. Mastyr, we've all been there. We've run maneuvers in Gem Meadow, we just never had a name for the place before."

Quinlan rested his hand on the map over the indicated area. "Damn, I think you're right. And it has several permanent open air tents, doesn't it?"

"With protective sun panels, yes."

"Okay, good to know."

"And we can't just fly there?"

He considered this option for a good long minute. "My instincts tell me that the caverns are the way to go. If nothing else, we won't be vulnerable in the open air."

"You have to go with your instincts." Henry shook his head. "This Lorelei, she's something very different, isn't she?"

"Yes, she is, but she's also a woman in need of protection which is all that really matters. The rest, the danger, Margetta's power, well, fuck it all."

Henry's spirit lightened once more. "Your bravado is outdone only by your bullshit. But yeah, fuck it all. The brigade we've built can take a few Invictus wraith-pairs, like the ones you described. We'll just need to be cunning and as you know, we trolls excel at that. We've had to in order to survive you vampires and shifters."

* * * * * * * * *

Batya stood in the hall, near the doorway to Quinlan's library. She'd heard most of the conversation and from the shadows had watched the man who had made love to her last night.

A north-facing skylight high in the roofline, set at an angle to keep true sunlight out of the room, kept the space from being oppressive. Her fae vision warmed up the area further so that she had a perfect view of the Mastyr of Grochaire.

But from the moment she saw him again, her heart had started thrumming in her chest, almost pounding with renewed desire. In all her life, she'd never desired a man so fiercely, as though nothing had meaning except being near him.

If anything, her independent spirit had kept her one or two steps removed from ever getting seriously involved with any man, even though she'd had a couple of decade-long relationships over the years. But she always grew dissatisfied with the demands. And she couldn't even begin to imagine how demanding Quinlan would be with anyone he settled on as 'his woman', Goddess help her.

Yet here she was, staying in the shadows for no other reason than by doing so she could just look at him.

He was already half-dressed for battle. He wore a long-sleeved woven shirt and what she knew to be his snug battle leathers. His thick leather boots ranged past his knees and were turned down at the top, drawing her eye to his heavily muscled thighs. Slim silver studs ran in a line down the outer seam of the boots, glinting in the autumn half-light.

With his hair pulled back in the woven clasp, the hard line of his cheekbones gave his features a dramatic turn, and created a sharp angle of dark and light. He had large round eyes, thick lashes and heavy straight black brows, a purely masculine collection of features that brought the air rushing out of her chest. Add the crooked line of his nose and she wished that Henry wasn't in the room.

But if his sheer physical beauty wasn't enough to tear at her feminine heart, what he'd just said about Lorelei and his determination to get her safely to Ferrenden Peace, spoke the truth of his character more than anything else he could have said or done.

Desire burst over her like a sudden thunderstorm, and her heart slammed around in her chest almost wildly. How had Quinlan done this to her in just a few short weeks, or maybe just overnight because he'd filled her with his seed and pierced her personal frequency, taking her hard, bringing her to the brilliant flash of ecstasy over and over.

The damn vampire was magnificent.

His brows drew together as he turned in her direction. "Batya?"

She stepped forward, leaving the shadows reluctantly.

One side of his lips curved. "Were you spying on us?"

Then his nostrils flared and his mouth opened as he dragged in a big gulp of air. She knew he'd caught her scent as well as the level of her sudden desire. He looked at Henry. "Would you excuse us for a minute?"

"Yes, mastyr."

Henry moved on his swift troll feet, grinning as he passed by Batya. He even offered her a salute of two fingers, then hurried from the room. Maybe he sensed what was coming and that he shouldn't be present for what would happen next.

But if Batya was in any doubt that she wasn't alone in her experience, Quinlan covered the distance in a few long strides and gathered her up in his arms. He held her tight against him as he kissed her and not even his snug leathers could conceal what her appearance in the room had done to him.

His tongue drove deep and moved swiftly in and out. She suckled his tongue, struggling to catch her breath. *What's happening?*

The hell if I know, but damn I want you and when your scent poured over me I thought I'd come apart, run you down, flatten you on the floor. Sweet Goddess I didn't think I'd feel this way just seeing you again.

Finally he drew back, but he kissed her eyelids, her nose, her chin. His hand pressed against her buttocks as he ground into her, letting her feel him. "What have you done to me, Batya? I was supposed to be the seducer here."

"It's not me," she cried, pulling out of his arms. "This is all your fault. You had to come to Lebanon."

Distance helped, even if it was only eighteen inches or so. Her heart labored in her chest and she struggled to breathe. That weird heaviness was back. "Are you in need of blood? We have a battle coming. I've been feeling it since I woke up, like a weight inside me."

"Soon enough." He searched her face. "But I don't need blood, not yet. But you'll donate again?"

Here was a hard truth, just how much she wanted to open a vein for him. "As long as we're doing this together, absolutely. You don't have to think twice about it. I know how hard it is for all the mastyrs, the toll the blood-starvation takes on each of you."

"It does. You've helped more than any other woman so far, I want you to know that. The cramping isn't nearly so bad." His half-smile appeared. "You've got rich blood."

"I'm glad. I'm glad I could do at least that because I don't know how much good I'll be in the coming days."

He caught her chin with his fingers and forced her to meet his gaze. "Hey, without you I couldn't have gotten the three of us here. You don't give yourself enough credit."

"But I'm not a fighter, Quinlan."

"Yet we wouldn't have survived without you. I'm convinced of that. Battle isn't everything."

"You're right. I know you are." She glanced at the table. "So what place was Henry talking about?"

He drew close, and with one hand on her waist, he leaned forward and tapped the spot on the map both men had been studying earlier. "It looks like a smudge, but it's a shallow dip in the land and apparently, it's the gateway to Gem Meadow and the rest of the passage to Ferrenden Peace."

She glanced at him. "You're serious."

"It's the only way."

"Are you saying we can't just fly over the mountains?"

He glanced over his shoulder. "Ask Lorelei."

Batya turned in the direction of the door and sure enough, Lorelei stood there, her expression solemn, concerned.

Batya asked, "Is this true?"

"I'm afraid it is." She joined them near the table. "There aren't that many places to hide in any of the realms and Mastyr Quinlan's stronghold is well known. Margetta will eventually make her way here and if we took off over the mountains, she'd catch us. The only way is to follow the journey that you already laid out for us in your paintings. My guess is that a certain level of enthrallment still covers most of this region and will make Margetta's search for us difficult. Not impossible, but a challenge even for her."

Batya tapped the map near the smudge. "There's a strong vibration here." She glanced up at Quinlan. "Do you know what this is?"

At that, Lorelei peered close. "I think it's a sinkhole leading to an underground river."

Quinlan leaned on the table with both hands, staring at the smudge. "That would make sense on every possible front. Then this is where we start. Right here."

"So what do we do?" Batya opened her hands wide. "Do we just go over there and stomp around for a few minutes? Maybe wait till the whole thing collapses?"

"Maybe."

Quinlan had a look in his eye, a dangerous spark that appealed to something inside Batya she'd never really known existed. He liked the idea that the unknown waited for them, that whatever lay outside his fortress carried a deadly edge.

She looked away from him, her gaze settling on nothing in particular. But inwardly, she wondered about herself. Who was this person who had become Lorelei's champion and who had slept with a Mastyr Vampire? She almost didn't recognize herself.

And yet, she did. Some part of her, lost perhaps in her independent pursuit outside of Grochaire Realm, had started coming alive maybe from the first time Quinlan had appeared outside her Lebanon studio-bedroom and touched her with his realm vibration.

Shifting her gaze back to Quinlan, she said, "Let's do this thing."

He lifted upright from the table and turned to face her, searching her eyes. He did that a lot, something he did with everyone, a sort of test, taking a person's measure. "All right, then." He glanced at Lorelei then back to Batya. "I want you both to pack some winter-gear. I have a storeroom full of every size of boots and coats. Nothing too serious since it's only October. We won't have any minus-degree weather and supposedly the meadow will be in the comfortable sixties. But we'll be camping."

"Camping?" Batya and Lorelei spoke at the same time.

With her nose wrinkled, Batya turned to Lorelei and found that a similar expression of distaste curled Lorelei's lips.

"Now who would have thought," Quinlan interjected, "that camping would be worse than falling down a sinkhole."

Batya just looked at him.

"It won't be as bad as you think. If we make enough noise, the wolves will stay at least fifteen feet away from the teepees."

"Teepees?" Again, Lorelei's voice joined Batya's.

"Not exactly teepees. More like open air tents." Quinlan shook his head, but he laughed. "Just be ready in twenty minutes."

But Henry appeared in the doorway, his active troll feet bouncing back-and-forth. "Mastyr, we've got incoming ETA twelve minutes out of the southwest. I think Margetta found us."

"Shit." Quinlan took Batya's elbow and propelled her toward the door. "Make that five minutes to get your gear together. Now run."

Batya took off with Lorelei on her heels as Quinlan shouted orders for the brigade and the support units to get to the courtyard on the double.

She'd never moved so fast as she gathered up a pair of boots, labeled by size, thank the Goddess, and a coat with a hood. Lorelei parted from her, heading toward her guest suite. Batya raced to her bedroom and grabbed her packed satchel. Everything she needed was in there.

With that, she glanced at the huge, fur-laden bed, the fireplace, the arched opening to the oversized tub. Would she ever be back here?

* * * * * * * *

Quinlan held both women in his arms as he levitated straight up into the air to the top the fir trees, then flew north and slightly west as fast as he could. The depression in the earth, surrounded by meadow and more trees wasn't far, ten miles, no more. He'd reach the location in less than a minute.

The brigade's medical and provisions support units came next, with ten powerful trolls who carried camp equipment as well as the women's satchels. The troll brigade, a hundred strong, brought up the rear and would engage Margetta and her force if necessary.

Both Batya and Lorelei remained quiet and alert, bodies tense. He would have expected nothing less, sensing in each woman a strong survival instinct.

He felt the air change as the sinkhole appeared. A grassy smell invaded the fir-tree scent and on instinct, he headed to the very center of what was, just as Henry had said, a rocky, barren stretch of land at the lowest point of the depression. He touched down.

Lorelei released his neck quickly, letting go of him to stand on the ground, as did Batya.

"Here." Lorelei pointed to a patch of grayish dirt. "This is the entrance, probably a shaft of some kind. I can feel it." She lifted eyes that glowed—shifter eyes.

Quinlan had these lapses, forgetting what she was for brief stretches. He nodded. "Good. What else do you sense? Can you break through?"

She rose up and sighed heavily. "The earth will have to do this for us. We can't violate her."

"What do you mean?" Batya moved up next to Quinlan, her hand grazing his, a touch that jumped-started a couple of extra heart-beats.

"This area of the earth is alive and has a will of its own. I can hear a river below. The sound is growing stronger."

"Then the earth is thinning, choosing maybe."

"I think so."

The women might be listening to the earth, but Quinlan had one ear to the sky and something wasn't right. He stretched his hearing as far as he could. That's when he heard the sounds of battle, of trolls screaming their war-chants, of energy released, of steel weapons engaging, and of wraith-shrieking.

Everything in the Nine Realms seemed to be changing, including the nature of battle and war.

Henry, can you path with me?

Yes, but I'm kinda busy. We've got thirteen Invictus pairs, one angry she-bitch of an ancient-fae and at least one of those uber-wraith-mastyr vampire pairs you mentioned. I've got three men down.

Do you need me?

Quinlan smiled, because he heard Henry snort.

This is war. Get those women into the earth. Margetta means business. Hold on. Yeah, fuck you, wraith.

Quinlan heard the shriek of a dying wraith and he smiled.

One more bites the dust.

Good.

We can hold these lightweights, mastyr. Just keep this line open and let me know what's happening, when we need to make tracks in your direction.

Lorelei says the earth is thinning.

Good. That's a good sign. But stick close. If the earth opens up, Lorelei might be in for a hard fall.

Quinlan turned to look at Lorelei and Batya and found them both on hands and knees, pawing at the earth. Then Lorelei stretched out, a sublime expression on her face.

Batya looked up at Quinlan. "She's communing."

Lorelei's eyes opened. "We'll have thirty seconds to get the entire brigade through before the earth closes up again. You should bring the trolls here now."

Quinlan nodded then relayed the message to Henry.

We're on our way.

In the distance, Quinlan heard a sharp whistle and the sounds of battle ceased. "They're coming."

Just as he turned back to the women he watched them both fall into a hole. Neither of them could fly so he dove in after them. He caught Batya's arm and pulled her to him, but her flailing movements, purely instinctive, didn't allow him to continue his descent.

"Lorelei, shift," he shouted.

In midair, the woman suddenly transformed into her wraith-self and ended up hanging only three inches above a massive jagged rock.

Quinlan breathed a sigh of relief, dropping down to set Batya on the floor of the massive cavern. A moment later, trolls fell, flew, or tumbled through the earth's doorway, one after the other, faster than he'd ever seen them move. The support crew came first, with all their equipment, then the Guardsmen.

The men were exceptionally well-trained.

"They only have seconds before the earth closes," Lorelei cried out. "Hurry! Faster!"

She began floating higher, while avoiding the stream of warriors. A hundred troops were a lot for the small space.

Quinlan glanced around. The entire brigade was there, except one.

He flew straight up, Lorelei not far away.

"Henry," he shouted, as the earth began to solidify once more. "Henry! Henry!"

He felt along the jagged shelf of earth, but no aperture remained. Lorelei once more pressed herself against the earth, petting the rocks, chanting softly. "We have one more. Please, mother realm. Do this for me."

Quinlan heard Henry shouting and beating on the lowest point of the sinkhole.

"Please mother-realm. One more troll. Please."

Suddenly the earth split, Henry popped through, and the stone closed up behind him.

Quinlan shot after him, because Henry was spinning hard. Something wet kept striking Quinlan and just as Henry would have landed in the rushing water of the river, Quinlan caught him, then carried him to shore.

The troll bled from his mouth and from a severe cut over his shoulder. He had burns on most of his face and neck. His eyes rolled in his head.

Quinlan called for medical assistance. He stayed close by as one of the trolls, trained in emergency quick-fixes, opened up his med-kit and went to work.

Kneeling, he stared at Henry and willed him to live. "Don't give up."

But there was no response.

Henry, you bastard, if you die now, I swear I'll chase you into hell and beat the shit out of you.

He saw Henry's lips curve, then his whole body went still and the medic drew back, both hands in the air. "I don't know what happened."

He felt a hand on his shoulder and looked up. Batya eased down beside Quinlan. "May I?" she asked.

He nodded, in shock. He could feel that Henry was right at the brink of death and that the medic couldn't help him.

Batya took his hand in hers, closed her eyes and that was when he felt her most essential faeness, and realized that she was a healer. "He needs blood. Now." She stripped off her coat and rolled up the sleeve of her shirt.

Quinlan stiffened suddenly, and a red hue covered his vision. His brained winked in and out as though caught in some kind of electrical failure, firing and misfiring. "Like hell you will." His deep voice reverberated around the massive cavern and a wind rushed through, blowing against Batya forcing her backward, away from Henry.

"Quinlan, he'll die otherwise."

"Not your blood, Batya. Your blood belongs to me."

Batya lifted both hands and then he felt her wind as she pushed back. "We must save your friend." She moved toward him and grabbed his face with both hands, staring fiercely into his eyes. "Quinlan, come back to me."

"I'll donate."

The words, uttered by Lorelei, brought sudden order back to Quinlan's mind. He turned and saw that the wraith, back to her fae form, had dropped beside the unconscious troll. The medic had already hooked up the necessary tubing, but waited for Quinlan's approval. In the realm world, all species could share blood. He nodded.

And the moment Quinlan saw Lorelei's blood flowing into Henry, he sat down. Batya moved so that she could put her hand on Henry's head, closing her eyes, and even from several feet away, Quinlan felt her healing power flow into the troll warrior.

He breathed hard, hating that she was touching another man then despising himself for even having the thought.

He pulled up his knees, angling his forearms to rest over the top of them, then dropped his forehead into his hands. What the hell had just happened?

A few minutes later, Batya's hand was once more on his shoulder. "He's going to live, Quinlan. See for yourself."

He lifted his gaze to Henry and watched as his chest rose and fell and his color took on a more normal hue. "I would have let him die. Sweet Goddess, I would have let him die."

"I don't believe that, not for a second. But what happened? I've never heard your voice like that before and you created a wind like Margetta's."

She drew close, then lowered herself to the ground to sit next to him. *Quinlan, what's going on?*

He couldn't look at her as he shook his head. "I don't know. I don't get it." He met her gaze. "What the hell is this, Batya? What kind of sick game are you playing with me?"

She leaned her head back as though he'd struck her. "I'm not playing a game. Why would you say that?"

"Because I've felt your power and I think you're using it to undermine who I am, to try to break down my commitment to Grochaire. You want to destroy me."

Embrace the Mystery

* * * * * * * * *

Batya stared at Quinlan unable to believe these words had just come out of his mouth. "You can't be serious."

"Why, not? You don't approve of Grochaire. You've said yourself that you'll never live in my realm again. Why not destroy me at the same time?"

Batya glanced around. The troll brigade had begun re-forming at a distance, taken in hand by several team leaders. At the same time, Henry continued to receive a healthy dose of Lorelei's blood.

"You're mistaken. I just needed something different, something Grochaire Realm or any of the other realms couldn't give me. And I have a purpose in Lebanon. A lot of realm-folk can't be part of things in the Nine Realms right now. Many of them fear the Invictus to the point of paranoia, so they live in the United States. That doesn't mean we hate Grochaire, not even a little."

He seemed to settle down, but he appeared distressed. She suspected he didn't like feeling out of control and that for a long moment, that's exactly what he'd been, making it impossible for her to give what she could have so easily donated to Henry.

But if Lorelei hadn't intervened, Batya also knew she could have reached Quinlan, helped him to tone down his caveman instincts. She also knew that his refusal to allow her to donate had more to do with their lovemaking last night than he understood.

"I can't believe I prevented you from helping Henry." Once again, he shaded his face with his hands.

"Quinlan, look at me."

He scowled, but he lifted his face to her. "You know damn well that if Lorelei hadn't offered, you would have relented."

He gripped her hand. "No," he said, shaking his head. "You don't understand. I wouldn't have. There's something inside me now that won't allow another man to touch you or to take from you."

The ferocity of his gaze tore at something inside Batya, something that recognized and really liked what Quinlan was saying.

Her fingers moved against his palm, a sensual stroke. *And I don't want any other woman to have even a drop of what you can give.* She stroked his hand again, running a finger down to the tip of his middle finger.

She heard a soft growl at the back of his throat, rumbling deep, something only a shifter or a vampire could do. The sound, full of vibration, went straight through her, forcing every ounce of her attention on him. No one but Quinlan existed.

With her free hand, she touched her throat, rubbing her thumb up and down her vein.

His gaze tracked the movement and his nostrils flared. *I'm smelling exotic flowers, heaps of it. Do you know that your blood tastes like that as well, like I'm drinking nectar from flowers that grow in the tropics?* His gaze slid past her, his brows low on his forehead as he watched everyone.

He pressed her hand harder. *I'm taking you tonight. Do you understand? When we're bedded down, I'm taking you.*

She nodded.

Good.

He rose and offered a hand to her, lifting her easily to her feet. He crossed to Henry, now sitting up, though he still looked pale.

But his gaze was fixed on Lorelei. "That's some blood you've got there."

Lorelei nodded. "Do you feel better, Henry?"

"You brought me back from the brink. Thank you, mistress."

"All right, you troll bastard. I see you'll live to fight another day."

"I will, indeed." He jumped to his feet. "The woman has restored me. In fact, I feel better than new." He glanced around. "This is one big motherfucker of a cavern. Which way to the meadow?"

Quinlan pointed in the direction the river flowed, amazed that in a very realm way, he connected with these unknown parts of Grochaire. "About fifteen miles north. According to the legends about the Pickerne Caverns, there's a well-worn, ancient path that tracks along this side of the river. I think we should walk, conserve our strength for later battle or necessary flights."

Henry glanced around. "I agree. What do you think? Fifty in front? The rest behind and the women and support teams in the middle, spears at the ready?" He glanced up at Quinlan. "Will that do, mastyr?"

"You read my mind."

He turned and issued a sharp whistle, delivered the split-force order, then waved his men forward. The first half of the troll brigade moved by at a brisk clip, and one of the team leaders set up a chant. Batya was taller than all of them, but something about their strong, soldierly manner, and natural troll charisma, made them a formidable force.

At Quinlan's direction, she and Lorelei fell into line just in front of the medic unit.

Henry, she knew, would bring up the rear, forever on guard.

* * * * * * * *

Quinlan followed behind Batya, watching her long, thick hair sway as she walked. She had a strong, elegant stride and kept up with the troops like she'd been made for camp life. Both women seemed oddly fit for this journey, another thought that kept him in a state of turmoil.

He wished Batya was a weak-spirited person so he could despise her, or maybe just plain stupid so he wouldn't respect her as much as he did. As it was, her character forced him continually into a state of frustration because, damnit, he liked her.

A lot.

And his thoughts kept drifting into the future, decades ahead of this moment in time. He had grandchildren clustered around him, a lot of them, or maybe they were great-grandchildren and he was Papa Quinlan to all of them.

The image made him gag. What the fuck was wrong with him?

Batya turned back and grinned. "Stub your toe again because I'm sure hearing a lot of cursing behind me."

He grimaced. "You just turn around and watch where you're going."

She chuckled and shook her head, then caught up with Lorelei. The women chatted more often than not. They'd been friends for two years. Each kept looking around at the river, the vaulted ceiling of the massive cave system, realm-made stacks of rocks indicating that at some point in time their ancient forebears had also been here.

He marveled as well that he marched through the Great River Caverns of Pickerne, a fabled underground river system that had until now belonged only to stories told to children.

The river and cave took many twists and turns. Though the ceiling sometimes crept lower, it never narrowed to an impassable point, not once.

After being on the march for several hours, a black expanse at the horizon began to grow and eventually filled with stars.

Batya dropped back to join him, walking beside him. "We've reached the meadow, haven't we?"

"Looks like it."

"This is wonderful." She took his hand and gave it a squeeze. "We've just made it through the second leg of the journey. But how sure are we that Margetta won't find us?"

"It's unlikely even though Gem Meadow was never part of the enthralled section. Henry and his troops have run maneuvers here many times, which is why there are several permanent tent structures. But Margetta will have no idea where we went and covering hundreds of square miles, even for her, and especially through mountainous terrain, will be extremely difficult. However, Henry will keep scouts in the sky the rest of the night and through the day. We're in good hands."

A few more steps and he walked out of the cavern for good. He breathed in the grass-scented air and watched as the brigade immediately began setting up camp.

"There are three large tents." He waved his hand in the direction of each. "One down river to the left and two higher up the feeder stream." Turning to Lorelei, he asked, "Which one would you like? You should have first choice."

Her gaze shifted to each one in turn, then chose the one highest up on the stream, the farthest point east.

Batya touched his arm. "Henry has the map. I think he's setting up a table in the middle tent."

"Yes, he is."

"Wow," Batya murmured.

"What?"

"Well, I'm amazed at the order and industry of your brigade. Some of your men are already bringing back kindling and logs from the nearby forest."

"Fires are important in any woodland setting, for cooking and for security."

She watched several take a different track. "Where are they off to?"

"We'll be dining on venison tonight. You'll see."

Two trolls, laden with packs, approached Quinlan. "Mastyr, we've been told to set you up down river, near where the stream joins the river."

"Yes, that will do."

The trolls headed toward the open-air tent.

"Wait, what are they carrying?"

"A couple of furs, some padding. Pillows."

Batya drew close and asked quietly. "Will Lorelei's tent be as nicely appointed?"

He nodded.

"And you arranged all this for our comfort?"

"Of course."

Lorelei offered her hand. "I want to thank you, mastyr, for all you've done for me. You've been incredibly kind."

But before he could take her hand, Batya stepped between Lorelei and Quinlan. She stared at the proffered fingers until Lorelei withdrew the simple, if very human gesture.

Lorelei chuckled. "Batya, you're much more than you know you are right now. Have a care." She then wheeled in the direction of her tent. When she'd walked ten feet away, she called out over her shoulder. "See you at dinner."

Quinlan stepped around Batya and saw the look of astonishment on her lovely features. She blinked several times before lifting her gaze to Quinlan. "Did you see what I just did?"

"Not quite as simple as you thought, is it, this thing between us."

"But why did I do that? I mean, I really trust Lorelei. That was just rude. I've got to apologize to her." She turned as if to move away, but he caught her elbow.

"She already knows and right now I need you."

Her gaze shot back to his and her hand went to her throat. "Your stomach is cramping, isn't it? I can feel it now." She glanced past him, down river. "The Guards have finished with the tent. We can be private in there."

Chapter Six

Batya walked beside Quinlan, surprised yet not, that he took hold of her hand. Whatever this was between them, seemed completely mutual and just as incomprehensible.

Earlier, he had blocked her from offering a vein to save Henry's life and just now, she would have clawed Lorelei to pieces if she'd touched Quinlan.

Neither spoke.

She remembered her father's word about 'embracing the mystery', but she swore if he were here right now and said the same thing to her, she'd punch his lights out. She felt controlled by things way beyond her understanding and Quinlan also resented this similar experience invading his world.

"You've grown very quiet." He squeezed her hand. "Not a good thing."

"I'm not a quiet person, am I?"

"No, not even a little." He smiled. "You have a wonderful laugh, almost boisterous and you voice your opinions freely."

"I guess I do. Oh, this is very nice inside. There's even a platform for the bed. It's not very wide, though, is it? One of us is likely to push the other off the side."

"I'll just have to prepare myself for a hard landing."

"Hey, I'm not that bad." But she laughed.

"The first night, when I was recovering from mortal wounds, mind you, I woke up with you draped over my chest and my thigh. I could hardly breathe."

Her heart seized at the memories, not just of waking up with him when he'd finally healed, but of having seen him fly through the plate glass window, of the depths of his burns, and that she knew he would have died without her help. "I'd apologize but I'm just too grateful you survived."

She sat down on the side of the bed and held out her wrist. "I'd offer a different vein, Quin, but I doubt we'd be able leave the tent after that."

When he didn't respond, she frowned. "What?"

"You called me, 'Quin.'"

"I did? Oh, I guess I did. You don't like it?"

At that, he dropped down to sit beside her, something that caused the wood-frame to creak. He was a lot of vampire to hold up anything on four posts of wood and a few one-by-fours.

"That's the problem, I guess, the thing I've been grappling with. I like a lot of the stuff you do and I even like you calling me Quin. You keep surprising me."

"Ditto." But she sighed heavily. She met his gaze, those large dark eyes of his now reflecting her own concern. "Does any of this mean *anything*? I just feel so confused by my behavior and yours. I feel desperately out of control."

He nodded slowly and without taking his gaze from hers, he picked up her wrist and began stroking the veins very slowly with his thumb. "The worst part of that moment for me was that it made me hot as hell. I knew you'd claimed me earlier, but right then you'd proved it. I'm the land you want."

She glanced down at his thumb, which had set up an erotic vibration at her wrist. Such a small movement, yet she shifted where she sat, needy for him all over again.

Lifting her gaze once more to his, she drew a breath slowly. "But I just reacted, that's what bothers me, like something new lives inside all that I am and keeps driving me toward you. I've never been in this place before and it maddens me."

He lifted her wrist to his lips and kissed where the vibrations had been touching her. His eyes closed. *Does this madden you?* He kissed her skin over and over, his sensual lips warm, soft and moist, increasing her desire.

You know it does.

He opened his eyes and met her gaze, his dark brown, almost black eyes piercing her as he drew back his lips. Her gaze fell to the sharp points of his fangs, glistening with purpose. She blinked several times and for the life of her she'd forgotten how to breathe.

He turned her wrist gently, then angled his fangs. He moaned softly. *Your mouth is open, begging for me.*

Then don't leave a girl hanging. Give me something of yours to suck.

He growled softly, then lifted his free hand and rimmed her lips with his thumb. She gave a soft cry as he penetrated her mouth and struck her wrist with his fangs at the same moment.

She suckled his thumb as he removed his fangs and attached his lips to her wrist. He groaned as he drew in her life's blood.

Desire flowed over her in heavy waves, up through her abdomen and into her chest, gripping her heart. How heavily her heart thudded as he sucked greedily, pulling into his body what she willingly gave.

But it was the level of her desire that confounded Batya. She'd always wanted Quinlan. What realm-woman in her right mind hadn't lusted after his extraordinary physique, his sexiness, his almost troll-like charisma, and that something very dark of his that spoke of dominance in the night?

I don't want to give in to you.

He met her gaze once more and his dark eyes flashed in the non-existent light of the tent. But her fae-vision held him in a glow. He sucked harder and thrust his thumb deeper into her mouth. *Then what do you want from me, Cha? Why are you here, in this tent, feeding me and sucking on me?*

She pulled harder on his thumb, her sucking sounds almost vicious in the enclosed space. *I want you moving over me and thrusting into me hard, but I don't want to surrender all that I am to you or to anyone.*

He released her wrist suddenly, and in flurry of movement, vampire fast, he threw her onto the bed and landed on top of her, pushing her thighs apart with his knees.

He pinned her arms over her head. "You're a fool to say things like that to me. You know what I am, the reputation I have. I take what I want where women are concerned." *And you will surrender.*

He kissed her once, invading her mouth with his tongue, letting her feel his desire. But just as she was ready to strip naked, and let him do what he wanted, he flew backward to stare at her hard from the open flap of the teepee, then disappeared into the night.

Batya lay trembling with a combination of fear and desire.

She understood something about herself as she continued to stare at the space Quinlan had just vacated: she'd always had the upper hand in every relationship she'd been in, that the men she'd chosen were, without question, men she could subdue or at least resist.

But Quinlan, sweet Goddess, who could ever command him and what would it be like to truly surrender to him, to be commanded by him, to be told what to do from one moment to the next?

She shivered, desire cascading over her in heavy waves. She didn't understand why she needed him so desperately, why she craved him, why she wanted him to come back and tear her clothes off.

Though he'd just taken a good portion of her blood, still her heart labored as though she wanted to give him more. Why? What was it about Quinlan that had turned her into such a shivering, lust-laden, heart-pounding female?

* * * * * * * *

Quinlan stood just outside the open-air tent, his thighs quivering like a stallion needing to run, or better yet, to mount something fast. He worked on his breathing, taking one damn breath in, releasing it, then pulling another labored draw into his overtaxed lungs. He wasn't sure his cock had ever been so hard.

Sweet Goddess what the hell was going on between him and Batya? He'd never been like this before. He'd wanted to strip her down and plunge inside of her. The scent of her sex still permeated the air, that rich exotic tropical fragrance that assaulted his senses and caused his nostrils to flare then retract, working like bellows.

She'd become life and sex to him, setting a fire in his veins.

The moment he felt he had himself under control, she'd looked at him and begged for something of his to suck. He wanted his cock in her mouth, but his thumb had worked almost as well and he'd been rock-hard for her.

He ached in his groin, a sensation that lit up his abdomen and chest. Even his pecs flexed and un-flexed wanting her large breasts against him, wanting them in his mouth. He wanted to feast on every part of her body for hours, to suck, tongue, nibble, bite, and drink from her repeatedly. He felt insatiable.

Yes, that's how he felt, as though no matter how many times he drank from this well, he'd come back thirsting for more.

And all the while, he despised Batya for having this kind of power over him, that though he'd ordered his feet to move at least a dozen times since leaving the tent, he remained right where he was.

A shout of triumph from the forest drew his attention away from Batya as several trolls, spears waving in the air, hauled a deer carcass between them.

The spell broken, Quinlan could finally move and he headed in the direction of the main camp, around which most of the brigade had pitched their tents. A waiting spit had been erected, a pot in which beans, onions and savory herbs cooked. The troll in charge of camp meals, as well as his minions, had the venison hoisted up on another tripod of poles and went to work, skinning and carving up the flesh for the brigade's meal.

Forty feet past the food-prep area, a steady stream of trolls hauled deadfall in and out of the nearby forest, feeding a growing bonfire.

A clearing kept the meadow safe and camp chairs had started appearing along with drums.

He hadn't been on maneuvers with the troll brigade for some time, but former memories always made him smile. The masculine bond among trolls spoke to something inside him, of what he loved best about realm-life, something apparently Batya didn't see or hadn't yet experienced. If she had, how could she have ever abandoned Grochaire in favor of free-clinic work in Lebanon?

A small cluster of trolls had already started up their music, with two guitars, several drums and even one lyre. The sound was magical.

He felt Batya move up beside him. She even took his hand and held it in a light clasp, though releasing a frustrated sigh.

I'm being a pain, he confessed.

Me, too. I'm sorry.

He turned to her and spoke quietly. "We'll part, Batya, I promise you that much, then we can leave all this nonsense behind."

She nodded but he saw tears brim in her eyes. "I've never felt so confused before, so overwhelmed."

"Me, neither." He released her hand, then drew it around his arm, setting them both in motion toward the musicians. "Have you ever heard bonfire music before, like this I mean?"

"No. It's wonderful." She glanced around. "Is it the meadow, with the mountain on one side and the forest on the other, because the sounds echo back and forth."

"The acoustics are great here, that much is true. But I really think it's more the musicians."

She held his arm tight. He felt her apology like a vibration against his skin, which only served to ignite his guilt. He'd started this whole damn fiasco by pursuing her in the first place and all because at his first attempt, when he'd caught her in the corner of her gallery that first night, she'd told him to 'shove it'.

No woman had ever told him to get lost before. And it wasn't his pride that made him come back, but rather those words had lit up his animal passion, a latent caveman-like need to possess, that kept him both sexed up and intent on having this woman repeatedly.

He wanted her and the slow, sweet scent of her sex drifted over him, alerting his body that she was ripe for him as well.

But where could any of this end?

* * * * * * * * *

Batya sat beside Quinlan because to be anywhere else gave her the shakes. She needed to be near him, a primal instinct that worked in her like a virus. She ate the savory beans and venison like she hadn't eaten for a week. Recent events had probably heightened her appetite, the stress of disappearing into a sinkhole, then hiking through an underground river and camping outdoors. Although keeping Quinlan fed also required nourishment.

How's your blood-starvation? Any cramps?

From the corner of her eyes, she watched him shift a hand to his stomach, then frown. *I almost feel normal, which is really weird. I can't remember feeling this way in a long time.*

She shifted toward him. *So you feel different? Because of my blood?*

He shrugged. *Maybe. Not sure. But I do feel better.*

That's a good thing, right?

A wary light passed through his eyes, of doubt and maybe a streak of fear, though she wasn't sure the cause of it. Whatever was bothering him, he said nothing more so she let it go.

The music never abated, though the musicians changed hands several times. Drums seemed an important component to the brigade, and the rhythm shifted constantly.

A keg of beer made an appearance. Quinlan left her sitting on a camp chair, slightly removed from the group of men. Lorelei had retired early to her tent, bedding down for the remainder of the night and what would become a good portion of the next day. No doubt Margetta would hunt through the night, then take her Invictus wraith-pairs home for the day, so with any luck, they'd have a stretch of peace before having to move through the Dead Forest.

She shivered slightly at the thought of the next leg of the journey. The name, 'Dead Forest', would normally have been enough to make her change course, but the realm part of her knew that in order to get to Ferrenden Peace, they had to go through the Dead Forest. All the reasons might not be known, but eventually they'd discover the purpose for the chosen route.

Quinlan would have no choice but to remain in the tent during the daylight hours, but in October, this far north, night came fairly early. Her own faeness also had a strong aversion to sunlight, but she could manage short periods of time without harm. Not so for her vampire boyfriend. He'd be toast within an hour of direct sunlight.

He brought back a tin cup for her, handing it to her carefully to keep from sloshing. She took a sip and a flavor of herbs, honey, and something she couldn't quite identify, rolled over her tongue. "Very nice."

He'd finished one off at keg-side and sat down beside her with a cup of his own in hand. As the drums filled the night air, she asked him about his life. "Tell me something most realm-folk don't know about you."

He leaned forward, his forearms on his battle leathers. "When I was young, I tracked every vale, gorge, and mountain-peak of this realm. I walked the rugged three-hundred-mile long coastline, repeatedly, searching out ocean caverns, seal beaches, and tide pools. I was crazy for learning every inch of Grochaire, long before I knew I had mastyr-potential in me. That's one reason I have an extensive map collection."

"I watched you touching the map." She sipped her beer, watching him over the turned rim of the cup.

His lips quirked. "Possessively, no doubt."

"More like love and affection, I think. It's given me a different view of you, who you are in that decadent core of yours."

He glanced at her. "Decadent?"

"Oh, yes, you're at least that."

He sighed heavily as he wiped the sides of his mouth. He looked serious suddenly. "There is something I want you to know, especially since we've been thrown together like this." He glanced at her. "You know those rumors about me, about killing my father?"

She nodded slowly, holding her breath.

"Well, they're true." In a quiet voice, he told her about the years of his father's drunken abuse, the enthrallment around their home that had kept his mother a prisoner, and finally her death, which had prompted him to beat his father senseless. He'd died not from the bruises, however, but from choking on his own vomit.

He fell silent, staring at the cup in his hands. He said nothing more, perhaps just remembering. She felt the heaviness in his soul and knew that these events had defined his life, set his future. How would he ever truly trust an intimate relationship?

Batya knew how hard it had been for him to talk about what must have been one of the most horrifying moments in his life, especially because he'd been so young, just a teenager.

"But you were innocent, Quinlan. He died because he was a drunk."

He shrugged. "I tell myself that, of course, but it doesn't change what happened or that I still imagine a dozen different scenarios in which I prevented my mother's death and somehow got my father into rehab. Of course, the concept of rehab didn't exist that many centuries ago. Still." He turned his cup in his hand over and over.

"Everyone deserves better than to be controlled and hurt. Everyone. I'd tell you not to feel guilty, but that would be as useless as it would be insensitive. I can't imagine what it must be like to carry that with you."

He met her gaze. "Thank you for that." He cleared his throat and straightened his shoulders. "And now, it's your turn. You never told me why you abandoned Grochaire."

"I didn't, did I?"

"Nope."

Batya knew the time had come, but she hated speaking about the triggering event that had forced her to leave Grochaire. Yet, Quinlan had a right to know, not just because he'd opened himself up to her but because he ruled Grochaire. "I was working in the north, late one night, closing up just before dawn. I was so tired and ready for my bed, but just before I opened the door, two Invictus pairs launched an attack on a passing car. They pulled an elven family out, the mother, father, three children, the youngest a baby.

"I got out my phone and called for help, but by the time your warriors arrived, which wasn't more than ten minutes, the family was dead. I can't explain what happened to me, but some kind of switch got flipped in my head, or maybe my heart, and I left. I just couldn't take it anymore."

"Was that near the wastelands?"

She nodded. "I'd been trying to set up a free-clinic there. But people kept disappearing or bodies would be found mangled and drained. But the children, Quinlan."

"I know."

He reached for her hand and gave her fingers a squeeze. "I'm sorry, Cha. I would have spared you that."

"I know. And I don't blame you. I don't blame anyone. I just needed to leave the horror behind. So, I moved to Tennessee."

"And you opened up your clinic and your gallery."

"I did."

When he released her hand, she fell silent and for a few minutes, he did as well, maybe letting the memories dissipate. The drums and music continued to fill the air.

He sipped his beer and glanced at her. "Since I told you two things, I think it only fair that you do the same." His lips curved.

Caris Roane

"So, tell me something no one else knows about Batya, about the daughter of Davido."

She thought back to her earlier revelation about the men she'd been with. She felt bad like she'd turned over a rock in her life and found a bunch of bugs crawling beneath.

She met his gaze. "All right, here goes. I'm not proud of the fact that I've always been with men that I could control. At the same time, you scare the shit of me for the exact opposite reason."

He shifted in his chair, and his eyes flashed in the night. A shiver went through her and suddenly his mating vibration was just there, on her thighs and forcing the air from her lungs.

Tell me to stop, and I will. His deep voice rumbled in her head.

But she didn't. Her heart hammered louder than the drums and suddenly she knew exactly where she wanted this to go. *I want to know what it's like just once.* She said nothing more, offered no further explanation.

He rose up from his chair, took her cup and said he'd be right back. He handed the cups over to the cook and bid Henry goodnight. A boisterous, suggestive chant rose into the air along with a lot of laughter.

He smiled as he returned to her, something that told her he was a man with a plan.

He took her hand, lifting her to her feet, then led her to a portion well beyond their tent. She understood. The farther downstream they moved, the less likely they'd be seen, not at this distance.

"I need a bath." She watched him strip, her vision adjusting. His boots came off first as he unzipped. His shirt came next, followed by his battle leathers.

And her heart pounded for more than one reason as he stepped into the waters. He was absurdly beautiful.

"It's warmer than I thought it'd be." He glanced up stream. "There must be a hot spring on some of that high ground."

The water tempted her. He tempted her. And the drums called to something very realm-like in her soul, a fateful sensation of belonging with Quinlan, belonging *to* him.

Just to be safe, she set up an enthrallment shield around them both.

"Nice," he said. "And I can see it better out in the open, like everything around us is slightly blurred." He found a deep spot and floated, knees up, arms sweeping backward.

She took off her shoes, her jeans and shirt, then unhooked her bra. She heard him growl as she stepped out of her thong. She eased into the stream, taking care not to slip on the rocks. He was right. The water temp made it easy to slide into the slow moving stream, stretch and swim, if just a short distance. It felt wonderful and for the craziest moment, she wanted to stay right there forever, in the stream with Quinlan, bathing and swimming, soon-to-make love.

She rolled in the water, and floated on her back, not caring that her hair got soaked. She paddled gently against the current to keep herself in one spot. The drums were muffled with her ears below the stream's surface.

Staring up at the stars and at the crescent moon, she let the stress of the past two nights drift away. She gave herself to the beauty of the moment, to the music and the pulse of the drums, to the starlight and moonlight, and to the soft feel of Quinlan's vibrations as he touched her through the water.

She smiled. *That feels nice.*

You're beautiful—a pale island of delectable flesh on a dark slate of water. May I come to you?

The dominant man requested permission?

She smiled even more. *Yes. Please.*

I have a condition.

Anything. She couldn't believe she'd said that. 'Anything'. Without thinking, without protesting even a little, she'd agree to anything.

He chuckled softly. He was closer than she realized.

She lifted her head and found him just a few feet away, moving toward her, the waterline a few inches below his navel, pecs glistening in the glow of her fae night vision. He'd removed his clasp and his long thick hair hung around his shoulders.

Maybe because he knew she watched him, he lifted his arms, flexing, as he pushed his hair behind his back. His chest rippled as well as his arms. He looked incredible. *You'll need to agree to this condition.*

She nodded, the water lapping at her shoulders. *Tell me.*

You'll have to do everything I say, when I say it. He drew close and held her gaze tight to his. *Do you agree?*

Batya stared into dark eyes that glittered with desire. His smoky, applewood scent floated around her, causing her nostrils to flare and her mouth to water. She nodded slowly, sinking her feet to the bottom of the stream and rising to meet him. The soft caress of his seductive vibration spread over her abdomen.

She didn't touch him, though. Instead, she waited for him to speak, to command, to do whatever the hell he wanted with her. Had she really agreed to this? What, then, would the vampire require of her?

Embrace the Mystery

* * * * * * * * *

Quinlan didn't recognize the sensation at first, the one that travelled through him head-to-foot and strengthened his muscles. Eventually, he hit on the name for it. She'd called it right, speaking of dominance. He wanted to rule her and his body loved the idea.

He also knew what he wanted from Batya, a kind of surrender she'd never given to any man before. She'd already turned over her will to him, and to some extent, her safety.

But there was more here, something he wanted to subdue and she wouldn't like it at first, he was sure of that. He took her hand and led her from the stream, picking up all their clothes as he went. Once inside the tent, he dropped the lot by the flap. Even though she sustained the enthrallment shield, he lowered the flap so that nobody wandering by would be able to see her if her shield wavered.

She was for his eyes, no one else.

The staff had made up his bed and laid out towels. He picked one up and dried her off, stroking her full breasts, narrow waist, and rounded hips. He turned her and took his time with her bottom and between her legs, parting them with his hands, rubbing the towel back and forth slowly and on purpose until she moaned.

She was a sensual woman and he loved it, that she responded to all kinds of touch and stimulation. That he'd made her come with his vibration alone had kept him on the hunt, made him hunger for her knowing that there was more.

Right now, he was about to find out how much more.

He pulled the furs back and told her to lie down on her stomach but to spread her legs wide.

She crawled over the stiff mattress.

"I want you spread eagle." He pushed the pillows out of the way.

The bed was small. Sleeping might be problematic, but he loved how her pale body filled the space over the black silk sheets. Henry had great staff and it showed.

He watched her breathing, the quick nervous rise and fall of her back, and his thighs tensed, his cock growing hard. He liked her in this state, the confident woman laid out, vulnerable, at his mercy.

He stretched out behind her, planting his hands on either side of her hips. What man didn't love the sight of woman's shapely ass and Batya's was about perfect.

He kissed her, soft slow kisses moving from one side to the other, then dragging his wet tongue over her skin, lapping at times. Even her skin tasted of her tropical flower scent. He got lost in the sensation, nipping at her, then biting hard so that she cried out. Her pelvis rolled and she moaned, but he held her down.

Just feel me, feel what I'm doing, but don't move.

Her breathing grew ragged, even rough. He watched her fingers clutch, then release the sheet repeatedly. But he wouldn't let her hips rise and fall.

He shifted backwards, inching his mouth lower, to the soft flesh of her inner thighs, working his way to the center, lapping, nipping, sucking. He lifted her hips and put a pillow under them to raise them up to reach her better. He wanted to do more French kissing between her thighs.

Once he got the right position, he used his hands to massage her bottom as he kissed her the way he wanted to, swirling his tongue in and out, sucking at times, plucking at her lower lips, always massaging.

Her breathing had turned to a soft pant. *Quinlan, I need to move.*

Stay put. He pressed her hips down.

She cried out in frustration, but he continued lapping at her, savoring the taste of her that flowed over his tongue, her scent rich, his cock hard.

He opened up his vibration, focusing solely on his tongue. He plunged inside and let the vibrations flow. She tensed, but she was right on the edge. He added more vibration and thrust faster. She let out a long cry and he could feel by her inner pulses that she was coming. But he held her flat as he punched his tongue inside her, thrusting hard, sending wave after wave of vibration into her and through her.

After a good long minute of writhing and crying out, her body finally fell lax. *Oh, sweet Goddess, that was amazing, and what you can do with a vibration and your tongue—*

He slapped her bottom. *No talking unless I give you permission.*

She moaned and her fingers once more squeezed the sheets.

"I want you on your hands and knees."

* * * * * * * *

Batya struggled to rise up because the orgasm had sent her to the moon and she'd still not quite come back to earth. What Quinlan could do to her with his tongue and just a little vibration.

Now he wanted her on her hands and knees.

She finally found her balance and looked back at him, the thick, damp mass of her hair falling over her right shoulder.

His fingers still played with her ass and she loved it. She loved his fingers on her, his tongue, his lips, even his teeth when he nipped her.

He positioned his cock behind her and began to push inside, holding onto her hips, easing into her. She watched his eyes close as he penetrated her depths.

She was so wet for him and he was so big. He pulled back almost the full length of her except his tip, then shoved back inside letting her feel his thick stalk the entire distance.

She could feel his body revving up and she gasped knowing what would come. The vibration through his cock came as a soft tingle then a rumbling as she pushed back against him.

"Be still." He slapped her ass again.

The sensation startled her. The sting remained, combining with the vibration and the thrust of his cock, to create something new, something electric, something she wanted more of.

She pushed back again.

Once more he slapped her, then leaned over her and bit down on the back of her neck, hard and not with his fangs. *You will obey me, Batya.*

She didn't understand what was happening to her, or why a strange vibration started up in her own body. She could hardly breathe.

That's it. I'm feeling it now, your mating vibration is accepting me. He rolled his hips, thrusting. *Damn that feels good.*

Batya couldn't help herself as she purposefully shoved her hips back hard.

No moving.

He bit down harder on her neck and reached around to pinch a nipple. He pumped in quick thrusts, grinding his teeth in to her neck and pinching her breast at the same time.

She cried out, wanting to tell him to stop because it hurt, yet not wanting him to stop.

She grew very still after which he eased up on the bite and the pinch, but increased the vibration deep inside. She moaned.

He rubbed her breasts now and licked the back of her neck, sucking in turns. He had big, fleshy hands and his touch sent a thrill through her. He added vibration to his fingertips and moved in slow circles as he thrust in and out.

Moving his lips to the side of her neck, he began to lick over her vein. She groaned, needing him to sink his fangs, to drink from her.

Do it.

He eased back and stopped the sensual thrust inside her.

She'd made a mistake. She'd commanded him and everything stopped.

Her body ached so deep inside for movement and vibration that she gave a groan. *I'm sorry mastyr.*

Say it again, but look at me.

She shifted once more to look back at him. His expression was hard, commanding and her breathing hitched all over again. He looked dangerous, lethal, like he could tear her apart with a thought.

Her whole body quivered. *I'm sorry, mastyr. I humbly beg your pardon.*

He wrapped the long, thick length of her hair around his forearm, and pulled so that she felt caught. Once more, desire rushed through her, of being pinned by Quinlan, held fast, unable to escape.

Much better.

Holding her gaze, he thrust into her again and once more let the vibrations flow through her breasts through his fingers and between her legs.

She moaned heavily, her own vibration seeking his and swirling over him. But he didn't seem to complain about that. If anything, his realm vibration moved with hers, a kind of dance that echoed the heavy pounding of the drums.

She realized that their joined vibrations had synched with the drums, another erotic layer that had her well squeezing and released his stalk.

I'm going to take your blood, Cha, and you're going to give it up for me. I'm going to drink until I've had my fill.

Yes, mastyr. She'd learned her lesson.

He released her hair to slide his arm around her waist. He held her tight against him in order to keep the upper part of her still while he continued to push in and out of her with his cock. She could have come but she held back, knowing that the slide to ecstasy was a mere thought away. She wanted to wait. She wanted the drums at the brigade circle rising to a crescendo, she wanted Quinlan sucking hard at her neck and his hips moving vampire fast. She wanted his vibration filling every inch of her body, then she'd release.

She'd never allowed a man to take her in this position before, not once. Now here she was letting the big hulk of a warrior vampire ride her hard, command her, and soon he'd drink, taking, as he said, his fill.

At the same time, and with great practice, his fangs sliced into her vein, then he began to suck. He sent another vibration through his lips on her neck so that chills rained down her side and over her breasts. He pumped his hips hard.

Mine, cha. His deep voice rumbling through her head, his body draping over hers, his mouth sucking down her life-force, his hips working her hard—all brought her mating frequency forward in a way it had never been before.

He had all of her, something no man had ever taken before.

And it felt so damn good.

His movements became brisk, even rough. She wanted to move.

Let me move, please, mastyr.

You've asked nicely. Move with me now.

She pushed against him, her hips rocking. The drums in the distance fed the rhythm. Ecstasy built as a wave pulsed through her, then another and another, catching her up as Quinlan thrust hard into her, fast now, the beat of the drums quickening, his vibration at full-bore. He was so hard and her body gripped him. She cried out as pleasure streaked through her well, her abdomen, and rushed upward, filling her chest, her heart.

Suddenly he released her neck, rising up behind her, grabbing her hips hard as he thrust quicker still, then shouted into the open air. Her screams joined him as the rhythm of the drums pulsed, finally stopping just as her own cries eased down and Quinlan's hips pushed in slower, final thrusts.

Her arms crumpled and she half-fell, half-tried to ease herself down onto the bed, her face pushed into the mattress, but she didn't care. She felt so damn good.

Quinlan followed her and because he was so big, he managed to remain inside her, his hands catching her hips so that he lay on top of her. He spread his arms out on top of hers, breathing hard.

In the distance, a new drum rhythm began and the lyre played the prettiest melody. Batya couldn't imagine anything more perfect.

She'd forgotten the difference in the realm-world and for a moment, a very brief moment, she thought she could live here forever.

Chapter Seven

Something felt very wrong to Quinlan, but he couldn't quite put his finger on what rubbed his instincts the wrong way. With his blood needs satisfied for a brief period and so many feel-good chemicals tripping through his veins, he should have been at ease.

Instead, as he rose almost groggily from on top of Batya, he secured the overhead protective sun-shield with a nagging sense of something critical left undone. He brought Batya a hand towel for cleaning and glanced around.

Finally, he slipped his leathers back on, as well as his boots, then stepped outside. He walked the entire perimeter of the tent.

The brigade's music had ended at last and most of the men headed toward their tents.

His vampire vibration, peculiar to his species, sent a warning straight up his spine and a shot of pain into his head.

He turned to the east. The horizon, even through a dense forest, showed gray. Dawn was coming.

If he stayed out here much longer, the pain would intensify, but he had to have one last look around. His body seemed to know exactly where Batya was and not just because she lay on the tent bed. A powerful call within his gut, demanding he protect this woman, seemed fixed on her like the needle of a compass always aiming true north.

He wondered if it was her faeness, or that she'd come from Davido's powerful troll stock. He didn't know. But she had a call on him that both energized and irritated him.

He tried to imagine the moment, after they succeeded in delivering Lorelei to the Ferrenden Peace, when he said his farewells to the woman. But the idea of parting seemed impossible, which also grated on his bachelor proclivities. What was it about this woman that called to him as though she was the moon and he the tides, that he'd always respond to her, always turn in her direction, always say yes?

When the sun broke through the forest skyline, his head throbbed and his shoulder blistered, he finally left his vigil, unsatisfied at having failed to draw even one conclusion, and reentered the tent, securing the flap behind him.

He lit up his vision, seeking out a tear in any part of the dense canvas, and at last satisfied, he drew close to the side of the bed.

Batya lay as he'd left her, on her stomach, naked, her arms and legs spread. She was already asleep, her back rising and falling. He got rid of his boots then his pants, but took a long moment to stare down at her.

He'd loved commanding her, savored how her fae vibrations had flowed over and around his, how she'd taken to his slaps and bites, his domination of her body, the intensity of her response.

His cock responded appropriately, despite how much he'd already left of himself inside her. He took his shaft in his hand. He fondled what had been pocketed between her legs, her strong nest that had pulled on him. He let the memory play out in his mind and somewhere in all of that, his vibration began to hum.

That's when he realized he was still joined to her, vibration to vibration. She awoke and turned her head in his direction. Her gaze fell to his cock and his hand rubbing up and down.

"I wasn't enough?" But she smiled.

His lips curved. "I'm just remembering."

She stretched and slowly rolled onto her back, her arms over head, her large breasts rocking as she turned. His gaze drifted the length of her.

She looked around. "It's dawn."

He nodded and took his time stretching out beside her. "We'll be stuck in here all day."

"And we won't have to think twice about the she-devil out there."

He shook his head, his fist still busy as he leaned over her body and drew a nipple into his mouth.

She made an encouraging sound, using a string of m's.

Then he was torn. Should he leave his cock so he could touch her breasts, or keep fondling what was hard and ready once more.

Her breasts won out and for the next several minutes he gave all his attention to both breasts until Batya was writhing and begging for more.

He made love to her again, taking her to the heights, falling back to earth. He dozed and she sprawled.

Once, he took a hard slap to his face as the woman turned in her sleep, so he woke her up and punished her with his mouth between her legs for a good long time.

When at last he woke up, with the sun waning in the west, he lay on his side, spooning Batya, his arm wrapped tightly over her chest.

And in that soft moment before coming fully awake, he felt her vibration laying over his. They'd never completely separated, not in all this time, something he'd never done with another woman. Ever.

But because he wasn't fully awake, he did something unexpected. He left the entwined vibrations alone, sinking into them and exploring all along their curved ridges.

He sent a heavier vibration along the joined frequencies and Batya moaned, grinding her hips against him.

"That's nice," drawled from her lips. "Do it again."

But he didn't because he came fully awake as shouts from the camp, of a desperate nature, brought him sitting bolt upright.

At the same time, he disconnected from Batya and it was a sudden painful moment that had her crying out as well.

"Sorry, but something's going on."

He jumped from bed and dressed fast. Batya wasn't far behind him.

The problem was he couldn't leave the tent, not yet. The sun hadn't set behind the horizon.

But Batya pulled her enthrallment shield close around her as she slipped beneath the flap. "I'll see what's going on."

She returned shortly. "Henry's coming. I'm going to bathe in the stream—a minute only."

He felt the strength of her shield, that she'd wrapped herself in a force as powerful as what had kept Margetta out the night before, so he nodded.

Just as he secured the belt over his shoulder, buckling it in place at his left hip, Henry begged entrance.

"Come."

Quinlan could feel the scowl on his own forehead and had his fears confirmed at the sight of Henry's three ridges drawn tightly together, a look of dismay in his eyes. "We lost a scout and the other has come in bloodied and half-dead. I've sent the healers on the trail to the northeast, carrying him out. Invictus wraith-pairs attacked them at the ten-mile western-most outpost. The survivor said there were twenty pairs, that one of the bound fae bragged that Margetta had brought a hundred with her, that she'd catch us in the Dead Forest, if not in the meadow."

Quinlan glanced skyward then folded back the upper flap. He squinted against the fading light. He had just a handful of minutes before he could safely leave the tent. He'd have to stay behind with Batya, but he trusted her enthrallment shield would get them to safety.

Glancing back at Henry, he frowned all over again. "How's Lorelei?"

"Good and she has all my men doing her bidding. One of them had just brought a bouquet of late-blooming wild roses to her, when the scout returned. We've rigged a harness that two trolls wear and she sits between them as they fly. We'll carry her at the front with several Guardsmen in the lead."

"I can always rely on you."

"Hell, yeah, you can."

Batya returned, naked, unbeknownst to Henry. Quinlan could easily see through her enthrallment shield now, maybe because of their recent connection. When she started to dress, even though she was invisible to Henry, he stepped between his brigade commander and all her female beauty.

"Where's Batya?"

Henry glanced around, his gaze skating past her. "She's bathing, cloaked with enthrallment."

"Oh, okay. That's right. She made it possible for the three of you to escape from Lebanon."

"Yes, she did."

"She's special, Quinlan. I can't put my finger on it, but she's got something"

"I would agree with you."

"No, I mean she's got something. Maybe it's her power or a layer to her faeness that hasn't revealed itself, but something's there, hidden maybe even from her."

He felt Batya go very still behind him.

Several more shouts from the direction of the camp set Henry hurrying back outside, but he called over his shoulder, "We'll be ready to fly in three."

"I've got a couple more after that inside. Set your men on the trail at will."

"Yes, mastyr."

Once, he was gone, Batya lost her shield and now, finished packing her satchel. "What do you think he meant, about me having another layer of power?" She glanced up at the open sky. A thin stream of clouds overhead caught the last pink-violet and quite deadly rays of the sun.

"I have no idea."

"Do you sense anything like that?"

He stared into her hazel eyes, searching. "I sense so many things, but I'm not sure what Henry meant. Did you know our realm vibrations remained joined all through the night?"

Her arched brows rose. "No. Are you serious? But I swear … Wait, you must be right because I felt the disengagement just a few minutes ago, and it hurt. I can't believe I wasn't aware. It all felt so natural."

"It did."

He drew back the overhead flap, the sky now moving to gray and darker. Each second that passed felt like an eternity.

He heard Henry's sharp call-to-the-air. The flapping of a hundred long coats as the brigade took flight, sounded like geese rising suddenly from a pond.

He glanced up. "Two more minutes but we'll need your enthrallment shield."

"Absolutely."

* * * * * * * *

Batya felt Margetta's presence and before a split-second had passed, she surrounded herself and Quinlan in a tight enthrallment shield. *She's here.*

I can feel her, too.

What's the plan?

Straight up into the air.

Got it.

He slid an arm around her waist and because he was so strong, she didn't bother with planting a foot on his boot. She simply wrapped her arm around his neck and leaned into him. *You smell like wood-smoke.*

He chuckled. *Let's go.*

She closed her eyes, but extended her senses outward, her realm vibration that mapped the location of Margetta and her forces. At the same time, she kept her enthrallment shield tight.

The swift rise into the air, the downward pressure on her head while her body lifted higher and higher, teased her stomach into a knot of excitement. She'd always enjoyed flight and wished it was one of her gifts.

But this, at least, was second best, flying at a terrific speed, straight up, in Quinlan's arms.

"I see them." Margetta's voice rolled through the enthrallment shield, but Quinlan kept rising. The air grew colder and colder. The shrieks from the Invictus pairs followed them.

Batya held on, knowing something was on his mind and sensing that to communicate at all, even telepathically, could somehow jeopardize their location.

Just as the tip of her nose started to freeze, he arced northeast, leveling out first, then beginning a slow descent.

She opened her eyes, startled to see that they'd entered a lower layer of clouds. But the mist broke and because she faced forward, she saw the strangest sight, a line of green forest, broken abruptly by a line of bright golden trees that went on for miles.

At first, she didn't understand what she was looking at, but the closer he brought them to the phenomenon, the demarcation point began making sense.

We can talk now.

I felt it as well, that Margetta would have located us with the telepathy right then.

Exactly.

Quinlan, we're looking at the point at which the Dead Forest begins, aren't we?

Yes, and I've already pathed Henry. They're only a few hundred yards away.

I can see them now. Lorelei's in the front. Is any of this going to work?

Sweet Goddess, I hope so, but Batya, they'll be on our trail. Can you place a shield around the entire brigade?

Batya swallowed hard. It was one thing to protect Quinlan or even her building in Lebanon because she'd been there a long time, but he was asking if she could wrap a shield around a moving brigade that didn't have either a solid front or an end point. *I don't know. I honestly don't know. I've never really used these muscles before.*

Your enthrallment rocked at the gallery. I'm still amazed.

But that's the point. She then explained her concerns about the nature of a moving brigade as opposed to a brick building.

His flying slowed as he eased down toward the brigade, flying above them. *All right. We'll take it one step at a time. Let's get everyone into the Dead Forest and see what you can do. I'll let Henry know.*

Sounds like a plan.

Batya essentially let her feet hang in the air as Quinlan flew her the final distance past the line of living forest.

But the moment he crossed that border, her head began to ring in the strangest way, as though a thousand vibrations crisscrossed the Dead Forest.

Quinlan dropped down to a shallow clearing a hundred yards in, marked by a dozen broad tree stumps. Batya realized suddenly that the forest was anything but dead.

He set her on her feet, but the physical battering of the forest's vibrations dropped her to her knees and brought her hands to her ears.

"Batya, what's wrong? Talk to me." She felt Quinlan's hand on her shoulder then his arm as he lifted her to her feet, but she could do little more than cling to him. *Don't you hear that? Feel that?*

Sorry, I'm only getting a soft sighing sound, wind through the trees, nothing more.

"I don't know what's wrong. I think it's the Dead Forest." Through the haze of her intense reactions to the unknown vibrations, she saw the brigade touch down in a half-circle around Quinlan.

Henry moved forward, his spear upright. "Mastyr, Margetta will be here in three minutes. Our scouts have sighted her force. They're on our back trail."

She felt Quinlan grow very still, the kind of stillness that only a vampire could do and if he hadn't been holding her upright, she would have thought he'd disappeared. She just didn't know what to do about the vibrations battering her or how long she could endure them.

* * * * * * * *

Quinlan had faced a lot of enemies in his day, but nothing like the one headed in their direction.

He held a shivering woman in his arms that he sensed had some kind of connection to the Dead Forest, but who also held the only viable form of protection against Margetta. He needed her to deploy her enthrallment shield and to do it now, or they'd all be dead and Lorelei captured by her brutal parent.

His ancestors had long-ago developed a stillness technique, a very un-dead quality. If he'd been alone, he would have appeared as a statue to those powerful enough to see him, but invisible to most. He couldn't imagine what Batya felt. He wasn't even sure she could feel him right now.

But stillness gave the mind opportunity to process faster, think clearer and with greater flexibility than an active vampire body.

So despite his impulse to *do something, anything,* he drew his breathing to just short of a halt, and let his brain work. Batya, Margetta, Lorelei. The three women's names flowed through his head over and over.

Batya.

Margetta.

Lorelei.

Lorelei the wraith-shifter, one of the most powerful realm-beings he'd ever encountered. Batya with a layer of power even Henry hinted resided within her realm-soul. Margetta, evil, manipulative, intent on her prize at all costs.

Batya.

Margetta.

Lorelei.

The idea sprang into his head, fully-formed, and he called out to Lorelei. "I need you here. Come here. Now."

Instead of jumping down from her perch slung between two troll warriors, she shifted suddenly into her wraith form, as though understanding. She floated in front of him, her eyes glowing.

She frowned at Batya. "The forest has enthralled her."

"I know. Put your hand on her back. I know you can do this, Lorelei, but you must block the vibrations so that she can settle her shield around us. Do you understand?"

The worried look in the woman's eye, told him she didn't believe herself capable, but she reached forward with the long, oddly shaped fingers of the wraith and touched Batya.

The fae body, holding tightly to him, arched once. Then a heavy sigh poured from her lungs and throat. "Oh, thank God."

"You mean I did it?" Lorelei's cheeks darkened with surprising color.

"Yes, you broke the forest's hold on her."

Batya drew back, blinking several times in a row. She stared at Quinlan. "I don't know what that was."

Henry intruded. "Margetta is half-a-minute out."

Quinlan took Batya's shoulders and searched her eyes. *Cha, we're in trouble here and I need you to do the impossible right now.*

She nodded. *The shield.*

As quick as you can. You can do this. I know you can.

I see her. Batya suddenly squared her shoulders. He felt the enthrallment shield emerge like a wave of warm water flowing thickly all around him, then past him.

Still keeping contact with her, he turned slightly to watch as the shield moved like a living thing past troll after troll.

Margetta, this time in her wraith form, flew swiftly, darting in the direction of the edge of Batya's wave. If she caught the edge, she'd be inside the shield. Quinlan was no fool and he'd waged war in the Nine Realms against a host of enemies. He knew Margetta's power. She'd destroy them all.

He shifted to look at Batya who tracked Margetta as well.

Batya's eye sparked with something he recognized and Quinlan smiled. She gave a sudden cry, her face twisted with a warrior's grimace, and with a sharp outpouring of her power she closed the shield and locked Margetta out.

The result was a wraith-shriek like nothing Quinlan had heard before as Margetta, having lost the advantage, screamed her frustration. She paced above them, flying in quick jerks over the shallow space of dry land, and he felt her battle frequency light up.

"Holy shit, let's get the fuck out of here. Henry, keep your men tight. Batya, hold that shield."

Lorelei shifted back into her fae form and her trolls rushed forward to catch her up in the sling. In turn, Quinlan slid his arm around Batya's waist and held her against him. He turned, heading up the path that led through the Dead Forest to their next destination, praying to the Goddess that Batya's shield, untried in a moving setting, would hold.

Quin, hold me tight even as I twist around in your arms. I have to see the brigade to sustain the shield. Tell Henry to keep the men close together.

Done.

He ignored the impulse to rush up the path but instead flew at a pace to track with Henry and the brigade. Batya pivoted hard in order to face backward so she could see the last of the trolls.

They're moving close. That's perfect. If your scouts fall back, I can't protect them.

Henry understands. Just hold it steady. Can I go faster?

As long as Henry's brigade stays close, speed is fine.

She sounded so damn confident, despite the fact that she trembled, and he loved that about her. But battle energy showed up in many forms and the shakes had come to him more than once as well.

There was something, however, he needed to know. *How important is Lorelei to this equation right now? Could you hold the shield without her?*

Yes, because she broke the forest's hold on me. Do you see Margetta?

She's ahead of us about thirty yards, but much higher in the air. I don't see her force.

I believe your shield has created enough confusion that they don't know where to go.

Why isn't she back with them?

I think she's waiting for a chance for the shield to weaken enough that she can grab Lorelei, or she may have some other plan.

What do you mean?

He ground his teeth. *Remember the map? We've got a series of switchbacks coming in about two minutes as we start climbing through the Pleach Mountains.*

I won't be able to see the brigade.

Quinlan frowned. *What if we flew over the mountains, in a straight line? You'd be above the forest.*

My instincts tell me the vibrations would probably return, but we could try anyway.

Let's at least give it a shot.

He pathed to Henry and a few seconds later, the entire brigade started rising.

But the moment they cleared the treetops, he felt Batya tense. *I can't do it.*

He dropped back, the brigade with him. He felt Batya relax against him.

The forest started screaming again. I knew I'd lose the ability to concentrate.

Quinlan glanced behind him. *What about using Lorelei at the same time to do the blocking like she did earlier?*

I've thought about that. But what happens if she can't sustain it, and we've gotten so far off the path we can't get back to safety? We'd be out in the open, vulnerable, and Margetta would take us down, you know she would.

Let met path to Lorelei and see what she says.

Good idea.

He switched pathing frequencies and sought Lorelei's but she told him she just didn't know.

Taking the variables into account, he knew he couldn't risk the brigade, not if Lorelei wasn't sure.

Returning to Batya's frequency, he related the conversation.

Then, we should stick to the path through the Dead Forest. We at least know we're safe here.

He set his gaze up the trail. *We'll just have to figure out how to do the switchbacks.*

Hey, I'm not getting heavy, am I?

He snorted. *As if.*

She laughed. *Yeah, yeah, vampires are strong.*

Well, we are, and I'm not your regular old vampire, either.

He felt her lips suddenly on his neck, right in the middle of a flight through the Dead Forest. *No, that you're not.* Something enormous burst in his chest, like a firework exploding and sending sparks everywhere. Sweet Goddess, a few words and she turned his world upside down.

He'd been content before Batya. Now everything seemed to be changing, morphing as fast as Lorelei could switch from shifter, to wraith, to fae.

Back to the problem, he pathed, but even in his head and probably hers, his voice sounded hoarse.

He turned his attention to the witch flying in front of them. Margetta. Power-on-power. He moved swiftly as Batya sustained her enthrallment power, holding his brigade together, keeping Lorelei safe for the present.

Screams erupted from behind him, toward the back of the ranks. *What was that*, he pathed. *Can you see?*

I don't know, but I have the worst feeling. A light flashed back there. Quin, I see smoke. Another round of screams erupted.

Sweet Goddess, Margetta's crew has found a way to launch some kind of fire bomb through the Dead Forest, across the path at random. I know they can't see through the shield, so they're guessing where your brigade is at, but they're hitting targets because of it. What are we supposed to do?

Let me contact Henry.

He drew in a deep breath, and switched pathing lanes again as he continued to speed up the trail just a few feet off the ground. *Henry, what's going on?*

The she-witch has had her wraith-pairs sending battle frequency blasts through the forest, the trees ignite, and fire shoots across the path. By all the Elf Lords, we've lost at least five of our force.

The enthrallment shield only disguised their position, but couldn't protect them from the fire blazing across the path.

Shit. He had to change things now so he made a quick decision. *Henry, we're going to speed this party up. You game?*

Hell-yeah.

Let your troops know.

Done.

Quinlan didn't wait for Henry, he just launched, doubling, tripling his speed. The dead would be left behind. There was nothing he could do about that. But changing up the flight would help.

Batya pathed. *Don't worry, the brigade is catching up.*

Henry knows what to do.

He loved his world, his troops, his Guardsmen, all his brigades. Losing even one of his men was a terrible loss and the thought of those left behind just plain hurt.

But he wouldn't think about that now.

He just had to get the women to the snowfields, cross them, and deliver Lorelei to Ferrenden Peace. But what was he supposed to do about the powerful, mastyr vampire wraith-pairs?

There didn't seem to be an answer any way he cut it.

* * * * * * * *

Batya's stomach turned as another flash burst through the forest in the distance and a third round of screams erupted from the troops in the back, despite that the column now moved at an incredible rate. Her shield held, but couldn't prevent the random fires that Margetta's force launched through the forest.

Men were dying and there was nothing she could do.

She felt Quinlan's determination in the taut state of his muscles as he held onto her and with the speed he moved.

Switchbacks coming up. How's the shield?

We're okay. Facing backward helps.

Lorelei's eyes were closed as she held onto the sides of the sling and the trolls in charge of her strove to keep a bare three feet behind Quinlan.

The snowfields were the next stage of the journey. While still watching the brigade, she focused her senses forward, on what lay ahead. All these experiences were so new to her that she felt disoriented and uncertain. She'd kept most of her fae powers in a latent state, except her healing gifts.

The one that moved within her now had to do with the path that Quinlan carried her over. She wasn't even certain what kind of fae power she possessed as she searched well ahead of Quinlan's position. She let the snowfields take shape in her mind and she saw them, vision-like, as clearly as the moment she'd seen the image for the painting the first time, before she'd ever laid a brush-to-canvas.

The mystery of it astonished her, that despite her desire to keep her faeness in severe check, it had emerged anyway and had laid out the route by which, hope-to-Goddess, Lorelei might be saved from her evil mother. Instinctively, Batya knew that if Margetta ever got hold of Lorelei, the ancient fae would gain a critical advantage over the Nine Realms.

As she continued to search into the future, what came from within her was a new kind of vibration. The Nine Realms was a world of vibrations and frequencies, all kinds, mating, battling, healing and so many more. But this one didn't yet have a name.

What are you doing now?

Quinlan's voice in her head comforted her and gave her a surprising kind of peace. At least, his increased speed had stopped the screams from the back of the troop line.

She tested the enthrallment shield. Though it held, Margetta still sensed enough about their position to be able to orchestrate the streams of energy that ignited the flash fires.

While holding her enthrallment steady, she turned in Quinlan's arms. *Something's going on up ahead.*

The trail's incline rose sharply. They'd reached the mountain and would soon begin a series of switchbacks.

Can you hold your enthrallment?

The funny thing was, now she knew she could.

Yes. But the troll part of me seems to think things are going to get messy.

Chapter Eight

Quinlan stuck to the path, his gaze searching every shimmer and twitch of the golden-leafed trees. He didn't know what to expect and even he could see that Batya's enthrallment shield held, but he had his battle frequency on full bore searching for the enemy.

He slowed as the first switchback came into view, a real hairpin curve, and as steep as the rocky banks were, the golden trees swayed in the constant breeze.

On he sped, Batya a warmth in his arms as he levitated and flew three feet above the ground, chin lowered

It's beautiful here. Her voice in his head eased him.

I think it's more than just a forest.

I do, too. But what?

Quinlan felt Batya's consternation, a soft vibration through his skin. There was another mystery, that he could feel her emotions, that she seemed to be communicating with him all the time, just not always verbally.

Right now, she seemed really intent on understanding her surroundings, which was not a bad thing.

He broke his telepathic link to her, then contacted Henry. *How we doin' back there?*

We haven't been hit in several minutes and I'm not seeing the enemy. Speed helps, but it'll be rough going up this mountain.

I know. And we're fifteen miles out.

Any orders?

Quinlan grimaced at the undercurrent in Henry's words. The whole brigade could come under attack at any moment, and all they could do was keep flying as fast as they could toward the Snowfields of Rayne.

How odd, though, that he could sense the snowfields now, the image of Batya's painting etched in his mind like a beacon.

The miles wore on, one after the other, through the mountains. He would need blood soon to sustain this pace, to keep the brigade moving.

And just like that, her words were in his head. *Need a tap while we fly?*

Did you just read my mind?

She didn't speak for a long moment. Instead, she grew very quiet, almost vampire still which also freaked him out.

Finally, her voice rang through his mind. *Quinlan, I'm not sure how I know what I know but I felt your hunger like a bell ringing within my head, or maybe my chest.*

If he hadn't been in motion, he would have scratched his head over this one. *I don't get it. How did you know? Why do you have a bell? Is it a fae thing? Or maybe a troll gift?*

I haven't got a clue except that things are changing within me and I am experiencing this vibration that looks forward, not into the future, not like a vision, but as though I can see or feel well up the trail.

So what do you see ahead of us?

She didn't speak, instead, she turned into him, slid her left arm more tightly around his neck, drawing herself higher up within the cradle of his arm, and lifted her wrist to his mouth. *Feed first.*

Quinlan wasn't stupid, so he didn't argue. Besides, his fangs had already emerged and using his free hand to hold her wrist steady, he struck then once more took her blood into his mouth.

The flavor, full of her scent, almost made him trip midair. But he adjusted, making a swift correction, and took in what tasted power-laden now. Maybe the new vibration she'd just mentioned had changed the quality of her blood, but whatever it was, he loved it.

As he drank, he felt nothing but gratitude that, while being pursued, she'd take care of his blood needs.

When he finished, he released her wrist, then readjusted his hold on her. *Thank you.*

You're welcome. There's only one problem now. I felt it a couple of minutes ago, but I thought I'd wait until you were done feeding.

What is it?

Something big. Not far now. I'm feeling dizzy.

Did I take too much blood? He couldn't have. He'd just barely topped off, taking only what he needed to sustain his power levels.

No, that's not it. I think… No, I'm sure it's Margetta. She's not far now. She's waiting for us.

Embrace the Mystery

As Quinlan rounded the next bend, the dizziness Batya had complained about hit him suddenly and his battle frequency kicked into high gear. He pathed to Henry, letting him know something was up, then slowed his speed. The trail curved.

We're coming up on an open stretch, a shallow valley. I can see it in my mind's eye.

She's waiting there?

Batya took a deep breath. *I believe she is.* He felt her tremble in his arms.

The dizziness became oppressive as he rounded a wide bend in the trail. The mountain gave way to a meadow, angling off to the northeast.

The grassy land had patches of snow but seemed to be a small valley in the middle of the range.

The trail climbed a small hill, then dropped down to a beautiful expanse that began to glow brighter and brighter.

He felt Margetta now and the distant spread of gold, glowing light, the same one that had been at Batya's gallery, almost blinded his vampire vision. Beyond the glow, he could see a large force of Invictus wraith-pairs hovering in the air, waiting.

Can she see us through the shield?

I don't think so.

And how did she find this part of the Dead Forest?

I think we cleared the entire Dead Forest from the enthrallment on the maps.

How far do you think we are from Ferrenden Peace?

Another hundred miles across the snowfields.

Oh, Quinlan, how are we going to cover so many miles?

Don't worry about that right now. This is the only battle we need to fight.

She was silent for a moment, then pathed, *You're right. Of course.*

Even though Batya's enthrallment shield held, Margetta blocked the path in a huge radius of light, at least sixty feet up, past the tree-top line, and twice that width, which spanned the narrow meadow.

He slowed to a stop, pathing to Henry at the same time, then dropped to the ground.

Batya released him to stand on her own. "What do we do?"

He didn't have time to answer, since Lorelei let out a piercing scream.

Turning in her direction, Quinlan saw Lorelei floating in the air, higher and higher and completely against her will. He left Batya, flying up into the air to catch Lorelei before she disappeared through the upper edges of Batya's enthrallment shield.

He could feel Margetta's hold on her. Still in her fae form, Lorelei wrapped her arms tightly around him, but Quinlan could barely hold his position in the air with her. The ancient fae increased her power over Lorelei. The frequency vibrated heavily so that he shook while holding Lorelei.

"Don't let me go, Quinlan, please. Kill me first. I can't fall into her hands. All of the Nine Realms will be in danger if she gets her hands on my blood and my power."

"I've got you."

"But we're still rising."

"Just hold on."

He needed to figure this out, but the situation was unfamiliar to him. If this had been a regular battle, he'd be issuing orders left and right to Henry and his brigade. He would have already set up a battle shield that would have protected the women from assault and capture.

But how was he supposed to battle a fae of incalculable power, who could operate an unknown frequency through Batya's enthrallment shield? The only thing he had going for him was that apparently there were limits to Margetta's power because right now, Quinlan kept Lorelei in a safe position within the shield. He just didn't know how long this would last or if the damn woman had something else up her sleeve.

* * * * * * * * *

Batya trembled, but not from fear. A terrible jealousy pierced her body and mind so that she could hardly move. She stared up at Quinlan, holding Lorelei in his arms, and inwardly screamed at him to let her go. Part of her knew he had to do this, had to hold her because it was the only way to keep her out of Margetta's hands. But the other part of her demanded action now. If she had flight capability, she would have levitated straight up into the air, ripped Lorelei out of Quinlan's arms, and beat her to a pulp for daring to touch him.

At the same time, thank the Goddess, her battle frequency had assessed the situation and given her enough self-control to think.

Quinlan needed help, as in *now*.

She'd helped him before and not just with the enthrallment shield, or her blood, or her healing power, but with her battling frequency.

She called to Henry who flew straight to her. "Can you get me up there? I need to support Quinlan."

"You got it." He called two of his strongest trolls and the next thing she knew, the men caught her beneath her arms and flew her to Quinlan.

As soon as she reached him she planted a hand on his shoulder and let her battle power strike home.

Instantly, he began to descend still keeping Lorelei tight in his arms.

Just as he reached the ground however, Batya felt Margetta's power flood the space. Batya flew backward and would have fallen hard except that the trolls, extremely well-trained, went after her and scooped her up setting her on her feet to give her a soft landing.

Once more, Quinlan battled high in the air against Margetta's hold just a few feet from the enthrallment shield. Whatever power Margetta utilized, would soon take Lorelei out of the safety-zone.

Several fires erupted again in the forest all around them but the width of the meadow kept the brigade safe, at least for now.

Batya didn't know what to do. She stared up at Lorelei, who had started shouting, maybe at Margetta, she couldn't tell.

She turned in Margetta's direction. She could see the beautiful ancient fae, her face twisted with effort, her arms outstretched, her energy aimed at her daughter and Quinlan.

The past two days once more shot through her mind, that Quinlan's desire had brought him to Lebanon, to her gallery. Surely, sex couldn't have been the only force. Surely there had to be more to this equation, something very realm, and no, she didn't want to explore it. She wanted to stay detached from this life, but right now she didn't have that option, not if she was to help save Lorelei, and whatever other ramifications her capture might have on the Nine Realms.

She was therefore going to have to do the most difficult thing of all, and she really didn't want to.

Henry had alluded to it earlier, some new kind of power that she possessed.

She focused inward, on her various frequencies, especially on her faeness. She picked up her most powerful vibrations that related to her fae ancestry, but nothing came to her as different, special, or even particularly powerful.

Quinlan inched toward the top of her shield, barely three feet away now.

Batya's heart hammered in chest.

Once more, she explored what lay inside her, the visionary power, so typical of the fae, but which had translated to her paintings, her healing power, her battle frequency, but nothing surged even a little to show her the way.

Her father's words came to mind, his parting thoughts about exploring her attraction to Quinlan as well as her heritage.

Henry flew high in the air, along with a force of four powerful trolls. They created a kind of flotilla above Quinlan and Lorelei, trapping them beneath the upper layer of the shield.

They'd stopped the upward rise, at least for a moment. But once again, Margetta's power rolled through, passing beyond the shield in the form of a great wind, and the trolls blew toward the south, like dry fall leaves.

Nothing seemed to be working.

She closed her eyes, setting her attention on her heritage, the entire breadth of it, all the years that Davido had raised her, cared for her, given her his troll wisdom.

Davido had been a rock in her life, troll that he was, so different from her faeness.

Yet she was part troll.

Her eyes popped wide. She might be essentially and genetically fae, but every species passed along recessive qualities here and there, like bright rocks forcing a stream to flow around them.

She turned inside once more, only this time, she planted her thoughts on Davido, on the mysteries that had surrounded this strange time with Quinlan, on the arrival of Margetta who had been stunned to find Quinlan in the gallery.

Quinlan was the true anomaly in this situation. Margetta would have known to expect Batya at her own gallery, but somehow, in all her preparations, she hadn't predicted Quinlan's presence.

Her mind began to work in a way that resembled her father, with a kind of instinctive troll-like precision that flowed from one thought to the next easily. Her faeness was all swirls, magic, and light, but this more rational part of her emerged with a kind of numerical precision.

She let the frequency flow, of instincts and calculation.

She stared up at Quinlan and stretched her vision to see him more clearly. He was only a foot away from the top of the shield. Sweat poured down his face and Lorelei wept.

Quinlan, she pathed to him.

Got any ideas?

One. You have the power to do this.

Not that I've noticed.

* * * * * * * *

Quinlan felt something new emanating from Batya, something unexpected. At first, he didn't recognize what it was, then he realized her words carried the feel of her father, of Davido.

He kept up his pressure on holding Lorelei away from Batya's shield, now inches away, but at the same time he focused on Batya, on the new vibration flowing into him. *What should I do?*

I don't know, Quinlan, except that it's important right now that you think creatively, outside-the-box.

He almost laughed. He'd never been a creative type. He liked maps where everything was laid out for him. He made war, organized scouting forays, ruled a realm. He even managed the politicking of the various town and city mayors fairly well. But what he didn't do was conjure up new and intriguing methods of doing anything.

So what could he possibly contribute to this situation other than his brute strength, which had failed him at Batya's gallery and which was failing him now?

He cursed beneath his breath, but Batya's trollish stream flowed stronger now, as though gaining substance as each second passed. *Quinlan, think opposites. If your strength can't beat Margetta, maybe something else can, something you've kept hidden from yourself in the same way I didn't know I had my father's instincts.*

Quinlan opened himself up to Batya's frequency. *Tell me more.*

There's a mystery here. How can Margetta reach Lorelei through my enthrallment shield? Except for the wind she can employ, why doesn't she just attack you? Maybe Lorelei needs to be a different kind of focus.

He had no idea what she meant, but he heard Lorelei gasping for air. With only half a foot separating them from the top shield, he was squeezing the life out of the woman he was trying to protect.

"Sorry, Lorelei." He eased up on his hold and for some reason, Margetta lost her grip and he and Lorelei dropped three feet in the air.

But the moment he began fighting Margetta's hold on Lorelei, he lost his advantage and started rising toward the shield once more.

Batya's voice once more entered his mind. *Tell me what happened.*

Quinlan didn't hesitate, but relayed the sequence of events.

The focus must involve Lorelei somehow.

A new strategy emerged like lightning and he knew what to do, maybe because Batya streamed her new energy toward him, or maybe he'd finally had a new thought. *Batya, train all your attention on Lorelei and I'll do the same. Use this new trollness on her.*

You got it.

Her quick affirmative response stunned him because it was very un-Batya-like.

When he felt her attention shift to Lorelei, almost at the same moment, Margetta's hold began to release. And as soon as he let go of his physical battling of the situation, and even loosened his grip on Lorelei, the descent began.

"What's happening?" Lorelei's doe eyes had a startled appearance.

"Change of strategy, and damn the elf-lords, but it seems to be working."

Lorelei glanced up. "It is. We're fifteen feet away from the shield now, at least. Thank the Goddess."

He'd been a warrior long enough to understand that he couldn't let up right now, that he had to keep his attention on Lorelei herself and not drift back into fighting mode again. Apparently, in that state, Margetta could easily overpower him, but not if he was simply looking at Lorelei and helping her to float back to earth.

The moment, she touched back down, Margetta's power broke completely.

Batya slid her arm around Lorelei's waist. "We have you."

Quinlan released Lorelei as well.

Henry flew in close. "She's up to something new. Do you feel that?"

"Oh, God," Batya murmured. "She's revving up her battle frequency."

Henry glanced around. "She'll fry us all."

Quinlan met Batya's wide eyes. *Any more ideas, Cha?*

She shook her head. "Haven't got a clue."

Quinlan was about to ask Henry for his take on things, but Lorelei turned to Batya. "Let the forest speak to you. I've been thinking about the effect the forest had on you and I have a feeling it was trying to communicate. Haven't you felt it as well, that the Dead Forest isn't really dead at all?"

* * * * * * * *

Batya turn in the direction of the ancient fae. She only had seconds to change what was about to happen.

Glancing up at the sky, she let go of her fears then glanced at Quinlan. "Get me up there."

"You've got it."

"But bring Lorelei as well."

He gathered up Batya in his right arm and Lorelei in his left, then headed skyward at top speed.

Batya closed her eyes against the sudden rush of wind, but as soon as Quinlan breached the tops of the trees, the maddening cacophony began, like a thousand voices all at once, shouting over each other, all trying to talk to her.

As she had earlier, though, she set aside her faeness and brought forward Davido's daughter, and the troll parts of her that might just be able to make sense of the situation.

She gave herself the same advice she'd given Quinlan. She stopped trying to fight against the sound and instead let it flow through her, a steady stream that soon softened and became an incredible internal melody.

Her vision altered at the same time and as she glanced around she saw the Dead Forest with new eyes, as a vast sea of iridescent leaves, glimmering in blues and green, yellows and purples. "It's so beautiful."

Lorelei whispered. "She's here, just beyond your shield."

Batya turned to face Margetta as she rose high in the air also. Her lips drew back in a snarl and her voice sounded rough. "If I can't have her, no one can."

She extended both arms and her power blasted toward them.

Batya had only a split second, so from deep within, that part that communed with the Dead Forest, she begged the extraordinary entity for help.

Just as Margetta's power reached them in a searing edge of fire, from beneath Batya's feet an answering cool wave, of enormous power, rose up from the Dead Forest and swept in Margetta's direction.

The profound wave gathered the ancient fae up, as well as her force of Invictus wraith-pairs, and swept them all away. Within seconds, they were nothing more than a speck in the sky. Another split-second, and they were gone.

Quinlan dropped them almost immediately back to earth and started issuing orders to send out patrols to find out where the ancient fae and her troops had gone. But Batya laid a hand on his arm. "Let me see if I can find out."

Quinlan raised his arm. "Hold!" Then the entire brigade stopped all activity.

She closed her eyes and withdrew the enthrallment shield. She opened up her troll sensors and focused on the chatter of the trees around her.

The vibration from the Dead Forest became a long string of sensations, but eventually shaped themselves into words that made sense to Batya. She translated for the forest. "The evil ones have been sent hundreds of miles from here, over the western realm ocean, Maris Sol. It will take them hours to reach land. We're safe to proceed to Ferrenden Peace."

A cheer went up from the troll brigade, from Lorelei and from Quinlan.

A portion of the brigade went down the back trail to gather the remains of those trolls who had died in the fire attacks. The rest resumed the trek northeast toward the Snowfields of Rayne, and Ferrenden Peace beyond.

* * * * * * * *

Quinlan held Batya against him, her head resting on his shoulder. She lay limp in his arms, asleep while he moved them both mile after mile, through the increasingly frigid night air.

Her peaceful slumbers gave him a lot of time to think. With her vibrations stowed, he was more himself than he'd been over the past several days.

Yet he felt restless and uneasy, not because he thought Margetta might suddenly reappear around the next switchback, but because he felt changed.

He'd finally realized something critical, though he hadn't yet mentioned it to Batya, but his stomach no longer cramped as it had for centuries. The state of chronic blood starvation for every mastyr vampire, had been his painful companion from the time that he'd arrived at mastyr status. Like Ethan and most of the mastyrs, he kept a stable of *doneuses* to take care of his blood needs. He'd needed constant donations, sometimes more than once a night when battling the Invictus,

And in all those decades, year after year, with a regular changing of his doneuses as one century moved into the next, he'd never been without the cramping in his stomach.

Until now.

Batya's blood had satisfied him, nourished him, and eradicated what had been horribly painful for most of his adult life.

To his knowledge, this extraordinary experience had only happened to two other mastyr vampires in all the Nine Realms, Mastyr Gerrod of Merhaine Realm and Ethan of Bergisson.

Sweet Goddess, if everything he understood was correct, then Batya was a blood rose, *his* blood rose.

Which at least explained why he'd been unable to stay away from her.

On some level, he must have known. Ethan had talked about his experience at length, about his erratic behavior, his craving for his woman, his need to protect Samantha as though his own life depended on her survival. Quinlan had also been drawn to Samantha to the point that he and Ethan had essentially fought over her in the Bergisson Guildhall.

But if Batya was his blood rose, then why hadn't he understood it sooner? Or maybe he had, but he just hadn't been able to face the truth until now.

Sweet Goddess, a blood rose. And his stomach didn't hurt.

But what the hell was he supposed to do with her? He didn't exactly respect her life choices since she lived as an ex-pat and had no desire to return to Grochaire Realm. In his view, realm-folk should have a commitment to their homeland above everything else, including family and personal happiness.

He'd lived by these values, so opposite to what Batya held dear. Although he did give her credit for seeing to the well-being of realm-folk in Lebanon. She wasn't a selfish person, just badly misguided.

But what was he supposed to do with her?

He had no room in his life for a relationship with a woman, any woman, even if she proved to be his blood rose. Maybe he could visit her occasionally in Lebanon, maybe she'd be willing to become one of his *doneuses*. Yes, that made sense.

With that much settled, he pulled her closer. The air had grown freezing cold, but he produced a lot of heat which he hoped kept her body temp at a reasonable level.

When he rounded a wide bend in the mountain range, suddenly a vista opened up before him, something he'd only read about in ancient fables, the Snowfields of Rayne.

Batya, wake up. You have to see this.

Hmmm?

She lifted her head and drew in a soft gasp. "Oh, my God."

He slowed his speed and one by one the troll brigade, with Lorelei, spread out in a single line to either side of him.

A soft, exquisite layer of snow, as far as the eye could see, rolled out before him, unbroken by trees or shrubs. The name made perfect sense. In the glow of his night vision, the snow sparkled beneath a black, star-studded sky. But it wasn't just the spectacular visual sight, but the essential power that emanated from the field.

"Do you feel it, mastyr?" Henry levitated beside him, head erect, eyes narrowed.

"Yes, a flow of power like nothing I've felt before."

"What do you think the source is?"

Quinlan shook his head. "I have no idea."

"Okay, so which way to Ferrenden Peace?"

Without even having to think about it, as though the map lived in him now, he pivoted slightly facing northeast. "That way."

"Can you reach Mastyr Seth? If Margetta finds us again, it would help to have reinforcements."

"Good question." He dropped to the snow and set Batya down, waiting for her to find her footing.

Her booted feet sunk just a few inches through a delicate crust with soft powder below. She leaned down and ran her hands over the surface. She even chuckled, like she was amused and delighted at the same time.

What do you feel, Cha? He needed to know. Batya, like Lorelei, had an unusual connection to the land. Maybe the snowfield would speak to her as well.

She rose up and met his gaze. *I'm just savoring this soft vibration of energy. It's lovely, even beautiful. Untouched.*

He felt it as well, that realm-folk had not walked in this land for a long time.

He withdrew his cell from the pocket of his leathers and found he had enough bars. Dialing, he was relieved when Seth picked up immediately.

"I've been waiting for your call, Quinlan. Do you have the woman?"

"Yes. The ancient fae gave us quite a bit of trouble and we've lost some warriors from my troll brigade."

"Very sorry to hear it." Seth spoke in a soft, clipped, careful manner. Of all the mastyrs, Seth held himself in tight control. He was extremely disciplined and though lean as hell, he had as much muscle mass as Quinlan. The vampire worked out with a passion and it showed.

He also had an organized mind that functioned like a computer, always analyzing. And he had one of the largest *doneuses* stables in all the Nine Realms and fed twice a day, rain or shine. He also had secrets. Some said he killed his brother in a rage over a thousand years ago. Of course, few still lived who could corroborate the story one way or the other. Maybe his sense of discipline came from keeping a volatile temper in check.

Whatever the case, Quinlan trusted Seth with his life. He gave him a rundown of all that had happened and that he now stood on the edge of the snowfields. "By my calculations, we're fifty miles from Ferrenden Peace. Do you have your map with you? Have you seen the enthrallment over this region roll back?"

"I have. Stunning. Impressive. I have half my Guard with me and we keep advancing in a northwesterly direction, according to your instructions. We've hit an exquisite light display in the sky, similar to the earth's northern lights. Do you see anything like that from your vantage point?"

"No, but I suspect it has something to do with the power this field radiates. I wish I understood more about our myths. I'll bet the answers to these phenomena show up in our oral traditions."

"You're probably right. So, what's your plan?"

"To keep moving in the direction imprinted in my mind until we meet up. Just keep an eye on your map."

"Will do."

When he returned his cell to his pocket, he saw Batya shiver. Without giving it a moment's thought, he pulled her into his arms then called for her satchel. As soon as she was bundled up in a warm coat, he ordered the brigade to move on.

He rose into the air, the brigade with him, and started across the vast Snowfield of Rayne.

Embrace the Mystery

* * * * * * * * *

With her head covered in a warm, furry hood, Batya savored the view as Quinlan flew her mile after mile across the snowfields. The vibrations soothed her and made her smile, even as the land sloped ever downward and the snow began to show more rocks and shrubs.

She realized she'd never been so happy in her entire life, a thought that startled her because it made no sense. After all, she'd just been through a series of harrowing experiences, including communing with the Dead Forest and watching Margetta and her force get blown clear across Grochaire Realm, over five hundred miles and then some. Yet, she felt content as though she belonged here, in Quinlan's arms, speeding above a white expanse that glittered like diamonds, toward an unknown destination.

How was this even possible, first that she was here and secondly, that she was content?

She'd always preferred her independent, self-ordained path to anything so full of realm meaning and purpose. Yet here she was flying toward a place from her world's myths called, Ferrenden Peace, a land supposedly ruled by a benevolent and very ancient virgin queen.

She wondered suddenly if that was exactly what they would find once they arrived, a strange kingdom ruled by a woman, also known to be an ancient fae called Rosamunde.

After another hour in the air, Quinlan drew his phone carefully from his pocket, a movement Batya sensed. He could easily upset their trajectory at this speed with a jerk of his wrist.

He'd already called Mastyr Seth twice before, each time checking to make sure that the enthrallment kept rolling back so that Seth and his Guardsmen would arrive at nearly the same time they did.

Quinlan slid his phone back into his pants pocket. *We're getting close, Cha. Seth has his map in front of him. He says the map reveals the border of Ferrenden Peace. He also said that another place name has appeared, the Kingdom of Peace.*

No kidding. Then she felt it, a wave of sensation that brought her breath up short. *I get it.* She laughed.

What is it? He adjusted her again in the circle of his right arm, still holding her tight.

Ferrenden Peace and Kingdom of Peace. I think our language changed the name over the years.

Quinlan smiled as well. *You may be right.*

And I'm experiencing a new vibration, something euphoric and I think it's coming from the town itself. You should slow down now. We're less than a mile away.

I see it. A wall of some kind. Mist maybe.

Right, but the town beyond is lovely, the streets rising to the crest of a hill, the castle on top. Sweet Goddess, this is a fairy tale.

All I see is the wall. He slowed down and after another quarter mile, came to a stop, dropping to stand on a cobbled street lined with trees and grass. "Is this the entrance?"

She didn't respond at first. So many sensations struck her at once, of awe and of great contentment, and of something like *coming home.*

Finally, she answered his question. "Yes, we've arrived. The gates are right in front of us, not thirty yards away." She stepped out of the circle of his arms and advanced forward, Quinlan moving to walk beside her.

"Guards," she called out to the two men posted at either side of the massive, black spiral gate. She sensed the power of the wrought iron, that the gate in one sense was purely ornamental. The mist would hold intruders out. No one simply flew over the gate into Ferrenden Peace. Admittance must be granted.

"Yes, Mistress. How may I help you this fine October day?" She smiled because he sounded like her father. Davido often used expressions just like that. The Guardsmen wore a uniform similar to Quinlan, except with a black leather beret angled over their heads.

"We request entrance. I am Batya, sired by Davido, The Great One, and this is Mastyr Quinlan, ruler of Grochaire Realm."

At her words, the mist rolled away from the gate and a soft exclamation rose up from the brigade ranks because now the kingdom was visible to everyone.

"You are welcome to enter, Mistress Batya. Indeed, you are expected. Queen Rosamunde gives you and your entourage, full access to our town."

Her first instinct was to explain that Quinlan and his Troll Brigade were hardly *her entourage*, but Quinlan gave her arm a squeeze, then thanked the Guardsman.

The gate opened wide.

Once the entire force was inside the city gates, she glanced back and watched as the mist and gate both closed back up.

Quinlan explained that Mastyr Seth would be arriving soon.

The Guardsman nodded. "We are fully informed. The queen has foreseen your visit and all is prepared. Mastyr Seth will join you at the castle in due course. In the meantime, accept the queen's hospitality. The Mistress of the Hall is here to settle all of you in proper chambers for the night."

A tall fae, in flight, introduced herself as Gizelda, her ease in the air giving Batya a pang of envy. She explained that she had made arrangements to home-host the entire brigade and that the ladies and Quinlan would be staying at the castle. "If that pleases you, Mastyr Quinlan."

"Very much so, thank you."

"Then follow me through the town and when we are nearly at the castle, I'll direct the brigade into the hands of my assistant, Myra."

Once Quinlan had them in flight, following the elegant Gizelda up the main street, Batya shook her head over and over. Many of the realm-folk waved to them as they passed by. Flower baskets hung from beautiful black light standards, set at twenty feet intervals. Blue shutters hung beside most of the windows.

At an intersection, a cheering group of troll females, many with low-cut tops, waved and screamed. The cheers became a roar as the brigade moved by.

Batya turned slightly in Quinlan's arms to watch as each Guardsman smiled and puffed out his chest a little more, spears in the air. Henry saluted the women, which caused another swift burst of shouting.

"We're definitely expected," she said quietly. "Those women are dressed to kill and I don't think they're working girls."

Because she was looking behind her, she met Lorelei's gaze and her friend smiled, tears in her eyes. Batya had been so caught up in her own experience that she hadn't realized what coming here would mean for the woman Margetta had been pursuing for decades.

"You're free," she called back to her.

Lorelei inclined her head. "Free at last."

Chapter Nine

Quinlan stood by the window in the room assigned to him. Some smart fae foresight had assigned Batya the adjoining bedchamber. She showered while he towel-dried his long hair.

The queen had already provided a meal, so they'd eaten, but Gizelda had made it clear Rosamunde wouldn't be receiving anyone until the next evening, which was just as well.

He felt like he'd been battling and marching for a week and a vibration up both arms told him he needed to feed soon. He'd spent a lot of energy flying Batya to Ferrenden Peace, known to the locals as the Kingdom of Peace.

He still couldn't believe he was here.

Ferrenden Peace

But dawn wasn't too far off. He could feel that vibration as well, the warning tingle up his spine, telling all vampires to seek shelter. He sometimes wondered how his ancestors survived without modern building materials.

Caves, probably.

He recalled one of his *doneuses* reading some kind of novel recently, a romance, where the vampires lived in caves and did some crazy stuff with chains.

No caverns in his world, just a variety of realm-folk needing his protection against the enemy.

He heard the revelers. The long window faced the main thoroughfare, and even at that distance he could hear the shouting and laughter. Henry and his men needed this time to let things go. They'd be mourning the loss of their fellow warriors when the next evening broke. Henry already had a brief memorial service planned for the fallen. Later, when the brigade returned to Grochaire, proper remembrance services would be taken care of by the families.

For now, getting drunk and well-laid would go a long way to healing the warriors.

"You're sure thinking hard. I've heard you sigh at least a dozen times."

He turned to find Batya backlit by the light from her bedroom, which had the happy effect of showing the outline of her womanly figure through the thin fabric of the nightgown she wore. Ferrenden Peace's weather, now that they'd left the snow behind, was relatively mild and the castle comfortable.

The queen had provided them with clothing. He wore a simple, but very soft, dark blue velvet robe.

He set the towel on the stone window sill, then crossed to Batya. She'd dried her long hair and it smelled sweet like berries as he pulled her into his arms.

She pushed underneath his robe until her arms flowed around his back.

You're hungry.

Yes, I need sustenance, but right now I need you more.

She hugged him, then lowered her hands to caress and fondle his ass. His cock loved it and stiffened for her.

She kissed his neck, her lips plucking at his skin, up and up, over his jaw-line to finally land on his mouth.

He crashed down on her, kissing her hard, holding her tightly to him. She slid one hand over his waist then his hip. He gave her just enough room to reach him, her fingers sliding around his stalk, a new kind of caress.

He drew back and looked into her large, hazel eyes. She was so beautiful, especially in the soft glow his vampire vision yielded right now. Emotion swelled in his chest, something unfamiliar, yet powerful. He felt strangely like he needed to say something important to her, maybe even to thank her for being so strong over the past few days.

Instead, he kissed her again and let all that feeling sweep through him. Her body responded, trembling.

After a moment, he picked her up and carried her to the bed. Holding her in one arm, he pulled the covers back then laid her out on the sheets. Her thick, blond hair fanned out on the pillows, just as he'd always imagined it would.

His gaze drifted to her large breasts and the three simple bows that held the gauzy gown together. He stretched out beside her and through the fabric fondled her breasts, teasing each tip into a swollen firm bud.

He dipped down and took her right breast in his mouth, sucking at her through the fabric. She moaned as she stroked his head, his cheek, and played with his lips while he worked her nipple.

"It takes so little," she whispered. "It's never been like this, Quin, not with any man. You take me to the edge in lightning speed."

Unwilling to stop savoring her breast, he pathed, *I love nursing on you.* He lifted his gaze while he suckled, to meet her wide hazel eyes, now dark with passion.

The scent of her sex, rich with her tropical-flower fragrance, hardened him even more. He arched his hips into her, pressing his cock against her thigh.

She pushed away his robe, her fingers kneading his shoulders and arms, then finding his pecs and rubbing over his nipples. Her moans grew louder.

He released her nipple as well, and helped her out of the gown then resumed savoring her breasts, fondling the size of her, the wonderful weight of each, enjoying her moans and coos and the way she worked the muscles of his arms.

He flexed his biceps for her over and over which kept her hips rising and falling.

Drifting a hand over her abdomen, he loved her soft gasps and the way her body jerked at his touch, as though his fingertips burned her.

Lower he crept. Only this time he massaged above her mound and across her pelvis. She breathed in deep gulps. Taking more of her breast in his mouth, he sucked harder.

Her coos turned to cries as he smoothed a hand over her mound. *Spread for me.*

Batya responded, easing her legs apart. His lips trembled over her breast as his fingers slid downward and found how wet she was. He groaned heavily as he played with her soft folds, just to feel her and to enjoy her.

She moaned again, her hips rising and falling, pushing into his hand. He slid two fingers inside and his cock jerked, wanting to be exactly where his fingers were. He slid in and out, suckling her nipple with the same rhythm that he used between her legs.

Her back arched, her body rolled.

"I'm in agony." Her voice sounded hoarse.

He moaned as he moved his fingers faster and faster. He felt her body tense, one hand digging into his neck, and the other into his shoulder.

A series of cries left her throat, then she shouted. He sustained the drive of his fingers as her body writhed and she cried out over and over. He felt her coming with strong spasms. He experienced her pleasure as well, like a second skin.

When her body eased back on the bed, and her breathing settled down, he withdrew his fingers, wiping them on the robe he'd taken off her.

"That was wonderful."

He rose up onto his elbow to look at her, at her flushed cheeks and swollen lips. He kissed her. "We've just started."

She nodded, then a soft smile spread over her lips. "I know. It's one of the things I like best about you."

He smiled as well and again his chest filled with an unrecognizable emotion, something that threatened to bust through his ribcage.

"What is it?" She rested a hand between his pecs. "You look like you want to say something."

He shook his head. "No. I'm just, I don't know, grateful to be alive, maybe. Hell, I should have died several times out there."

She huffed a sigh. "I know. I feel the same way."

He wondered if he should tell her that he suspected she was a blood rose. But somehow the moment didn't seem right, mostly because he knew she wouldn't be happy about that on any level, so he let it slide.

* * * * * * * * *

Batya let her gaze feast on Quinlan, on his dark, almost black eyes, his powerful cheekbones that looked chiseled from granite, his thick, straight, black brows that made him appear so serious and determined all the time, and the super sexy crooked line of his nose. Somehow, that imperfection made him perfect, almost too beautiful to look at.

Yet, she couldn't look away. She traced the line of his cheek with the tip of her finger, then followed each of his features, memorizing them perhaps because soon their strange adventure would come to an end.

She drifted her fingertip down his neck, then lower to smooth a hand over his thick pecs. He had an elegant body, a vampire warrior's body, strong and fit, lethal in its ability to slay the enemy. She knew there resided within his soul a sense of unworthiness, which she now understood. He'd grown up in a brutal home that had ended with the deaths of both parents on the same night. And he'd never truly forgiven himself for what happened, that he'd been unable to save his mother and that his violent outburst against his father had led to his death.

But it seemed a great irony that though he felt this way, undeserving of love, he was perhaps the most deserving man she knew.

She wanted him to know, but doubted words would make a difference so she coaxed him onto his back and, stretched out on top of him, and began to kiss him. She took her time, using slow, lingering kisses one after the other, all over his face and his neck, licking over his veins which caused him to writhe and moan.

She scooted a little lower so that she could track the line of his collar bone with her tongue, then descended to worship his beautiful, thick pecs one at time. She used her hands, her tongue, her lips, kissing at times, then nipping at him, to finally take a nipple in her mouth and suckle him.

His cock was a hard ridge against her abdomen and his hips flexed to grind against her. He held her in place with his fleshy hands caressing her bottom. Everything about the moment felt so right and so good.

She worked her way down his abs, using her hands and tongue again, to ride the swells and dips of his stomach, then descended to lick her way down the line of hair that ran into his trimmed pubes.

She took him into her mouth, sucking lightly because she didn't want him to come, not yet. She wanted to build him up to the moment so that he roared while pounding into her.

But she also felt that turnabout was fair play, so she opened up her mating vibration and while she held him in her mouth, she let the vibration float down his cock. Two could definitely play at that game.

She didn't think she'd ever forget the heavy, guttural groan that left his mouth and brought his upper torso rising off the bed.

Releasing him immediately, she sat up and stared at him. "Did I hurt you?" But she smiled.

He shook his head. "I've just… It was… Oh, Sweet Goddess, do it again."

"Are you telling me that no woman has ever done this before?"

He shook his head, his dark eyes wide. "Not even a little. I mean I've felt a few vibrations before, but honey you've got something no one else can do."

Batya felt absurdly self-satisfied. "Then lie back down and let me try it once more."

He panted and moaned as she drew him again into her mouth. She took her time and let the moment build, finally releasing the same vibration so that it flowed down his cock.

He didn't lift off the bed, but his back arched and he groaned like a bear in pain. It was an awesome sound.

She didn't dare keep it up, however, or he'd come too soon.

So she released him gently, and using her palm, she made a path back up his abdomen and met his gaze. She kissed his nose. "I love this curve."

"It's always bugged me."

"It's monumentally sexy."

He laughed, then teased her left nipple with the crook of his finger. "I love being here like this with you. I knew we'd be good together, but it feels like more than that."

"I think we bonded over the trauma of the last two days."

He smiled again, then leaned up and kissed her, rolling her onto her back. She thought he'd attack her breasts again, because she was stacked and she knew he liked the way she looked.

Instead, he knelt beside her and let his gaze rove her body, head to foot, every inch, maybe memorizing her the way she'd done earlier.

She didn't say anything but waited and somehow she wasn't surprised when, using his left hand, he began caressing her face, sliding his fingers down her neck and in careful, gentle swipes, back-and-forth, he mapped her. He'd done something similar with the map of Grochaire, remembering where he'd been, and savoring what he'd come to love.

He moved over each shoulder, his gaze following the line of his hands as he touched her, and petted her in soft swipes. He continued over her breasts, her stomach, her waist, her hips and mound, then down her legs all the way to her ankles and feet. He left no part of her untouched.

When he'd done the front, he turned her over and began from the soles of her feet, and worked upward.

His touch was firm, warm and gentle, more like who he was deep in his heart than who he believed himself to be.

She spread her arms straight out so that he could reach every part of her. By the time he was done, she felt known as she'd never been known before.

She rolled onto her back once more and looked up at him. He seemed awestruck as he stared into her eyes. "What is it?"

He shook his head. "I don't know. You confuse the hell out of me."

She nodded. "I know what you mean. I really do. But there's one thing I know for sure." She slowly swept her hair away from the right side of her neck.

"What's that?" But his gaze settled on her throat.

"Take what belongs to you, Quin. Take it now."

* * * * * * * * *

Quinlan was fully erect and now his heart pounded. He hadn't realized how much he needed to feed until she'd exposed her throat. His vision focused on her neck, narrowing and sharpening, until he saw her beating pulse.

"My heart feels weighted with what you need."

Again, he wondered if he should speak to her about being a blood rose, but chose against it.

He moved between her parted legs, and using his hand, he positioned himself at her opening. He wanted to come like this, filling her up while he took her life's blood into his mouth.

Her moisture flowed over the tip of his cock as he pressed into her. She gripped his shoulders with both hands. "Oh, Quinlan. That feels wonderful." Her hands rubbed up and down his arms and over his back. She took pleasure in his body and that pleased the hell out of him.

He held her gaze, willing her to look at him while he pushed inside and joined his body to hers in the age-old union that made man and woman one being.

She wrapped her long legs around his ass and he arched his hips, letting her feel all that he was and savoring how tightly she held him inside her body.

Her lips parted as she worked to draw breath. He leaned over her thrusting, then kissed her. She rolled her head so that he could see her neck. He licked in a long line from the base of her throat almost to her ear.

He felt her pulse, the heavy beating of her heart and he smelled her blood now, another sign that she was more than she understood herself to be. He looked down at her breasts, rising and falling as her body moved and writhed under him.

His fangs descended, growing longer as saliva flowed, anticipating the feast.

He paused in his movements and gathered up his hair, twisting it, then shoving it behind his back. He didn't want anything to interfere with this moment.

"Do it, Quinlan." Her body tightened around his cock as he drew near her throat.

He bit down once, let his fangs retract, then settled in for the best suck of his life.

He couldn't explain why this moment was different from before, but it was, maybe because of all they'd been through. He worked his hips at the same time, moving in and out of her slowly, letting her feel him while he drank down her elixir that tasted of heady tropical flowers.

Power flowed into him at the same time, so different from his regular *doneuses,* that which he'd been needing from the time he attained mastyr status. As the blood reached his stomach and began to feed him and nourish his body, his muscles strengthened. A kind of euphoria worked in him at the same time, telling him that he needed to do this again and again, the rest of his long-lived life.

But he wouldn't think about that. Instead, he savored the taste of her. Something he'd wanted from the beginning.

She cried out, enjoying the experience as much as he.

Batya, I... He almost told her loved her.

I know, it's too much isn't it? This much pleasure? Sweet Goddess, Quinlan, your cock is unbelievable and chills keep racing up and down my body.

I'm going to add to that.

She gasped. She must have guessed.

As he continued to suck, and to roll his hips, he let his mating frequency release, just a small vibration at first.

Batya groaned. "Oh, Quinlan. Heaven. Just heaven. And you smell of wood-smoke." Her voice was hushed with passion.

He reached a point when he'd had his fill, and now he could take Batya the distance. Only this time he wanted to rock her world with the vibrations.

He released her neck and watched her head thrash back and forth over the pillow.

He drew the vibration very carefully into his groin. The sensation almost made him come, but he wanted to do this for her, to have the vibration take over her inner well.

He focused hard and began to release the vibration.

When she first felt it, she arched her back, which tipped her pelvis and created a tight hold on him that almost brought him over the edge again.

He took a series of strong breaths and held on.

"Quinlan, how the hell are you doing that? Oh, My God."

He moved slowly, focusing on her face. He leaned down and kissed her, small touches of his lips to her chin, to the faint dimples in her cheeks, to her eyebrows. Focusing on her features helped.

Her hands once more gripped his shoulders, then fondled his muscles as she squeezed his arms. Every touch was a beautiful fire on his skin, igniting his desire for her.

He increased the vibration, which parted her lips as a cry emerged from her throat.

He thrust faster now and added more vibration. He watched the ecstasy building on her face. Her fingernails sank into his shoulders and he loved it, loved that she was caught up in the experience, savoring his body, his cock, his vibration which only he could give her.

He became one with the vibration as pleasure built. Heat flowed through him, the power from her blood anchoring his muscles in tremendous strength. *Cha, look at me.*

She struggled to focus on him, her breathing in harsh gasps. *I see you.*

Do you want it faster?

She offered three small jerks of her chin, almost trembling. "Yes. Please. Faster. Vampire fast. And Quin, your vibration." He saw tears leak from her eyes.

Then he understood. His vibration had spread through his body and through hers. He now mingled with her mating frequency which lit a fire in his chest.

He thrust faster and faster, holding her gaze, watching the tears fall, knowing that this would explode between them.

"I'm coming."

Her words, her voice, the rapt expression on her face, tightened his balls and he began to release, to fire his essence into her in hard, tremendously pleasurable bursts.

He flung his head back and roared as ecstasy gripped him, flooding his body with fire, as her well tugged on him in rapid succession, as her body thrashed beneath his, as her cries left her throat until she screamed with pleasure.

He slowed, then felt another round rising within him. *Again, Cha.*

"Oh, God, Quin." She opened her mouth and screamed once more, the vibrations flowing back and forth, streaking through every part of him and enhancing the pleasure as his cock delivered the goods. Another roar left him, the vampire part of him that loved battling and dominance.

He sustained the drive, savoring every ounce of pleasure until his woman, his blood rose, lay beneath him, breathing hard and finally coming down from the heights.

His vibration eased up and his cock relaxed, but his body still experienced waves of ecstasy as though his blood kept releasing pleasure on pleasure.

Batya twitched and laughed. "It's the most incredible aftershock."

"Like smaller versions of the big show."

"Uh-huh." She worked hard to catch her breath.

He followed suit, then settled his forearms beside her. Once more, his chest filled with that strange, inexplicable sensation and words rushed into his mouth, words he didn't recognize, so he swallowed them.

She pushed at damp tendrils beside his cheeks. "That was beyond extraordinary. You were right; we are good together."

"I know I said it at the time, but I never dreamed it would be like this."

"Like what?"

"Like if we kept going we could solve all the problems of the Nine Realms, just the two of us."

She smiled, her two faint dimples making an appearance. She had a beautiful smile so he kissed her again. "Thank you."

She nodded. "Ditto."

After cleaning up, Quinlan cradled Batya in his arms until she fell asleep. He remained awake even after dawn crested the land. His thoughts had turned to his journey with Batya, trying to understand what was really happening between them.

Just as his eyelids grew heavy, the strange, impossible thought pierced his mind: Could he have a life with her?

* * * * * * * * *

Late that afternoon, Batya dressed for her audience with the queen in her throne room. Quinlan had already left, needing to confer with Seth who had arrived with a contingent of the Walvashorr Guard.

Having showered, Batya donned the woven gown that Gizelda had provided for her. Ferrenden Peace held to ancient protocols and though Quinlan could be presented in his Guard uniform, she had to wear a long gown made of traditional realm fabrics, the same material that made up the Guard uniform shirts.

Many aspects of the Nine Realms had remained in previous centuries, one more reason why she liked the modern world of Tennessee.

Once dressed, she regarded her reflection in the mirror. She'd braided a portion of her hair and wrapped it in a circle on top of her head, also an ancient tradition for unmarried women. She'd already noticed that many of the women in the main street wore some kind of head-dress, whether a scarf or a hat, indicating they were married.

She added the silver linked belt that gave shape to the gown and hung at a pretty angle over her hips, the attached, decorative chain dangling, no doubt on purpose, to the juncture of her thighs.

She shook her head and laughed. She thought she looked ready for a costume party more than anything else, but these were the rules of the castle. The queen had given her shelter, and dressing in old-realm costume offered in return a small measure of gratitude.

Gizelda had given her instructions as to the location of the main receiving hall, so Batya made her way there with some confidence. Two troll guards stood to either side of an arched stone doorway. The guard on the right informed her that Mastyr Seth was within but that Mastyr Quinlan had gone down to Main Street to see his brigade commander.

She'd met Seth decades earlier when he had visited her father. She had thought him an overly serious type, not given to having fun, or enjoying life.

But when she entered the room, something shifted for her so suddenly that she gasped, even though she didn't exactly know why.

He stood on the other side of the massive, vaulted chamber, a thumb hooked over the cross-belt of his Guard uniform, his free hand holding a map. His brows were drawn together as he studied what looked like an ancient realm-document.

But he'd never looked so attractive. He was tall. All the mastyrs were.

He turned to meet her gaze, but didn't smile. If anything, his brows formed an even harder ridge as he stared at her. His nostrils flared and he groaned.

The map fluttered to the floor.

But she was feeling it as well, a need to go to him, to feed him as she'd fed Quinlan last night and for the past several days.

He wore his brown wavy hair held back by the woven clasp. His cheekbones stood out like the sharp edges of a statue, leading to a strong angled chin. His green eyes had the look of a hawk as he stared at her, a predator ready to pounce.

The trouble was, she wanted him to pounce.

Her heart pounded heavily in her chest once more, as it had from the time that Quinlan had started coming around and bugging her.

"Come to me." His deep voice pulled her toward him.

Batya knew this was wrong, on some level she knew she betrayed Quinlan, even though neither had spoken words of commitment. Still, she shouldn't be longing for mastyr Seth like this.

She rubbed her throat. Her vein pounded for the vampire.

Just a few feet more.

He pulled her into his arms and she bent her neck. "Take what you need." The same words she'd spoken to Quinlan.

She felt saliva drip on her neck. He'd strike soon and it would feel wonderful. She needed him to feed, as though somehow her own life depended on feeding this mastyr vampire.

In that moment, she finally understood all that had happened over the past several weeks and more importantly, exactly what she was.

A blood rose.

Oh, Sweet Goddess, no.

"What the fuck is going on here!" Quinlan's voice rumbled through the lofty chamber.

Mastyr Seth released her, setting her off to the side and behind her as though protecting her.

Uh-oh.

Quinlan launched, but Seth did too. The next thing she knew, the vampires grappled midair, two of the toughest mastyrs in the Nine Realms. A fist caught Quinlan on his chin, jerking his head and his body backward toward the floor, but he'd been a warrior a long time and righted himself.

Flying at top-speed, he plowed into Seth with a hard shoulder to his abdomen. His momentum sent both of them hurtling toward the tall arched cathedral window that overlooked the town's southern aspect.

"Oh, Sweet Goddess, no!" she screamed, stretching out a hand, but to do what?

At exactly the same moment, she felt a rush of energy sweep past her and both men ended up hanging in the air, frozen in place. Seth's head was flung back, his body almost parallel to the floor, Quinlan above him, twisted, his face red with rage, but still as death.

"I must say, this wasn't the welcome I'd expected."

Batya turned slowly and met the gaze of one of the most beautiful women she'd ever seen in her life. "You're Queen Rosamunde."

"I am." A wry smile twisted her lips. She had exquisite dark violet eyes, unusual even among realm-folk, and she stood at least an inch taller than Batya. She wore her red-violet hair in several braids looped and twisted elegantly on top of her head.

"And you did this?" Batya asked, turning back to point at the men, still unable to credit that the queen, or anyone, had that kind of power.

"Come chat with me for a few minutes. Once I remove the stasis, the focus of my efforts will have to be on them." She climbed three stone steps to her throne, turned, then sat down. "So, how long have you been a blood rose, Mistress Batya?"

The question startled Batya because on some level she supposed that the queen, living behind an enthrallment veil, wouldn't be aware of what was happening in the Nine Realms.

"So you know about the blood rose phenomenon?"

She nodded. "I do. I might have kept Ferrenden peace from the rest of the world, but I have several spies and have always remained current on everything happening beyond our borders." She smiled. "I believe the blood rose marks the beginning of a new era. So, how long have you known what you were?"

She moved toward the throne. "I think I've known for a long time, but I couldn't believe it." She put her hand to her chest. When had her heart started feeling so weighed down with blood?

She remembered now. The day Quinlan had trapped her in the corner of her gallery and kissed her neck, licking above the vein. That's when the whole thing had started.

"Tell me everything." The words were spoken in the same way Vojalie spoke to any realm-folk she meant to enthrall. Rosamunde clearly had the same gift because Batya began to talk. She told the queen about her gallery and Lorelei, about Margetta and the attack, Quinlan's burns and healing, then their entire journey to Ferrenden Peace.

Rosamunde frowned slightly, biting at her lips as her gaze drifted to the two vampires hanging in the delicate balance between time and space.

Batya looked at them as well, but the experience proved difficult since she once more felt an overwhelming need to offer up a vein to each.

Steadying herself, she turned back to the queen. "May I ask a few questions of my own?"

Rosamunde shifted her gaze to Batya and smiled. She had the delicate features of the fae and softly pointed chin. Her ears were beautifully peaked and curled, well-studded with diamonds and gold. "Let me tell you about Ferrenden Peace first and about myself. Then if you have questions, you may ask them."

"That would be wonderful."

"First, I have been dreaming about you for two months now, which I believe is about the time Mastyr Quinlan sought you out."

"Yes, it is."

"Ah, that explains so much. You see, your presence here is fulfilling an epoch prophesied centuries ago. We've been waiting for your arrival and for Lorelei's for some time, and I for one am grateful that the enthrallment has finally rolled away from this area. I have missed communion with the Nine Realms, and with Walvashorr."

Batya listened enrapt, but suddenly all she could feel was the powerful depth of the queen's loneliness, that she'd been in a position of solitude for longer than Batya could even imagine.

Rosamunde offered a brief history of Ferrenden Peace, that the fables mostly were true though much more elaborate than reality, that she'd ruled for a very long time, and that her kingdom was entirely self-sufficient and, like the namesake, peaceful.

She then turned the subject slightly and spoke of the time over a thousand years ago, before the creation of the terrible Invictus wraith-pairs, when wraiths were a natural and welcomed part of realm life, when peace reigned throughout all the realms.

Given the eras she covered, Batya said, "Then you must know my father."

"Davido? Yes, of course." She smiled, her violet eyes full of affection.

"But you haven't spoken with him."

She shook her head. "Not in all these years."

"Will that change now?"

"In the coming era, yes, but not right away and now I think it's time to bring the men back to earth."

Rosamunde waved a hand, which sent another powerful vibration streaking through the air. Batya turned and watched as both men, rather than continuing forward through the window, dropped a hard four feet to the stone floor, although Quinlan landed on top of Seth.

He quickly pulled away, almost flying backward. "What the fuck?"

He turned and saw Batya first, then the queen. "I beg your pardon. But what happened? Ah, hell we would have gone through that window."

Chapter Ten

Quinlan stood halfway between Seth and Batya, glancing back to his fellow mastyr then turning to look at Batya. His memory returned in a sudden flash, of Seth preparing to bite down on her, to take her blood, and his former rage returned, a flow of heat and anger so sharp, so sudden, that he was turning once again in Seth's direction, when Batya suddenly appeared right in front of him.

She took hold of the front of his coat, gripping the soft leather in her hands and staring up at him. Her gaze kept him frozen in place, though fury still boiled in his veins. She leaned up and kissed him, not a simple touch of her lips on his, but a full, warm kiss that had him piercing her mouth with his tongue and enfolding her in his arms.

You're not to feed him.

I know.

He drew back. "Then why were you going to?"

"Because I didn't know what I was then. I'd hidden that truth from myself. Did you know I was a blood rose?"

He sighed heavily. "I figured it out while I flew you over the snowfields and you slept in my arms, why I pursued you like I did, why I couldn't keep away from you, why I desire you so much. But I couldn't tell you. I was waiting for the right time."

She nodded. "I can appreciate that." But tears touched her eyes. "Then none of this is real? We're just caught in some kind of strange realm phenomenon?"

He shook his head slowly. "I don't know. I don't know what any of this is."

The queen intruded. "Are you done trying to kill the Mastyr of Walvashorr?"

He turned toward Seth, aware that his ire had diminished, then nodded.

Once more, the queen spoke. "And you, Mastyr Seth. Are you calm enough to speak with me?"

"Yes, my queen."

"Good. Then will all of you approach because I have commands to give you from our kingdom's prophecies."

Quinlan felt disoriented as he slid his arm around Batya's waist then moved with her to stand before Queen Rosamunde. Seth joined him on his left and for that he was grateful. If the vampire had positioned himself next to Batya, the battle would have started all over again.

"Mastyr Quinlan, your troll brigade must remain behind for two weeks to enjoy a period of revelry with our maidens." She shifted to meet Seth's gaze. "Your force as well, Mastyr Seth."

Quinlan frowned. "May I ask why?"

But Batya whispered. "The town needs an infusion of what only these Guardsmen can give."

"Your blood rose has spoken correctly. We need new seed in our population, so let your troops know that they may give freely, without need of protection."

Quinlan couldn't help but smile. How many times, over the decades, had he been required to negotiate parents-rights issues because of accidental pregnancy. "Are you saying this would be without repercussion should children be born of this arrangement?"

"You have my word."

He couldn't help but glance at Seth. If Ethan had been next to him, he would have exchanged a wink with him. But Seth was cut from a different sort of cloth. "With all due reverence, my queen, I want your command in writing."

Queen Rosamunde lifted a hand. "You shall have it, of course. These modern times require written contracts. And you, mastyr Seth, may remain as well or return to Walvashorr. The prophecies were not specific to you except that you would arrive to support the Mastyr of Grochaire. I have no specific command for you."

"Very good, my Queen."

She shifted to meet Quinlan's gaze. "As for you and Batya, you are both commanded to leave within the hour. You must return to your worlds to continue your good work as you see fit, but I must warn you that trouble awaits you and that you must find a way to compromise and to work together if you are to survive."

"You refer to Margetta?"

She glanced upward as though mentally reviewing earlier notes-to-self. Finally, she returned her gaze to Quinlan. "I'm not sure, but please take care to tend to one another diligently."

Quinlan met Batya's gaze. When she nodded to him, he spoke for them of both. "We will."

Batya took a small step forward. "And what of Lorelei?"

"She will remain here and I will teach her how to withstand her mother's various powers."

"You can do that?"

Rosamunde lifted a brow. "I will ignore that you've questioned my abilities."

"I'm sorry," Batya added hastily. "But from the time that Margetta made an appearance, I became convinced that she was the most powerful woman in all nine realms."

Rosamunde drew a deep breath. "I can see that you're a good friend to Lorelei and though what I'll teach her won't be absolute, it will be more protection than she's ever known. Then she will begin her own journey." Her gaze skated in Seth's direction for a brief moment, then back to Batya and Quinlan. "That is all I have to say."

"I'll want to speak to my brigade." Quinlan wouldn't leave without addressing his troops. "And my men will have their dead to remember."

"Of course. And you will find Henry at the Troll's Delight." She smiled. "The shutters are a very pretty pink. You can't miss it."

* * * * * * * *

Batya hugged Lorelei and wished her well. The fae-shifter-wraith, part vampire, had already spent time in Rosamunde's company, knew of the queen's commands, and remained quietly in her suite, also by the queen's orders. Lorelei didn't seem to be minding at all.

"I feel hopeful for the first times in decades."

Batya tried to comprehend what Lorelei's life had been like. Her own appeared so mild and uninteresting compared to a life lived on the run. Batya had been hounded by Margetta for three days and it was already wearing on her nerves. What had a lifetime of pursuit been like for Lorelei?

"Come visit the gallery when you can."

"Of course I will, but what will you do if Margetta and those wraith-pairs come after you and Quinlan?"

"She won't have a reason now."

"My mother is vindictive. Remember, she wanted me dead rather than let me live my own life."

Batya tried not to think about that, about what could happen now that Lorelei lived behind the safety of Ferrenden Peace's veil of mist and she and Quinlan would soon return to their respective worlds.

"We'll be all right. Don't worry about us."

Lorelei smiled. "I won't. You guys are amazing. Just, be patient with him, Batya. I think he might be a keeper."

"I'll try. I just never expected all of this, or any of it really." She didn't explain about her blood rose status. She hardly knew what to do with the information herself, nonetheless try to explain it to someone else.

Lorelei hugged her good-bye and Batya returned to her room to change out of the gown and to remove her braids. She really wasn't used to the formal look.

Just as she finished packing her satchel, Quinlan returned to the rooms smiling.

"What?"

He shook his head, hands planted on his hips. "Nothing."

"Okay, now you have to tell me."

"I just saw Henry and he had an arm around two women and more love-bites than I'd seen in maybe my whole life, right here." He skated two fingers up his neck.

"Something tells me some of the women around here have been love-starved for a long time."

A cheering sounded from the window. Batya crossed and glanced down. In the distance, she saw the troll brigade and what was probably Seth's force celebrating. When drums started up, and lights went on all over the town, she was pretty sure this occasion would be celebrated in two realms and one kingdom for a long time to come.

Quinlan joined her by the window, sliding his arms around her from behind, holding her tight. "Wish we didn't have to leave." He nuzzled her neck. "I'd love a repeat performance of last night."

The thought of all that they'd done together, especially the thrilling climax with his vibrations flooding her body, made her body grow weak as she leaned into him. He kissed her neck several times then sucked on the vein. She bloomed beneath his touch, his words, his lips.

"We have to go. The queen said we did. But when we get to Lebanon, you can share my bed."

"We'd break that bed."

She had to work to catch her breath. "We probably would."

"We could go to my stronghold."

She turned in his arms and he kissed her hard, his tongue pummeling her mouth in the best way. *We should do that, at least once more before you take me back to the States.*

Okay.

She pushed him away and shook her head. "Really, we'd better stop. The queen said we needed to get going."

"You're right."

* * * * * * * * *

With Batya held tight against him with one arm, and her satchel held in his free hand, Quinlan took off, rising high above the city. He didn't want to delay their return by traveling through the town. No doubt Henry and his cohorts were already lost in song, dance, and the company of women so that nothing could be gained by saying a second good-bye.

Once at the entrance to the city, the Guards rolled back both the gate and the mist. He flew through and began the long ascent that would lead them to the snowfields and back to Grochaire Realm.

He'd made his apologies to Seth and had taken a few minutes to share his blood rose experience with him. Given the current trend making its way through the mastyrs of the Nine Realms, Seth would do well to be forewarned.

Seth had in turn expressed his own remorse for having taken advantage of Batya but was bemused that she'd come to him so readily.

Quinlan released a sigh. "We're not bonded. Right now, she would feel driven to serve any mastyr vampire." From what he understood, the bonding process had many avenues, sometimes occurring over a period of time, at others with a strong decision of the will, and even Gerrod had said that his bonding with Abigail had taken place during captivity and had involved a sharing of each other's blood.

Seth had frowned. "Everything I've heard from you or from Ethan and Gerrod sounds nightmarish. I lost control with Batya. That's unforgiveable."

Quinlan tried to encourage him, but until Seth experienced a blood rose for himself, he wouldn't really be able to relate.

He'd left him with the promise to call soon in order to discuss the future of the Nine Realms.

As Quinlan flew, he tried not to think about the hard truth that once he left Batya in Lebanon, she'd be fair game. He recalled what his own attraction to Samantha had been like just six months ago before Ethan had completed the bond with her. He and Ethan had done serious damage to the Guildhall when they'd fought over her. And now with Seth, he'd been on the receiving end of that hellish reality when he found his fellow mastyr ready to sink his fangs.

He shuddered.

What's wrong?

Just thinking about walking into the throne room and finding you in Seth's arms. Sure enough, he shuddered again only this time rage erupted. *Why did you do it?*

She stiffened in his arms. *Why did I do it? You mean why did I go to him?*

By now, they flew over the snowfields, but he took little pleasure in the soft vibration of energy that worked through the land. Instead, he ground his teeth. *You heard me. Why the hell did you go to him? Did our time together mean so little to you that you couldn't restrain yourself?*

She fell silent, but not necessarily in a bad way. He was pretty sure she was thinking hard about the situation, a quality they shared in common.

I don't know why, she pathed at last. *One minute I was standing by the doorway, and the next I was crossing to him like he had me enthralled, which wasn't possible. I'm sure it's the whole blood rose thing, but Quin, I'm pissed as hell about this. I don't want to be a Goddamn blood rose.*

And I don't want to be a mastyr vampire.

But you can't help being a mastyr vampire. You were born that way. You must have known early on that you'd rise to mastyr status.

I did, but what's the difference? Clearly, you were always meant to be a blood rose.

Well, I didn't exactly know that I'd one day have this lovely job description of satisfying your blood needs. Sweet Goddess!

He huffed an impatient sigh. *So what if you're a blood rose? Suck it up.*

Well, fuck you very much. And exactly what do you think will happen if one of those wraith-pairs, you know the ones that Margetta created with mastyr vampires, decides to come after me in Lebanon? What am I supposed to do then?

Well, you can call me, of course.

But what good will that do? As I recall, it was my enthrallment shield that saved your ass.

He had a strong desire suddenly to drop Batya and her satchel down on the snowfield and suggest she find her own ride back to

Tennessee. Breathing hard through his nostrils, he pathed, *Then I guess you'd better get really good at creating those special shields of yours.*

Fine.

Fine.

He didn't like that she'd raised some solid points, especially since he didn't have the answers, so her silence worked for him. It also gave him time to think.

Two questions rose to the surface. Exactly what was she supposed to do as a blood rose? And how was he, or any of his Grochaire Guardsmen, supposed to battle these uber-wraith-pairs?

Wanting an answer to that, he had Batya hold her satchel for a moment while he phoned Rafe. His second-in-command assured him that Grochaire was fairly quiet and no reports of the kinds of wraith-pairs Quinlan described to him had made an appearance.

Reassured, he told Rafe he'd be back in Grochaire in a couple of hours and would talk to him then.

Taking the satchel back, he headed west, using a different route back in order to avoid the Dead Forest. He thought it possible Margetta might have left scouts on the back trail waiting to strike.

An hour later, of covering mile after mile, Batya pathed, *Sorry, Quin. I'm a bit edgy and I didn't need to speak to you that way.*

I'm sorry, too. We definitely need to talk about what happened and about the future, and hammer out some details.

I just want you to know that I'd be happy, at the very least, to become your doneuse. *I know it's made a difference for you.*

I appreciate that. Oh, damn, his chest swelled up again with all that strange, bizarre sensation, like he had a cloud in his rib cage that kept expanding.

He carefully kissed the top of her head as he flew west, hoping to hell that he wouldn't encounter the wicked witch before getting Batya to safety.

* * * * * * * *

The trip across the snowfields had given Batya plenty of time to think. She recalled what Rosamunde had said, and that she and Quinlan needed to work together. Quarreling had only served to reveal the problems they faced, but nothing more.

And what was she supposed to do with her blood rose status?

Quinlan had asked an important question: Had their time together meant so little to her?

Of course not. If anything, the nature of their relationship overwhelmed her with its depth and the sheer excitement of being with him was like nothing she'd ever known before.

Her thoughts turned to Lebanon and the life she'd built for herself there. She loved the ex-pat community. She could never give up her healing work there. The local realm-folk depended on her and her service made her happy.

She shared this quality with Quinlan. His devotion to Grochaire, which had been his life's work as well as his life's sacrifice, matched her own love of her community. Her efforts might have been on a much smaller scale, but the desire to serve equaled Quinlan's, so at least in that way, she understood him, she got him.

But exactly how they were supposed to make all of this work escaped her.

We're not far from the border between the snowfields and Grochaire. I can feel the vibrations thinning.

She could as well, but the thought of reentering their old lives caused her heart to lurch. Yes, she loved her life, but she didn't exactly want to leave Quinlan behind and she definitely didn't want another mastyr vampire chasing after her.

Yep, they had a lot of issues to resolve.

An odd vibration went through her as the snow disappeared and grasslands arrived. A forest of fir trees came next. They were still high in the eastern mountain range. At least now that Margetta wasn't around, they could take a direct route up and over.

But almost as soon as that thought went through her head, two things happened at once. She sensed that Margetta was near and something flashed near the edge of the forest, not a bright light, something duller.

She started to ask Quinlan if he'd seen the flash as well, but something struck her and threw her out of Quinlan's arms and into the air. She tumbled, bouncing against Quinlan then away, then back.

She didn't understand what was happening until she started falling to earth and nothing Quinlan did could stop their descent. At the last second, he pulled her on top of him as he landed with a thud on the hard, grass-covered ground.

"Shit. Oh, shit."

She pushed off of him but got only so far as rolling on her back. When she looked up, she saw the dark night sky through a jute web, something laced with fierce preternatural power and the trap had a familiar scent of rotting garbage.

"She caught us."

"She did." His deep voice rumbled and she heard his despair.

Margetta appeared surrounded by a much smaller entourage than before. She hadn't brought along her regular force of Invictus wraith-pairs, just the two powerful couples who each radiated a strong desire to slay the enemy.

She scooted closer to Quinlan and he slid an arm around her, holding her against him.

"Now isn't that sweet. Lovers to the end." Margetta hovered just a few feet away. She lifted her gaze toward the east, in the direction of the snowfields and Ferrenden Peace. "I can't see beyond the mist barrier. I can't move beyond it either. But I know my daughter is there as well as that damn woman who calls herself a queen."

Margetta shifted her gaze back to Quinlan. "So tell me, has she finally taken a man into her bed? The Great Mastyr and I call her the virgin queen." She laughed, a brittle sound that shattered the silence of the cool mountain air. "She's my nemesis, but one day there will be a reckoning. One day." She blinked several times then turned her attention back to her trap.

She still bore a golden glow, which Batya thought must be a shield of some kind.

"So, Mastyr Quinlan, here you are, exactly where I want you. There's nothing either of you can do to break the spell I have over the net. You're trapped and both of you will die here. I could send a single fire ball in your direction right now and consume you both, but that's not good enough for what you've cost me, and all because you couldn't resist a little fae tail."

Batya's turn to blink. Was it possible Margetta didn't know that she was a blood rose?

"What is your intention?" Batya asked. "If you don't intend to fry us, then what?"

Margetta's gaze settled on Batya and she felt the ancient fae's power in a painful vibration over her skin. "That you both endure horrific deaths, of course. Mastyr Quinlan's will be brief but excruciating and will occur within the first hour after dawn."

"No," Batya whispered.

"Oh, yes. But yours, my dear, for having saved him and for having helped get Lorelei to Ferrenden, will be far worse. I've left instructions to have a shelter built for you around the net. You'll be stuck in this cage with your lover's rotting corpse. You'll die slowly and painfully from starvation with only the bones of your beloved for company."

She smiled, glancing from one to the other again. "I believe my work here is done."

As she turned away from them, Batya couldn't restrain herself. "Go to hell."

The ancient fae whirled and within a heartbeat hovered above the netting. Her beautiful features twisted into an expression of fury as she began to shriek, sounding more wraith than fae. Louder her shrieking sounded until Batya's ears thrummed with pain. Batya's back arched and as the decibels rose, her vision faded until finally she blacked out.

* * * * * * * * *

Quinlan awoke slowly, first to the smell of meat cooking over an outdoor flame and then to the fact that his right arm had fallen asleep. He was very weak and had a hard time pulling his arm out from under Batya who was still unconscious.

Margetta had caused them both to pass out.

But how much time had passed?

Thirty feet away, one of the mastyr vampire wraith-pairs lay on furs in the mountain grasses, naked and coupling, grunting like animals. The other talked in quiet tones, tending the fire and roasting what must have been a mountain goat over the flame. The woman turned a spit, then reached in a bucket and poured something savory over the flesh. A strangely homey and erotic scene combined.

He slowly flexed his arm, not wanting to draw attention to the vampires. Sometime during his unconsciousness, they'd erected a day-shelter with a sun-blocking canvas. Clearly, Margetta had left them here to guard the prisoners until they both perished.

Batya stirred beside him and moaned, the sound loud enough to draw the attention of the mastyr supervising the goat. He rose from his camp chair and made his way over to the net and dropped down on his haunches near Batya.

"She's pretty." He reached through and fondled Batya's breasts. "And built. Nice. Too bad you won't be around to enjoy her, but once you're gone, maybe I'll release her for a few hours just for fun."

At his touch, Batya awoke completely, and pushed his hands away, scooting closer to Quinlan.

The last of Quinlan's confusion left as rage flooded his body. He launched across Batya to reach the bastard, but the mastyr just stepped back as the net did its work. Fire burned over his skin and he fell to the ground next to Batya.

He lay trembling, old feelings returning of the powerlessness he'd felt as a child, watching his father, in his drunken rages, pounding on his mother, beating her senseless.

"Mastyr Quinlan, let me give you a taste of what your woman will get when you die. I'll take her out of this net for extended periods and fuck her till she screams, but it won't be a gentle scream, because I like to use knives when I work a woman. So eat that, you fucking bastard."

The vampire walked away laughing.

Quinlan turned his back to the fire and stared at Batya. She lay shivering, so he drew her into his arms, the only real comfort he could give her. When dawn arrived in two or three hours, she'd be left alive to endure torture for who knew how long.

He would die soon, but he'd be leaving Batya behind to endure the whims of a sadist who intended to carve her up while he raped her.

His whole life, all these centuries, he'd been battling evil, but what good was that if he couldn't save the ones closest to him, the ones he loved?

And there it was, his deepest truth, the one he'd shunned the entire time he'd pursued Batya, that he loved her, that he'd fallen hard maybe from the first time he'd caught that tropical flower scent of hers.

As she shivered again and he pulled her closer still, he thought about all that had happened over the past several weeks and he drew one conclusion. He didn't care what had brought them together, only that he held her in his arms and he loved her.

He loved her.

She'd gone against the grain, risking realm-censure and disapproval, but she'd lived her own life, gone her own course, and performed an admirable service at the same time. He knew from his own experience that realm-folk needed compassion, something he gave freely in his duties as Mastyr of Grochaire.

But so did Batya. In that way, they matched each other point-by-point.

And he loved her.

He loved her.

But just as this revelation washed over him in a sublime wave of sensation, he glanced at the net that held them captive. How the hell could they escape this prison? The sun would rise in a few hours and he'd fry.

* * * * * * * *

Batya trembled, but not from cold as she was sure Quinlan thought, but from a rage so pure she could hardly think.

How dare that piece of shit vampire fondle her breasts.

Yes, rage ruled her right now, but not a new rage, something very old that had lived in her for most of her life, from the day she'd seen that Invictus pair kill a whole family of elves.

Those images had burned in her soul all her long-lived life, eventually driving her to live outside of Grochaire, to create a better life in Tennessee.

Yet here she was, drawn back into the fray by the strange ability she possessed to serve a mastyr vampire with her blood. Even now, even with death on her heels, her heart labored because she sensed Quinlan's need.

She wished so much that she wasn't a blood rose, but she couldn't help that.

Another chill swept through her that had nothing to do with how cold it was in this mountain forest meadow. Rage, yes, but something more.

She focused within herself and recognized that her battle frequency had come alive, the one that Quinlan had tapped into, giving him enough power to escape Lebanon with a woman under each arm.

Quinlan. He'd surprised her at every turn. She'd thought so little of him, that except for his dedication to serving Grochaire, he was little more than eye-candy.

Now, as he held her and rubbed her back, all his actions of the past several days had served her or Lorelei or his brigade. He was one of the most generous men she'd ever known.

Her chest constricted and tears rushed to her eyes. She didn't want her time with Quinlan to end. She'd worked so hard to separate herself from Grochaire, yet in the end, she had fallen in love with the ruler himself.

She blinked, aware that she'd just used the 'L' word.

Sweet Goddess, she loved Quinlan, with her whole heart, with every inch of her body and every tremor of her soul.

She loved him.

Sliding her arms around him, she hated the thought that in a few hours the sun would rise and she'd lose him forever.

She couldn't let this happen. He couldn't die now. They'd barely gotten to know each other. "I love you, Quin. I just didn't know it, but I think maybe I fell hard when you walked in wearing that red-sequined Mardis Gras shirt."

He chuckled, his hand still massaging her back. "I love you, too. I never thought this would happen for me. I didn't deserve it."

She drew back and looked into his eyes, caressing his face. "You idiot, no man deserves love *more* than you. I've seen the truth of who you are, that every action of yours is built on serving your people. I just didn't get it until you took care of both Lorelei and myself. You could have left us anywhere along the way."

He looked shocked. "No, I couldn't have. Don't even think it."

Her heart melted. "There, you see? You've just made my point." She kissed him and set up an enthrallment shield. The last thing she'd let those fucking wraith-pairs see was the affection she felt for Quinlan.

* * * * * * * *

Quinlan pulled her close and once again that powerful sensation filled his chest, but this time he recognized the source— his love for Batya had taken him over.

He loved her. He let this truth flow through him, swell his chest, his heart, his mind until his mating vibration came alive and reached for her.

She opened her frequency in return and he let his love flow into her. She moaned softly, rolling on top of him, and kissing him. *Your vibration isn't like before.*

I want you to feel my love, Batya, that this isn't a small thing for me.

You fill me up, Quin. I've never been so happy, even caught in this net, I've never known such joy.

She drew back and looked down at him, her lovely hazel eyes tear-drenched, yet she smiled. "I love you so much."

He nodded and wiped the tears from her cheeks.

A new force rose inside him. He let go of the past, of his feelings of unworthiness, barely recognized in his own life, and he opened himself to this woman, to love, to believing himself worthy of this kind of happiness.

One thought rose above all else, that Batya couldn't die. He couldn't let her perish in this super-charged net. She had to live.

Loving her had become the biggest surprise of his life, but now that he'd acknowledged this tremendous truth, he couldn't just lie here waiting for the sun to claim him and he definitely couldn't let either of those bastards use her body.

But the more familiar ways of battling wouldn't work. He needed new thoughts in this situation, a new approach.

"Quinlan, what is it?"

"I'm trying to think outside the box, get outside my head. There has to be something we can do."

"I don't want you to die, Quin. You need to live, for the sake of the Nine Realms."

A profound sensation of love swept through him once more and he knew what he wanted to do, what needed to be done.

"Bond with me, Batya, right now. There's a reason, as strange and bizarre as this whole journey has been, why we've come together. Bond with me. Now."

She smiled. "I want to more than anything, but how do we do this? I thought it required time."

"The last time I spoke with Vojalie, she did say time would create the bond, but a decision between us could do it as well. And even Gerrod and Abigail bonded by sharing blood. Our land is in a constant state of flux, including the magical elements. And right now, I'm thinking well outside my usual grid of action and I believe we can do it." He put a hand to his chest. "That's what I feel here, right now."

Her eyes searched his. "You think we have a chance, don't you?"

He smiled. "If we work together, just as Rosamunde said."

She nodded. "I'm in."

He opened up to her, letting every one of his frequencies reach for her, his mating frequency, his battling vibrations, and that place where he kept what he treasured most, the soft waves of his devotion to Grochaire and now his love for Batya. All flowed.

She arched, taking it in. In response, he found a waiting nest inside her of all that she was in her faeness and power.

Her vibrations returned to him, throbbing waves of desire, and of her love for the ex-pat community in Lebanon, of her artistry, and even her newly discovered battling frequency. All swirled inside him.

Look at me.

She opened her eyes. *You're so beautiful inside me, Quin.*

He nodded. *And you're like a banquet I could feast on for centuries.*

I join myself to you, Quinlan, now and forever. He felt her decision as though she'd just opened a door and walked through.

He followed after her. *And I bind myself to you, Batya of Lebanon, the woman I love with all my heart, who I give myself to without reservation. All that I am, now belongs to you.*

Staring into her eyes, he felt a great miracle happen.

"Do you feel that? Our vibrations are swirling around each other, over and over."

"Growing closer and tighter."

She nodded. " I can feel the bond forming."

"Like ropes braiding together to become even stronger."

"Yes, exactly like that."

The moment the bond solidified, a flash of light exploded outward, a surge of power that felt like a bomb going off.

Batya reached out her hand. "Would you look at what we've done? We blew the net apart."

Quinlan glanced in the direction of the roaring fire. "But they can't see it because of the enthrallment shield."

"Exactly."

"Why do you think they haven't noticed we've disappeared?"

"Arrogance. They have no fear we can escape, so they're not paying attention." He shifted his gaze back to her. "How about we join forces and take these assholes down."

"Hell, yeah."

Quinlan loved the look in his woman's eye. No fear, just a determination to do what needed to be done.

Chapter Eleven

As Batya rose to her feet, she couldn't believe she and Quinlan had accomplished the impossible, that they'd broken free of Margetta's super-charged net.

They could also just fly out of the meadow, over the forest, and down the mountainside to civilization. But that would leave two super-powered wraith-pairs free to exact whatever vengeance they wanted on the first realm-folk they encountered.

Quinlan rose as well.

Batya couldn't believe how different she felt in her own skin, as though everything had changed. The bond between them felt like a steel cable.

He drew close and pulled her into his arms. She'd never been happier or felt more fulfilled, as though life boiled down to this moment, to a deep connection, and everything else took second place.

"You can fly," he said.

Batya pulled back. "What do you mean?"

"You can fly now. I sense it in you, in the same way that I'm moving along your battle frequency and I can feel the level of your power and what you can bring to an engagement. Batya, you can fly."

She saw the hard warrior's light in his eye, something she'd always seen in him. She glanced down at her feet, as though expecting them to rise on their own.

He took her arm in a gentle clasp. Glancing back up at him, she saw that he smiled. "Go ahead. Give it a try. I'll steady you."

But in that moment, she felt it as well, an innate ability that had always been there. She thought the thought and slowly began to rise, very controlled, levitating as though she'd been flying since childhood. *I must have gained something of your knowledge in the bonding because this feels very natural to me.*

You look like a natural.

He rose beside her and they were both now five feet off the ground and her enthrallment shield held. She twirled in a circle midair and felt completely competent. Unbelievable.

She turned to face him. *So how do you want this to play?*

He glanced over at the campsite where all four captors sat with plates on knees eating goat and beans.

I want you to stay focused on your battle frequency. Let it run wide open and just go with your instincts. When they come for us, take the wraiths and I'll engage the vampires. How does that sound?

Fantastic.

Ready?

The question surprised Batya in its simplicity. The answer was simpler yet. "Yes."

"Then go ahead and release your enthrallment shield. After that, I thought we'd fly straight up."

Batya let the shield melt away. "Now what?"

Her words, however, brought their captors turning to look at them. "What the fuck?" the nearest mastyr called out, rising to his feet, his plate sliding off his knees to the ground.

The two vampires shot into the air. Quinlan took off as well, and without thinking, Batya followed him. Her instinctive response surprised her as she waited for her mind to catch up with her body.

She didn't waste time, however, in over-thinking what was going on. Her wide-open battle frequency had put a smile on her face and her limbs trembled with adrenaline as she tracked with Quinlan.

The first mastyr reached them along with his shrieking wraith lover. Batya didn't give it a second thought as she lifted her hand, and let what proved to be a stunning ball of fire explode in the wraith's direction. The wraith streaked toward a nearby stream, her gauze-based gown in flames.

Batya headed after her and knew exactly what she would do. The wraith dove into the water and came up screaming in pain. She held her palm toward the wraith. "Now sit on the bank or I'll hit you with another one."

The wraith, her dripping, burned gown, hanging on her strange, lean body, stood up in the shallow water. She moved to the bank and sat down, shaking from head to foot.

Batya drew close and extended her healing frequency to the woman. The wraith's eyes rolled with agony. She'd probably pass out in a couple of minutes, as blistered as her skin was. Batya decided to help her along and planted her hand on the woman's forehead, sinking her into painless sleep.

Wraith, coming up behind you. Quinlan's words rang sharp in her head, but even if he hadn't warned her, Batya sensed the enemy. She bolted to the right then shot into the air, whirling at the last moment. The wraith's stream of killing energy went wide of the mark.

Batya aimed her palm at the enemy and let another ball of fire release from her heavily vibrating arm.

The wraith tried to move out of the way, but Batya waved her hand and controlled the trajectory. A few seconds more and the strike hit home, causing the second wraith to perform like the first, heading straight to the stream.

Batya repeated the drill until both wraiths lay side-by-side, sunk into oblivion, at least for the present.

She flew straight up to a parallel position in the air with Quinlan. He fought both mastyrs at the same time, so that lightning-like energy flowed in streaks of red and blue, back and forth.

Each of the men had been wounded and she felt how hard Quinlan fought to equal these men. If she'd killed the wraiths, the battle would already be over because the shared Invictus power faltered when one partner died. But the wraith-pair bond still fed the mastyrs because their mates lived.

Killing the wraiths outright hadn't entered Batya's head. She'd brought all that she was into this battle, which meant she was a healer first. She also knew that Samantha, serving as Ethan's blood rose, had developed the power to dissolve Invictus bonds. One or all of the Invictus could be saved, given extensive rehabilitation.

She stayed at a distance, and focused on connecting with Quinlan's battle frequency. When she tapped in, she let her power flow to him.

The change in Quinlan erupted like a volcano. The width of his strikes broadened and the vampire on the right shouted his sudden pain, tumbling through the air to land hard on the earth. He didn't move.

The remaining vampire wheeled, heading toward the nearest tree-line.

* * * * * * * * *

Quinlan followed in his wake. He needed to reach him before the vampire disappeared into the forest and he'd never find him. He doubled his speed and just before he reached the trees, Quinlan let loose with a powerful stream of energy and caught the bastard in the kidneys.

The vampire arched his back as he shouted in pain, tumbling toward the earth. Like his counterpart, he hit hard and fell unconscious, exactly the way Quinlan wanted him.

As soon as he'd made sure that both Invictus pairs were out for a good long while, he headed slowly in Batya's direction, rising once more back into the air.

He drew his cell from his pants pocket and called Rafe. "How about helping me out with something."

"Name it, mastyr."

Batya flew toward him and he opened his arm. When she drew close, he pulled her tight against him, the way they'd spent most of this journey together.

"Just get your ass to my GPS location. I'm in the Ashur Mountains, just below the snowline." He glanced around. "You'll find me about thirty miles east of Saddleback Vale."

"You been hit in the head? There's no such place."

He smiled, thinking about how all the maps would reveal more of both Grochaire and Walvashorr Realms than most realmfolk had ever seen before.

"Trust me, Rafe. Find a map and have a look." He then detailed the need for a portable prison.

"I've been stationed along the eastern border with twenty of your best men and I've just picked up you signal. See you in about thirty minutes."

* * * * * * * *

The Grochaire Guard detail arrived within a half hour and during that time, neither of the wraith-pairs reached consciousness. For that Batya was grateful. Quinlan might have helped open her battle frequency, but this part of her nature worked in opposition to her healing gifts and she would be very happy to leave this part of the journey behind her.

As she watched the last of the Guard head into the west, with both wraith-pairs chained in two separate steel cages, she glanced around the meadow. The fire had been extinguished and the tent carted away as well. The campsite looked pristine. Quinlan had even sent Margetta's net to be studied by one of the shifter-scientists who excelled in breaking down the components of preternatural phenomena.

Still incredulous that she could fly, she levitated into the air just to try it out once more. The journey had given her so much, including the ability to fly, a concept that had many layers and brought a smile to her lips.

"You're enjoying the idea of flight."

"I am. I still can't believe it."

"You look good in the air."

Quinlan rose to match her position then took her in his arms and kissed her. She drew back suddenly and looked around, but they remained stationary. "For a moment, I forgot about flight and got lost in the kiss. I thought for sure I'd fall out of the sky or we both would. Do you do this often?"

He chuckled. "No, and I probably won't make a habit of it, especially not with you. Way too dangerous."

"My thoughts exactly." He seemed so changed as she stared into his dark eyes. A new man. Some of the darkness that had clung to him had drifted away.

"Do you have any objection to returning to my stronghold? Spending the next few nights with me?"

For a moment, she could hardly speak, but finally managed, "I want nothing more."

"Good. I thought about taking you to my beach house or to my main residence near Buckner, but I want you to myself for just a little while longer and I also want to see you lying on top of all those furs again."

A shiver travelled through Batya, head-to-toe. She would get to be with Quinlan again, to share his bed. But it would be different this time.

His lips curved in a really smug smile. *I can smell your sex, my love. The idea appeals to you.*

And you have that smoky scent, too.

Want me to fly you?

Let me fly part of the way. When I get tired, I'll gladly accept your arm. And one more thing, I know you need to feed. Want a snack first?

I'm tempted, but we're only an hour away, maybe less. I'll wait.

The images that rushed through her mind crippled her ability to sustain the levitation and she collapsed against him. *I take it we just shared the same visual.*

Can't wait. Cha, let me fly you. Just like this. Let me hold you against me, just as I did all the way to Ferrenden Peace.

She sighed deeply as love filled up her heart. Leaning her head against his shoulder, she pathed, *Let's go.*

* * * * * * * *

I'll want to get your satchel first, then make a phone call.

With Batya held close, Quinlan searched the ground for several hundred yards. The satchel had been knocked from his hand when the net caught them. Finally locating the flowered bag, he touched down to retrieve it.

At the same time, he pulled his phone from the pocket of his battle leathers, called ahead to his housekeeper, and informed her about the brigade's two-week absence. He asked her to create a simple meal for them, then promptly gave her the next three nights off. He couldn't imagine leaving the stronghold one moment sooner than that and he definitely wanted some alone time with his bonded blood rose.

With Batya tucked closed to his side, he picked up her satchel and rose high in the air. He needed to feed, but he'd wait because he wanted the complete experience right now. He also needed to get to his stronghold because it was closer to dawn than he'd realized. He already felt the first warning twinges up and down his back.

He flew over the mountains, letting his heat keep Batya warm as she snuggled against him. She didn't say anything, nor did he. Words seemed unnecessary.

The journey back to his stronghold became a time of reflection and amazement on so many levels. He now viewed his life as having taken place in two parts, before he'd begun his pursuit of Batya, and now after.

From the time that he'd buried his mother and killed his father, he'd truly never believed this day would come, that he'd have a woman in his life, that he'd feel in any way capable of protecting her because of all the ways he'd failed to protect his mother.

And the harder truth was that he couldn't always protect Batya, not so long as terrible evil forces, like Margetta and her kind, existed in the Nine Realms. Life held no real guarantees except for the two inescapable realities: change and death.

Well, change had come and this time change rocked his world.

And he would spend his life making sure that Batya knew how much she meant to him, blood rose or not.

By the time he reached his fortress of wood and iron, and entered the fortified courtyard, a line of gray on the horizon had his spine aching.

Once past the massive, arched wood door, however, he breathed a sigh of relief. Nothing sounded better than the lock clicking into place.

"That was close," Batya said, stretching out her arms and legs. "You're shaking."

"Well, we're here now. You must be hungry."

"Only for one thing."

He growled as he drew her into his arms. He kissed her for a long moment, but he sensed something in her, not a hesitation exactly but something. He pulled back. "What is it?"

She had a blush on her cheeks. "Quin, there's something I'd like to do with you, that I've never done with any man before and really couldn't because only a vampire could do this, but…"

He liked the sound of that because she'd just referenced his fangs, and he loved that she was just a little bit embarrassed. He leaned close and whispered into her ear. "You want me to bite you someplace special?"

He felt her shiver. "I want you to bite me everywhere."

He couldn't think for a moment. The thought of obliging her had hardened him almost painfully. "Oh, Cha." He stayed close to her ear, rimming his tongue along the curves that had a lovely fae peak on top.

She purred as he slid along the folds then finally dipped inside. He plunged in and out.

So, you want me to nibble on your ankles, where else?

The back of my knees.

He groaned again.

And… Once more he could tell she was shy about making the request.

Where else, Cha?

My breasts. All over my breasts.

The thought of slaking his vampire thirst on her large, beautiful breasts just about robbed him of breath. She had a lot of territory to cover.

She drew back. Her eyes had a dazed look. "I want a bath first."

He nodded. "I'll meet you in the bedroom. I'll just fetch some food from the kitchen."

She grabbed the front of his Guardsman coat and pulled him close, kissing him hard on the lips. "Good idea."

She turned and walked in the direction of his master suite, then with a giggle rose into the air and flew down the hall.

He smiled as he headed in the other direction.

* * * * * * * * *

Batya filled the boat-like tub, then climbed in for a good long soak. Quinlan returned with a beautiful branch of grapes and small, crust-less sandwiches cut into small heart-shapes. "Well aren't these precious."

Quinlan rolled his eyes. "I'm going to kill my housekeeper. She's taunting me because of you. She must have known I'd bring you back here."

"Smart woman."

"But the white wine is good."

"The best."

She took the small glass, leaned back and sipped. She watched his gaze drift down the length of her body. His eyes took on a hooded look and his smoky, applewood scent got tangled up in the warm air above her. She was pretty sure she'd died and gone to heaven.

Food needed to be the priority, however, so she focused on the meal and the wine and encouraged him to do the same.

When he'd finished eating, he hopped in the shower. She finally eased from the tub, toweled off then used his blow dryer to get some of the dampness out of her hair.

She slid beneath the furs to wait for him, her body thrumming with life and desire, and she wondered if their recent couplings would make a vampire-fae-troll baby. She then realized with a start that for the first time in her life, the idea of having a child actually appealed to her. Amazing what changes the right man could make in the life of an independent woman.

When he appeared in the doorway, she sighed.

"You are freakingly good-looking, Quin." He'd pulled his hair back in a clasp but that was the only thing he wore.

He paused and planted his hands on his hips. "Well, you're not arranged quite as I'd hoped."

She giggled, threw the covers back and hopped out of bed. "It's cold in this room."

"Not for long."

She knew what he wanted.

She rearranged the covers then stretched herself out on top of the furs.

"Much better. Exactly the way I wanted to see you."

He moved with all the strength of his vampire genetics, muscles flexing and quivering, until he stood beside the bed and looked down at her. His gaze took her in once more, as it had while she'd bathed.

She held her arms out to him and he came to her, stretching out on top of her.

She caressed his face. "I can't believe we're here."

"I know." He looked so serious suddenly.

"I was afraid we wouldn't make it back alive, but you got us there."

"*We* got us there."

She smiled. "I guess we did. Is this really happening?"

He leaned down and kissed her, a full, moist kiss that melted her hips and legs. She parted for him, feeling his rigid stalk as he glided lower. He was heavy on her in the best way.

He kissed her for a long time, stroking her arms with his hands, grinding against her, but he didn't try to enter her.

Easing his tongue out of her mouth, he licked her lips. She was ready for more, when she felt a shift in his vibration and suddenly his fangs struck, stinging just her lower lip.

She cried out, but he retracted his fangs and began to suck and the pleasure flowed.

Her breaths mingled with his. She felt his chin quiver and his cock twitch as he drank from her.

He drew back slightly, staring down at her mouth, his eyelids at half-mast. "I love seeing blood on your lips. Sweet Goddess." He flexed his hips and his cock pressed against her.

She touched his face with her hand. "Do you want inside now?"

He shook his head. "No. I've just gotten started."

To prove his intention, he nuzzled her neck then her ear. A second later, a fang pierced the soft flesh of her earlobe above her pierced earring. He took the lobe in his mouth and drew from her what had to have been the smallest rivulet of blood possible.

Oh, Cha, even a few drops is like heaven to me.

Her hips rolled on the bed. She shifted around trying to find a way to capture his cock between her thighs, but he kept just out of reach.

He let go of her ear and met her gaze. "No, you don't. You made your request and I intend to deliver."

Another shiver went straight through her.

His lips and tongue made a slow progression down her neck, over her collar bone, then lower.

* * * * * * * *

Even Batya's skin tasted like her tropical-flower scent, something rich, heady, more than he'd ever dreamed of.

He marveled that his stomach no longer hurt, not even a little. How had this extraordinary thing happened—a woman in his bed at long last, covered in furs, and writhing to the feel of his lips, his tongue, his fangs.

He watched her beneath hooded eyes and every arch of her back or rock of her hips, brought another moan from him. Her mating frequency played over his skin and even flowed over his cock so that he was as close to coming as ever, but somehow managed to hold back.

He wanted to pump his seed inside her, nowhere else, at least not right now. Maybe she was ripe and ready to bear a child, maybe that factor was in play as well. He just didn't know.

But he wanted her full of his child. That much made perfect sense to him now. He wanted to parade her in front of as many other men as possible, to show them what he could do to his woman, to prove all that he was in a tradition as old as time.

He suckled her first, taking turns and delighting in how she'd flex each breast when he nursed on a nipple, forcing more of her into his mouth. He took more, until his own body called a halt. How many times had he almost come?

But he moved to the side for what he needed to do next, the one thing she'd asked of him.

Her hand found his arm and she squeezed his bicep, so of course he flexed for her, then turned to meet her gaze.

Her eyes were full of love. That's what he saw, and what came to him in a wave of powerful emotion. He felt his life meet full circle in this moment, of having known love in the early years of his life, then lost it for centuries, only to have the blood rose phenomenon bring him home again.

He leaned over and kissed her. "Thank you, Batya. Thank you." He wanted to say more, but simply didn't have the words.

But she nodded, caressing his face.

His gaze drifted, as it often did, back to her full breasts.

"Give me what I need," she whispered.

He didn't require another invitation, but settled his lips over the upper swell of her breast, struck, then sucked once more.

At the same time, he fondled the other breast, teasing the tip into a tight bud, stroking the low fullness and weight. *Your breasts are so beautiful.*

They're yours, Quin. Only yours. All yours.

Quinlan took his time, and worked over every inch of her breasts, biting and sipping, and with each strike, her trembling increased. He could feel her pleasure which fueled his own.

She healed fast, but when he knew she'd reached her limit, he rose up and stared down at least two dozen puncture wounds, all healing quickly. Her nipples were hard beads and her labored breathing caused her breasts to rise and fall.

He positioned himself again between her legs, his cock a hard and ready missile. As he pushed inside her, gliding easily along the wet pulsing channel, she groaned.

Had sex ever been better?

No. He thrust three times, just to feel her well and to seat himself deep inside.

Then he let the real magic begin as he supported himself on his forearms, stared into her eyes, and opened up his mating vibration.

* * * * * * * *

Batya lay poised on the edge again, ecstasy hovering just a breath away. She stared into Quinlan's eyes, the man who'd teased her mercilessly and delivered a thousand times over what he'd promised all those weeks ago.

He'd repeatedly said, 'we'd be good together, Cha'.

And they were good together, more than she could believe. How far they'd come. How much they'd achieved, opening up most of the enthralled lands around Ferrenden Peace.

But here she was trembling from the exquisite pain and pleasure of his bites, of his suckling and fondling, ready to have him take her to the heights once more, while looking into his dark eyes.

How she loved him. How much she treasured all that he was, especially knowing what he'd endured as a child and how he'd tried to defend his mother, almost losing his young life in the process.

Now she was here caressing his face as he drove into her, his vibration flowing through her well and into her abdomen so that she could hardly breathe.

She didn't want this moment to end. She wanted to stay like this with him forever.

He turned his head slightly to plant a kiss on the palm of her hand. *Let me drink from you, Cha.*

Yes, please, yes.

He smiled as he met her gaze. "I love you so much."

She nodded, then showed him the depth of her love by simply turning her head and exposing her neck. He jerked inside her, which caused her to tighten.

He grimaced, leaning away from her and closing his eyes. *That felt too good.*

I know. She remained very still to let him recover. She knew him by now, that he wanted to drink from her and if possible, come at the same time.

He licked a slow line up her throat, yet kept moving into her from long practice.

She waited, trembling, eyes closed. His vibration flooded her, while his hard cock drove into her.

He struck.

She cried out and her body seized, just on the brink of orgasm, yet holding steady.

He began to swallow down her blood and she wrapped her arms around his shoulders, amazed by his strength and his stamina.

She breathed hard and groaned as the pleasure built, rising fast. He grunted as he drank.

He curled over her and while he swallowed her essence, she felt him start to release, which pushed her over the edge.

So many sensations arrived at once, that she howled at the ceiling, his mouth still fixed to her neck, her blood still leaving her body, his cock jerking inside her while he thrust faster and faster. He grunted against her neck, his vibration at full bore.

A second orgasm barreled down, carrying her away on a streaking comet of passion. She tumbled through time and space, not knowing where she would land.

Stars flew before her eyes as her body spasmed within and as her heart filled with so much joy she could no longer breathe, or think, or do anything.

When at last she returned to herself, Quinlan lay on top of her, breathing hard, a heavy bountiful weight, something she would know over and over again for years, decades, and hopefully centuries to come.

He was the man for her, the mystery her father had told her to embrace, and how grateful she was that despite her stubbornness and her independence, she'd engaged when she would much rather have stayed behind in Lebanon.

"Where did you go?" He mumbled against her shoulder. "You got so quiet."

"I think I visited another galaxy just for fun. That was amazing, Quinlan."

He lifted up off her and chuckled. "What do you mean?"

"The amazing part?"

"No. I get that." He thumbed her cheek. He was still inside her, his girth making it easy to stay put at least for a while. "The galaxy part."

She reached back and undid the clasp, freeing his hair. "I'm afraid if I tell you the truth, you'll preen too much."

"What are you saying?" He actually frowned like he didn't get it.

She shook her head. "I think I lost consciousness."

His lips parted. "You're serious."

"I saw stars."

"Sweet Goddess. Are you okay?"

"Oh, Quinlan." A wave of affection flowed through her. "This is why I love you so much. You didn't boast about fucking me till I passed out, you asked if I was okay." She curled toward him in order to plant a kiss on his lips.

Which of course heated things up all over again, and because their vibrations were still entwined, and he was still inside her, he made love to her again and again.

* * * * * * * *

Quinlan stood while Mastyrs Gerrod, Ethan, and Seth sat at the round table in his stronghold dining room. The ladies had left so that Vojalie could feed Bernice and Davido had accompanied them. Ethan had taken charge of the mastyr-based wraith-pairs and Samantha had effectively broken their bonds, but no one yet knew whether any of the four realm-folk could be rehabilitated. Only time would tell.

Quinlan had been right about one thing, his bond with Batya had ended Seth's drive toward her, in the same way that he'd shown no interest at all in Samantha after she'd bonded with Ethan.

Gerrod, the most conservative of all the mastyrs turned in his chair toward Quinlan. "I still cannot believe that you of all mastyrs are proposing earth, access-point bases. You've been the most vocal about holding to our traditions, keeping our worlds separate."

"I won't say that I'm not concerned, but I can't predict the future and the one thing I believe we need is a means of communication, one realm to another, apart from our world. How many times has Margetta shut down our communication? Too many times, making it impossible for us to warn each other or even to ask for Guard support."

"He's got a point," Ethan said. He wore his long brown-blond curls in a braid, something Samantha had done for him. The handsome bastard could wear the look, he'd give him that much. "We all could have used a fallback method of reaching each other in the past and who knows what Margetta and the Great Mastyr will have in store for us in the future."

"Yes, I think you've spoken the dilemma exactly right." Seth frowned. Of all the mastyrs present, Quinlan knew Seth the least, only that he ruled Walvashorr with precision and care, making use of his profound, analytical mind. He also had a quiet voice that carried a lethal edge. "I for one am in favor of the idea."

He wondered if somewhere Seth had a blood rose waiting for him.

Maybe. Probably.

He felt Batya reach for him along his telepathic vibration and turning slightly, he pathed, *Hey.*

Hey, yourself, my love. He'd had three blissful days and nights with Batya and during that time his love for her had deepened to a place he'd never thought possible.

And what can I do for you?

Um, that's a loaded question. I'm thinking fangs.

He smiled and turned away from the table. *And I'd love to oblige you by sharing in explicit detail what I'd do with my fangs, but I'm with three mastyrs who will know exactly what I'm up to if I start in.*

He was sure he could hear her chuckling. *Vojalie wants to speak to us. Just you and me, for a moment. Can you come to us yet? We have coffee ready for everyone in the lounge.*

He glanced back at the table, intending to ask the other men what they thought, but both Gerrod and Ethan had crossed their arms over their chests and now grinned at him. Ethan then pretended to crack a whip in Quinlan's direction.

But he just didn't give a good Goddamn. He shrugged. "Batya says they have coffee ready for us. What do you say to giving my earth-access bases a shot?"

Gerrod nodded. "I think we're all agreed." He rose as he spoke and the other two mastyrs joined him.

To Batya, he pathed, *We're on our way. Love you, Cha.*

Ditto, Quin.

He closed the conversation down and moved up next to Seth as together they followed Gerrod and Ethan from the room.

"So what's it like?" Seth asked quietly, holding Quinlan back with a slight pressure on his arm. "This whole blood rose thing."

There were so many things Quinlan could have said, but finally he just shook his head. "You wouldn't believe me if I told you. But if fate contrives to send such a woman your way, just embrace the moment, the passion of it, and let go."

His frown deepened. "Let go?"

"Yeah. It's a concept you'll have to get used to."

* * * * * * * *

Batya wept. Vojalie, perhaps the most powerful fae in all the Nine Realms, had just given them the news.

"You're sure?" Quinlan asked. He stood beside his library table, the one that had held the combined map of Grochaire and Walvashorr not even a week ago. "We're going to have a daughter?"

Vojalie spread her hands wide. She was one of the most beautiful fae women Batya had ever known, one of the kindest souls, and right now had given them the best possible news.

But the woman's gaze was fixed on Quinlan. "I have dreamed of your mother repeatedly in the past several weeks. I don't have great rapport with the spirit world. I believe life is for the living. But in these dreams she spoke of Viola. Do you know whom she meant?"

Quinlan nodded. "My grandmother. She was killed by the Invictus a long time ago."

Batya shifted slightly to see Quinlan's expression better. He looked like he'd taken a blow to the chest, a sensation she felt within the bonded state of their mating vibrations.

She slipped her hand in his. He met her gaze, searching her eyes, then squeezed her hand in response. "What are you thinking?" she asked.

"That there's something more here, something I'm trying hard to remember about Viola. Mother always thought she'd been targeted by the Invictus. She had so many stories of near-escapes."

Batya put her hand on her lower abdomen. "I think I know. I think Margetta tried to end the line well before either you or your mother arrived. She didn't want you born or maybe she didn't want this child born."

"That would only make sense if my mother had been targeted as well, but she wasn't. She was—" He couldn't finish the thought because another hard truth about life surfaced.

Quin, what is it? Tell me. Tell us.

He glanced from her to Vojalie. "Sometimes life is so hard it's almost unbearable. But I've just realized that the only way I would ever have been born, and now this child with us, is if my father hadn't been a brutal, controlling bastard.

"He kept my mother under lock and key. He'd bought illegal protective spells from a fae, who also put an enthrallment shield around our house. I'd always believed it was to keep her inside, but now I don't know. What if he'd known on some realm-level that her life was in jeopardy?"

Vojalie shook her head. "Sometimes the great paradoxes of our lives are the hardest to bear. But you can still despise what he did to her."

"I think my mother understood the gift he gave her, even while hurting her at the same time. She always forgave him and I don't mean a kind of docile relenting, but she forgave him."

"He kept her safe then." Vojalie frowned slightly. "A great paradox, indeed, because look at the gift he created in you, that you would grow up to serve Grochaire as no other mastyr ever would have.

"You've done well, Quinlan, beyond what your terrible background should have allowed you to do, better even than you will ever believe you've done."

"I agree," Batya said, squeezing his hand firmly.

Quinlan turned to her. "This is a lot to take in, but from the time that we bonded, I've felt a sense of closure, of life righting itself in a strange, miraculous way. I have no doubt that because of Margetta and the Great Mastyr, the Nine Realms are in for it. But right now, in this moment, with a baby we've made together, I can be grateful that you've come to me, that your presence in my life has changed me, and that I can know love. Beyond that, we'll take life as it comes."

She knew how hard these words were for Quinlan to speak, so she spoke her own hard words. "I secluded myself because I saw too much of death. I never thought I could come back to Grochaire, to have a life here, but you made that possible."

She would continue to run the free-clinic in Lebanon, especially now that Quinlan had a new plan to open up a Grochaire base in Tennessee. He'd already applied to the state government for permission and had meetings lined up with the Governor on the following week to hammer out regulations and protocols.

But her bond with Quinlan had brought her full circle as well so that she would create a new free clinic in the poorest section of Grochaire Realm. She'd wanted to for decades, but her fear of the Invictus had sent her fleeing her birth-realm instead.

Now that the enemy's intentions were better understood, Quinlan and the mastyrs here tonight were building better defenses. Her realm-clinic, for one thing, would have two Guardsmen on duty all through the night, when the Invictus were most active. During the day, a squad of Guard-trained shifters would take over.

As Quinlan continued to hold her hand and gaze into her eyes, she turned her thoughts toward him and the new life within her.

"I think we should call her Viola." The name just felt right.

Quinlan slid his arm around her waist and pulled her close. "I think my mother would have liked that."

Vojalie nodded. She then raised her arms high and spoke a string of blessings for the child whose life had just begun.

Batya held Quinlan's gaze as Vojalie's voice rose and fell in the poetic cadence of the ancient words. She willed him to understand her love and knew she'd succeeded when a smile curved his lips and an affectionate expression lit his eyes.

I love you, too, he pathed.

An image rose in her mind, of a young girl flying a kite on a windy evening down a long sloping hill. She had dark eyes and hair as black as night. The colors arrived, of the green grasses on the hill, the girl's red dress, and the purple kite, splashing over the image, bringing the beauty of the scene to life. This would be her next painting, the one she would execute long before her daughter came into the world.

But the inscribed brass plate at the bottom, the letters in a lovely script, stunned her the most, *Viola, Queen of Ferrenden Peace.*

She almost said something to Quinlan and Vojalie, but a mysterious instinct stopped her, that to do so would jeopardize not just her child, but Rosamunde as well. She remained silent. And when she drew within once more, the same image remained, but the brass plate had disappeared. Her daughter's future was hers alone to know.

What an incredible turn in the journey of her life, that she would stand opposite one of the realm rulers, bound to him as his blood rose, now pregnant with a future queen.

Her father had told her to embrace the mystery.

And so she had.

The End

About Caris Roane

As of November, 2013, and with the publication of EMBRACE THE MYSTERY, USA Today Bestselling Author Caris Roane has published fourteen paranormal novels and novellas and one contemporary romance. Writing as Valerie King, she has published fifty Regency works. In 2005, Romantic Times gave her a Career Achievement award in Regency Romance. As Caris Roane, she currently writes paranormal romance for St. Martin's Press and is also self-publishing several series set in different paranormal worlds.

To learn more about Caris Roane/Valerie King, and to see her current releases, please visit her website: www.carisroane.com

Titles by Caris Roane

THE GUARDIANS OF ASCENSION SERIES

Ascension
Burning Skies
Wings of Fire
Born of Ashes
Obsidian Flame

THE BLOOD ROSE SERIES

Embrace the Dark
Embrace The Magic
Embrace the Mystery

THE AMULET SERIES

Wicked Night
Dark Night
The Amulet Series: Wicked Night and Dark Night

Now Available!

EMBRACE THE PASSION, Mastyr Seth's story!

And find out what happens to Lorelei!

To get updates on all Caris Roane releases, be sure to sign up for her newsletter/mailing list from the Home Page of www.carisroane.com

Finally, if you enjoyed this story, please take a couple of minutes to leave a review at your favorite online retailer! And you don't have to be a blogger to do this, just a reader who loves books! These reviews help tremendously to get the word out for your favorite authors!

CPSIA information can be obtained
at www.ICGtesting.com
Printed in the USA
FSOW02n1104090217
30618FS

9 781499 501353